AGAINST THE DARK

AGAINST THE DARK

Stanley
Middleton

HUTCHINSON
LONDON

© Stanley Middleton 1998

The right of Stanley Middleton to be identified
as the Author of this work has been asserted by Stanley Middleton
in accordance with the Copyright, Designs and Patents Act 1988

1 3 5 7 9 10 8 6 4 2

This edition first published in 1998 by Hutchinson

Random House (UK) Limited
20 Vauxhall Bridge Road, London SWIV 2SA

Random House Australia (Pty) Limited
20 Alfred Street, Milsons Point, Sydney.
New South Wales 2061, Australia

Random House New Zealand Limited
Poland Road, Glenfield, Auckland 10, New Zealand

Random House South Africa (Pty) Limited
Endulini, 5A Jubilee Road, Parktown 2193, South Africa

A CIP record for this book is available from the British Library

Papers used by Random House UK Limited are natural, recyclable
products made from wood grown in sustainable forests.
The manufacturing processes conform to the environmental
regulations of the country of origin.

ISBN 0 09 1800617

Typeset by Palimpsest Book Production Limited,
Polmont, Stirlingshire
Printed and bound in Great Britain by
Mackays of Chatham PLC, Chatham, Kent

These are the arcs, the trophies I erect,
That fortify thy name against old age;
And these Thy sacred virtues must protect
Against the Dark, and Time's consuming rage.

Samuel Daniel (1562–1619)

1

The couple walked, swaying, arms about waists in the darkness.

The B-road along which they made their way was narrow, and at this point it climbed gently uphill, with the trees of a copse on either side. Footsteps clanged on the surface more noisily now that they had entered the wood. Headlights briefly lit the sky, then the road, as the pair stepped aside into the grass verge. Two cars, one closely behind the other, passed too quickly, they thought, and then another perhaps a hundred yards behind, but less smoothly.

'Piccadilly Circus,' he said. She looked at her watch.

'Ten to eleven,' she answered. All rested quiet round them, without a breath of wind. The night air struck cold.

'We ought to have brought the car.'

'We're not sober enough. We'll be in bed before midnight.'

He kissed her, deeply, satisfying himself.

'Onward,' he said, breaking away. 'Ever upward.' He took her arm, marched her strongly forward. 'Excelsior.' He sang the last word, loudly, dramatically, badly.

They reached the top of the hill, and began to descend, still between trees. Halfway down, the wood began to peter out.

'Somebody still up at the big house,' she said. Two windows shone in the distance.

'Yes,' he said. 'You can see it quite well from here. The whole place. You can't see it at all further along. Just the front gate.'

'What sort of period?' she asked. He loved handing out information.

'Early nineteenth century, I guess. Been altered, enlarged, they say. I've never been inside.'

They had now reached the stone bridge over the stream and began to ascend between hedges. The big house had disappeared from view. They did not speak again until they stopped at the white five-barred gate between ramparts of holly ten feet high. He pointed this out.

'Change from hawthorn,' he said.

'If not much. At night.'

They prepared to set off at their good if erratic pace, but for a moment hand in hand now they stood, swinging arms, delighted.

Today, part of his February half-term holiday, was a Monday and the third day of their honeymoon. They had planned it exactly. Married first thing on Saturday morning, they spent two nights in a hotel in Stamford in the next county, and had returned this morning to his cottage. He had seen to it that the refrigerator was well stocked, the central heating turned on and in working order, the bed-linen clean and ready in the airing cupboard. His new wife had been slightly suspicious, asking him mildly facetiously what might have gone wrong.

'Nothing,' he'd answered loudly. 'I hope. But that's marriage. I do my best for you, but I can't promise perfection.'

'You should know,' she had said.

Thomas Tyler, the husband, now almost fifty, had been married before. The bride, Elizabeth, was his junior by more than twenty years. They smiled at each other and kissed again in front of the white gate. A car passed at speed. They could see stars.

'What's the name of this place?' she asked.

He pointed at the name-plate, in tasteful metal on the top bar.

'The Hollies.' His finger traced the gothic lettering, barely discernible on this night of the new moon. 'Before that Spinney House. Alias Suicide Hollow.'

'Why?'

'Some man hanged himself from one of the big trees.'

'When?'

'Just before the '14–'18 War, I believe. For love, they say.' He laughed, then coughed.

Suddenly they were startled by a light inside the grounds of the house, and then the beam of a powerful torch shone into their faces.

'Who's that?' a voice called. A woman's.

Thomas Tyler pulled his wife forward so that they stood right up to the gate.

'What's wrong?' he asked.

2

The torch shone blindingly into their eyes; they could not make out who was holding it.

'Who are you? What do you want?' The voice croaked, but the torch was steady.

'We're on the way home. We live in the next house along the road.'

The torch approached, played rudely on them, then was as suddenly extinguished.

'I know you,' the woman's voice said, and stopped, irresolute.

'You have the advantage over me,' Thomas said.

'You're that schoolmaster at New Orchard Cottage, aren't you. I've seen you about.'

They could by this time make out the shape of the woman behind the gate. Tall, with a mass of grey hair, she seemed dressed in a nightgown over which a dark overcoat had been tightly buttoned.

'Is anything wrong?' Tyler asked.

'I heard something moving in the house. Then a crash. I put lights on, and went round all the doors and windows.'

'And?'

'They all seemed securely fastened. All the bolts. Double-locks. Everything.'

'I see.'

'Nothing broken. I opened the door, and I heard your voices. I came out.' The woman gave a creak of a laugh. 'I know what you're thinking. That it wasn't wise for a woman to unlock her front door and then come wandering about. I'd have done better to ring the police, and then waited for them. That's what you think, isn't it?'

This exactly described Tom Tyler's mind, but he said nothing. The woman now forced herself right up to the gate, where she switched on the torch, and directed it not exactly at them this time, but closely enough for her to give them another examination.

'Can I ask you to do something for me?' she asked.

'Within reason,' Tyler answered.

'Would you walk round the house with me again? To set my mind at rest?'

'Right.'

The woman opened the gate, and Tyler eased Elizabeth through first, and followed. The heavy wooden gate banged

3

behind them, and the three stood together in the drive, strong man in the middle. They advanced, turning right under an arch of dark trees, then left again.

'Hold this, please,' the woman said, handing Tyler the torch. Its size and weight surprised him. 'It does as a weapon,' she said, as if reading his thoughts, 'at a pinch.'

She rattled keys and unfastened a Yale lock.

'I'll go first,' she said, banging the door shut, 'and put some lights on.' They advanced through a glass porch to a second larger door where the woman fiddled again with keys. It opened without a sound. Lights came on, upstairs and down, and the woman having signalled them forward into the hall, took a semi-circular course round them to close the front door.

'There we are,' she said returning.

'Thomas Tyler.' He introduced himself, voice formal. 'And this is Elizabeth, my wife.'

The woman offered no reciprocal information, did not speak. Inside, in the light, her most striking feature was a mop of grey-white hair, so tangled and upstanding that it seemed to Tyler that she must deliberately have so misshapen it. She wore a mannish dressing-gown, cord pulled tight, over a nightgown. On her feet she had what looked like a pair of army boots, with thick rubber soles, but neatly laced and tied to the top. The effect was not so startling for in these days he had seen otherwise well-dressed teenage girls, sporting equivalent heavy footwear.

'If you'll come round the back windows with me first,' she said. They followed her first into a kitchen, with pantries, and three almost empty, shelved store-rooms. Every window was secure, either screwed in or bolted. She expressed satisfaction, and led them back into the hall and then into two large drawing rooms where they examined windows and furniture. They could see no sign of an intruder. Two further smaller parlours and a long gallery seemed intact.

Back in the hall the woman showed slight signs of embarrassment, waving her arms about and asking, 'You don't think I made it up, do you? I heard a crash. I wasn't dreaming.'

'Upstairs?' Tyler asked. It was almost as cold inside the house as out.

'If you'd go through the studio with me.'

'Surely.'

4

Elizabeth had taken Tom's hand, and it pleased him. The woman looked about her, in agitation. She led them by a wide, solid staircase to the first floor.

'In here.' She posed in front of a door which stood at the end of a narrow corridor. 'This faces north, of course.' She led them in.

The size of the studio surprised them. Bare bulbs lit the place haphazardly, leaving corners of shadow. In the wall opposite them the one huge window was covered with a venetian blind, closed. Tyler immediately was reminded of nautical matters; he could not think why; the sail of a Chinese junk perhaps. He looked about him. Two long tables, littered with pots and tubes of paint, brushes, bottles, rags, a pleated smock, palettes, saucers, knives. Chaos abounded, dirty disorder. The table-tops were jabbed and smeared with paint, as was the floor-covering. Against the walls of the room pictures leaned, singly sometimes, sometimes in stacks of three or four. Others hung, not in any pattern but as if a blind man had knocked nails with abandon over a larger part of the surface, and some half-sighted person had slung up pictures at mad random. Again Tyler battled with his prejudices. Artists should opt for, demand, fix an order, not only in the pictures but in their display.

'There are only the three windows,' the woman said. She hoisted the blind. Tyler examined the locks, then stared out into the rectangle of light thrown into the garden. He could not see properly in a dim glimmer; crooked trees, bushes, clumps clustered but unmethodical.

'It all looks pretty secure,' he said, rattling a bolt.

Elizabeth wandered about the room. Suddenly she gave a little exclamation of surprise.

'This is it,' she said. 'It must have fallen.'

The other two stepped briskly across. A large classical head lay on its side. Tyler picked it up while the woman shone her torch. A splinter had been freshly chipped from the square base, under the inscription which read ΠΛΑΤΩΝ.

'Very handsome,' he said.

'Supercilious,' Elizabeth added.

'Who's that?' the woman asked.

'Plato.'

The head had fallen from a small shelf which still housed another, this time bearded, carving.

5

'How could it fall?' the woman asked.

'Perhaps you dusted it and replaced it too near the edge.'

'Dust?' Scorn crackled. 'What, in here?' She looked solemnly at them. 'I'm not allowed up here. On my own. Except to bring Mr de la Tour messages up. He won't have a 'phone in here, though it would save him no end of time. Why would it fall off?'

'One or two cars raced by,' Tom answered. 'They may have shaken the shelf.'

'Why one but not the other?'

'Heaven knows,' Tom said, 'but there'll be a perfectly rational explanation. One screw put in more loosely than the others. Shelf not quite straight. Head had a bit of a knock while something was being shifted.'

That satisfied the woman. He walked the perimeter of the room, as nearly in straight lines as the debris allowed.

'Anywhere else?' he demanded.

'No, thank you. That will do. My mind's set at rest. I thought somebody had got into the house. It's lonely and out-of-the-way to be here on your own in the daytime never mind the dark-hour.'

'Yes.'

They made their way downstairs.

'You'll be all right?' he asked.

'Yes, thank you.'

He felt in his pockets, dredged up a biro.

'If you've got a slip of paper I'll write my name and phone number for you.'

She pointed at a block of paper; its sides were decorated with what looked like hand-scribbled music. He tore off the top sheet and wrote.

'Thank you. Mr de la Tour is coming back tomorrow.'

Once outside the Tylers stood in the cold until they had heard the locking of both doors before setting off at a smart lick.

'Who's Mr de la Tour?' Elizabeth asked.

'The painter.'

'"*The*"?' she said. 'I've never heard of him. Is he well known?'

'Yes.'

'Oh, yes I know now. One of the Sunday magazines did a thing on him, recently. Big nudes. I didn't know he lived here.'

They were swinging along the road, glad the journey was so nearly over.

'Let's hope you, we've had no thieves,' Elizabeth said.

'Nothing worth stealing. Burglars don't want books.' He laughed. 'That would make a good title.'

'For your memoirs?'

Twenty minutes later they clattered through the gate and into the cottage. It smelt warm, and was intact. He helped himself to a small whisky; she refused. His fingertips were black with dust from the studio.

2

Chords clanged through the Tylers' cottage on Wednesday morning. Thomas, dusting round the dining room listened with unalloyed pleasure to his wife as she played the piano in the other room. She had closed the door but the instrument was powerful, could fill, flood the whole house with sound.

Thomas Tyler smiled, hummed, lifted knick-knacks, like some housewife or skivvy, as he dusted and polished. When he had moved into this place twelve years ago on his appointment as second master at the Captain Albert Ball Comprehensive School his father had presented him with this Bösendorfer upright and he determined to learn to play it. He had changed jobs not with any notion of bettering his career, for he had been happy as head of the history department of the Beechnall Boys' Grammar School and would have been happy to see his time out as a teacher there. He had made the move because his wife had left him. This had hurt him badly, though he said, on the few occasions he made a public pronouncement about the matter, that he did not blame her.

Janet Tyler (née Foulkes) had been clever, forceful, good-looking. The professor of law at the university had always made something of a favourite of her, had openly said that she was wasting her talents as a solicitor in a provincial city, and had made it possible for her to join a large London office. At first Tyler had thought she'd refuse. The offer was tempting, the prospects and money excellent, but Janet had seemed happy enough with him. They had married comparatively late, he at twenty-nine and she at thirty-two, and had lived in some style in a beautiful, small Regency house tucked away in a terrace of three amongst the Victorian and Edwardian mansions of businessmen, consultant surgeons, high-ranking administrators. In their street two knights, a medical professor who appeared often on television, their MP, a junior minister on the way up, and a millionaire bookmaker had settled. All would speak to the Tylers.

The house had been small, but convenient with light rooms and polished floors. Janet had carefully but sparsely furnished them from sales over six years. Pictures, large gold-framed water-colours, decorated the walls. The whole place shone, gleamed, seen to advantage on a late Spring morning, always newly furbished. They had no children to ruin the effect.

Both regretted this. They had married for love, and a love that seemed not to grow less. The young schoolmaster, new to the town, whose first post had been at Shrewsbury School and his second at York, and the handsome, slightly older lawyer admired each other and were, he would have claimed, sexually fulfilled. Nevertheless as soon as Janet became certain that the London offer was firm, she decided to accept. It was a magnificent opportunity; she'd be given a partnership in a few years and now that she approached forty, such openings would be infrequent. She planned her future with precision.

'What am I to do?' Thomas had asked her modestly, at the end of a long, cogently-argued account of the advantages of a move to London.

'You'll easily get a job there,' she said. 'It's one-way traffic. Schools are crying out for well-qualified people.'

Thomas listened. Janet's case seemed watertight; no counter-claims existed. She'd be a fool not to go. He saw at once that she had determined on the move, and that was the end of it. He had felt disappointment insofar that she clearly considered him as a minor figure in the drama; and that settled the matter. She had decided that they were unlikely to have children; she had never before admitted this, had spoken hopefully.

Two years before this time, the High Master had called him in, had told him that Matthew Dodd, the head of his department, had decided to retire, and had offered him the senior history post. He had never expected this; Dodd, a very successful teacher, had not once mentioned leaving. It came out later that he had inherited a considerable sum from his father, and had decided to retire to Italy where he'd hoped to write a book on finance in mediaeval Florence. He had recommended Tyler over the heads of two more senior men.

'I shall have to advertise nationally,' the High Master said to Dodd. 'You know that.'

'Yes. And I see you may attract someone who seems more

suitable to you. I understand that. And it will, of course, be up to you.'

'What is so good about Tyler?'

'He's something of a scholar. Did well at Oxford. I know his tutor. He's a good teacher. Has no disciplinary troubles with his classes, works them hard and can make the subject interesting.'

'Perhaps they're connected.'

Dodd raised his eyebrows, but had no intention of bandying educational points with the head.

'Moreover, he's a rugged character. He'll fight his corner.' Dodd had seen to it that the history department had acquired a lion's share of the cleverest boys in the sixth form. Science and the Classics had done well enough in the past; but history now stood supreme. The whole staff accepted this, realised where the largest part of the school's Oxbridge places came from.

The High Master offered the post to Tyler, without public advertisements. His governors supported him. The older men grumbled, but not to the faces of either protagonist. Dodd offered congratulations and gobbets of advice.

'I don't need to tell you what to do. You've been with me long enough. If somebody lets you down, let him know. I don't need to mention names.'

In fact they all supported him, and the two new men he helped to appoint had worked harder than anyone expected. Tom Tyler quickly learnt that no power resided in the position; he decided who taught whom, who marked this exam or that, but for the rest the success of the department depended on him and his efforts. He did not mind this. It was as it should be. He prospered.

During Janet's first year in London, he visited her often, and they took two short holidays together, one in Rome, one in Paris. They made love enthusiastically in the bedroom of his wife's rather dreary flat.

'I shall move out of this place before too long,' she informed him. That did not surprise him. This plain, if roomy apartment, with its unmatching furniture showed nothing of her taste. 'It suits me now. It's close to work, and it'll do until I'm on top of my job. Then I'll decide where and how much to spend. And perhaps by that time you'll have moved up here, and will want a say in it.'

The marriage with two homes suited both well, so that it came as a shock nearly a year after they'd lived apart when on the occasion in January that he was up to discuss the summer holiday, she said bluntly that the marriage no longer meant anything to her and that they should divorce.

She made the pronouncement with her usual confidence; she had worked it all out, weighed snag against advantage and now waited either for his complete agreement or for a statement of his objections which she would then dispose of. Upright in her chair, right hand on the arm, head slightly tilted to the right, smiling, she now gave him the opportunity to speak.

Tyler had sat silent.

He had been in the flat for half an hour and had noticed no difference in her reception of him. A warm embrace, a hospitable cup of Earl Grey, inquiries about his health and his work, and then suddenly this hardening of voice with the announcement that their marriage was over. It seemed unreal, then uncouth. He could find nothing to say; no anger burnt in him; breathless emptiness unmanned him so that he faced her, his mouth open, not even groping for words.

His silence was the best defence.

Janet had learnt from experience that he could argue a point, grow robust in his own defence, knew when he should debate cleverly and when to shout his opponent down. But this mute man, this creature with pale face and staring eyes, frightened her. He was strong and now, at a loss for words, might physically attack her. They kept to their chairs making not a sound for perhaps five minutes, though it seemed longer.

She spoke first.

'It's true, isn't it?'

'What is?' Aggressive, brusque.

'That our marriage is over. It means nothing to either of us.'

'No.' He could barely choke the word out.

Again silence drained him.

'We don't live together. We don't write often. Or even phone. We're both determined to go our own ways.'

'Are we?'

'You know we are. You've not the slightest intention of coming up here to live in London.'

'I'd be a fool to come to any old job. I've taken on work that interests me, that I can prove myself on.'

'That's what I mean.'

'But that's nothing to do with our marriage. If I were a serviceman or in the merchant navy then I'd see less of you than I do now. But that wouldn't mean our marriage was over. We'd expect some alteration at some time.'

She argued that it seemed foolish to hang on to the present ragged arrangements in the hope that something better might eventually appear. That seemed unlikely. They met now for perhaps three holidays a year, and every other weekend. There should be more to a marriage than a score of meetings, a hundred sexual couplings, fifty 'phone calls, a dozen letters.

'Such as?' he asked.

'The making of a home together. Physically. The actual building and its interior decoration, its garden. We were doing that in Beechnall. We were creating a place, a set of circumstances, based on bricks and mortar. True, we had no children. We both, I think, regretted that. True, we made our separate ways career-wise, but we entertained friends in a home that bore our joint mark. That is no longer possible. You must see that.'

He did not. He loved Janet, a woman, not a 'set of circumstances'. The phrase made no sense. He wanted her to do well at her career, and was prepared to make some sacrifice to ensure this, but this conception of marking themselves on the world by the possession of a house had never occurred to him. His mind shuddered. He had been propelled into a country where the laws of nature or custom no longer applied. She seemed changed. This elegant woman, so coolly stating her case, was snatching his pride, his amour-propre away from him. Had she been reasonable, rather than merely appearing so, she would have asked for a probationary period, a time of testing, during which they could have forged, or tried to find, a *modus vivendi*. If she had made a demand that he changed his job and came to live with her in London, he would have been angered, but he would at least have understood her. There would be the shreds of reason visible, a pattern for change that gave him an element of choice.

This present proposition seemed so arrogant that he could barely believe his wife had made it. She had exactly decided what she would do, be like, want in the next few years, and had done the same for him. He had not been considered; he'd

12

been moved like a chess-piece. It was beyond comprehension. She must be hiding something.

'Is there somebody else?' he ground out.

'What do you mean?' She straightened, playing for her own advantage. She knew what he had in mind.

'Is there some other man?'

She waited now, as if she gently racked her brains to come up with the name of some unobtrusive, eminently forgettable character who might just, if she pushed the limits of meaning wide enough, fit his description. She puckered her brow, prettily.

'No.'

'Do you mean that?'

She dismissed the question with a wave of the hand.

For the next half-hour they trampled over the same ground. He, now more capable, advanced his view that they would do better to have a period of trial, three months, say, to see if they could come to some accommodation. She acted as if she could scarcely believe her ears.

'What's this last fourteen months been?' Janet asked.

'What do you mean?'

'That was the period of probation. We both had the opportunity to see how it worked out.'

'I didn't look on it like that.'

'No. Apparently not. So much the worse for you.'

'And you're not prepared to extend the period?' he asked.

'For a month or two, yes. Though I doubt whether it will make much difference. This last three months I've looked carefully at this marriage, and I have found it as I have described it. I cannot think that you would be able to convince me otherwise. But I am willing to postpone our final decision, say, until the end of next month. That gives you six weeks.'

She barely raised her voice, spoke as if she were making some abstruse legal point to a committee of experts. He knew despair. In the end she gathered the tea-things on to the tray, said she must go out to shop for one or two essentials, and declared they would eat at about six-thirty. After that they could talk again, if he so wished, or go to a pub or wine-bar, or visit the cinema. She handed him a list of films available. He could stay the night, if that suited him better; the spare bed was already made up for herself. He wondered where. She'd be grateful if he'd leave sometime in the morning as she had a lunch appointment at one.

'Occupy yourself, can you, for the next couple of hours? There are plenty of books and magazines,' she said over her shoulder. 'Or go out if it suits. I don't want you to feel that I'm neglecting you.'

She balanced the tray with neat speed, and closed the door behind her.

Thomas Tyler felt numb. The shaking anger had disappeared, the cold of despair. Now he sat in a chair, unable to run two coherent thoughts together. Even his limbs seemed uncoordinated. He crossed his legs, expectations low. In the end, after he had heard her call and the outside door bang shut, he pushed himself to his feet, looked open-mouthed at a shelf of paperbacks. He would have claimed to have read each title, but when he reached the end of the row he could not recall a single one. This surprised him; he pulled a book out at random, an old, discoloured Pelican, the edges of each page brown: S. Körner on Kant. He read the epigraph from Schopenhauer, looked at the picture of the author. The book must be forty years old. He wondered vaguely where it had come from. He did not know that Janet studied philosophy or even read round the subject. He replaced the book with difficulty in the jammed row, and looked at its neighbours. D. J. O'Connor on John Locke, Ruth Lydia Saw on Leibniz, Richard Wollheim on F. H. Bradley, Stuart Hampshire on Spinoza, G. J. Warnock on Berkeley, F. C. Coplestone on Aquinas, Austin Duncan-Jones on Butler's Major Philosophy, all of an age, with blackened dusty tops. A job lot from a jumble sale? Perhaps they came from Janet's father's books; he had plenty, but from time to time had a furious clear-out. Thomas himself had profited from his history shelves. One never knew. Never knew what? His head reeled. What would be useful.

He stared in disbelief at the dirtiness of his fingertips.

In some dumb way these books represented careful thought. Today he had suffered from a complete lack of rationality, felt it like a punch. Janet, the clever lawyer, who owned these books and gave them shelf-room even if she never read them, had acted as if he were a child to be ordered off for its own good, without appeal. Or worse to be treated like a stereotype, with no compunction, in a world where

14

the enormous variations of human behaviour went unrec-
ognised.

Thomas slumped back into his chair.

He looked again at his dirty hands, and stumbled his way out
to the kitchen where he swilled them under the cold tap. Now
they smelt of scented soap, like those of Dickens's Mr Jaggers.
The kitchen was tidy, but as ugly as the rest of the house. He
had made his mind up. From the notebook he always carried
he tore out the last page, jaggedly, annoying himself by his
clumsiness, sat at the table and wrote in biro:

'Janet, you seem to me to be acting irrationally, so that
I doubt whether any further argument today will change
your mind. If I stay until tomorrow it will only make matters worse.'

He looked at his complex sentences. They expressed the
truth, if baldly. He started on a new paragraph.

'I døn' døn do not wish our marriage to break up. I think you
know that. I am going back home now, but am willing to see
you at any time. I still love you. I had no idea that the marriage
was so near breakdown. It's not so on my part. I want it to
continue. I can't stress this strongly enough. I feel so low that
I am going to walk out now. Forgive my bad manners. With
love, and I mean that. Tom.'

He propped the note prominently on the kitchen table, found
his bag in the hall, put on his coat and let himself out. It had
stopped snowing. Defeated, by tube and main line he made
his miserable way home. One week later Janet sent him typed
proposals for the sharing of their property. He judged, as did
his solicitor, that it was utterly fair, slightly generous even.
Nevertheless he made one more appeal to her to keep the
marriage intact, but she made no reply. In the end he allowed
the divorce to go through.

During this interim he found his life almost unbearable. It
was as if he'd not only been dismembered but blinded. He tried
to work himself out of his despair, but to no avail. He took on
further A level marking, not because he was short of money,
but his sense of self-worth had been irreparably damaged.

In the end he decided that he must leave school, house,
town, start again elsewhere. He was by no means optimistic
that this would cure him, but he grew more desperate by the
day. He consulted the High Master, who advised him not to

15

move. Thomas reluctantly described the effect of divorce on him. His senior listened gravely.

'It won't be nearly so bad in a year's time. We've had two divorces in our family recently.' Tom had heard nothing of this. 'People recover. More quickly than I'd ever believe.'

'People vary,' Tyler said grimly.

'And you think you'll grieve for the rest of your life?'

'I shan't ever forget.'

'No. But it won't seem to matter so much.'

Tom Tyler examined his superior. He was no more than fifty, and had held this position for fourteen years. His appearance was thoroughly old-fashioned; he wore a grey suit with a waistcoat, a faintly striped shirt and a silk tie. When he drew back his sleeves, a gesture to convey thought, one saw his cuff-links. Socks matched the tie, and his black shoes were highly polished. His gown hung on the study-door ready for official expeditions into the school. The hair, touched with white only at the temples, was held neatly in place but cut short at the back. The hands were shapely and brown. Only the hooded eyes suggested that there was more to the headmaster than a good appearance and an ability never to put a foot wrong.

'Stay here, Tyler.' No Christian names sugared the precise voice. 'You're doing well. Better than Dodd. You're as efficient, but you're more of a human being. You've taken the department over without trauma or drama and improved it. Don't give it up for another year or two.' Dr Thackeray touched his smooth cheeks, approvingly, with the tips of long fingers. 'Give yourself a dog's chance.' A wolfish smile apologised for his odd metaphor.

Some weeks later when the High Master had instituted further inquiries and had made up his mind that Tyler was determined to leave, he suggested that the young man apply for the post of deputy head at a large comprehensive school further north in the county. Tyler would be able to drive there from his present house, and this would give him the opportunity to look round the district for a decent place to live.

'Let me outline the advantages. I know the headmaster. He has twice been a junior colleague. He's a man who cares about standards.'

'What's his subject?'

16

'Like me he's an ignorant scientist. Chemistry.' Dr Thackeray was a physicist. 'But he wants to build up a strong sixth form. He's doing that for science and maths, but he'd welcome a historian. The arts side has been ramshackle, but he's appointed a new head of English and is currently looking for a good modern linguist. I guess you'd be responsible for sixth form history teaching, so you wouldn't lose touch with your subject. He seemed interested, very interested when I spoke to him about you.'

'And the disadvantages?'

'You won't find the high-fliers and achievers you deal with here. That's for certain. That's not to say the pupils won't be worth teaching. And Stephen Miles is determined to raise standards. He's been there five years, and he's pleased with the way things are going. Or so he says. Teaching is his priority. Results. Nowadays heads of schools are responsible for budgets in a way they never were, but that won't bother him. He can do mathematics, and he can make his mind up.'

'It would be a good move, you think.'

'No, I don't. You'd do better to stay here and concentrate on history. That's what you're interested in. We give you just about enough administration to keep you abreast of the world. I know you're doing work outside. I read your last two articles in the *Portland Magazine*, and they were both entertaining and intelligent. You, unlike most of your colleagues in local history, don't work from the assumption that I have to be interested in something because it happened in 1390 and not 1990.' Thackeray waved his hand. 'Oh, no. I know what you're going to say. Don't let's argue the point. Your stuff was good. Your fellow-scribes prove their assiduity, and that's better than nothing. You have real flair.'

Tom cynically wondered who Thackeray had been talking to. The High Master was a member of the Portland History Society, Dodd had seen to that, but giving expert judgements on the quality of articles in their quarterly magazine showed him in a new light.

'You could apply for headships now. In my day one went straight from head of department to head of a school. Now it seems the fashion to have an intermediate step, as deputy. You watch somebody else making mistakes, I suppose, or that's the idea. I don't see much sense in it. At the top you need somebody with a good academic record, ambition, common sense and ability to know what's happening, and where, and who's responsible. Before long boards of governors won't appoint you unless you can flash an MBA before their dazzled eyes.' Dr Thackeray closed his own, looking formidable.

Tom Tyler enjoyed these interviews, which were always kept short. Thackeray was rumoured to be a lonely man, but he did not fill up his time with small talk. He had the qualities of a cultured peasant, if such existed, crafty, three steps ahead, mind-bogglingly quick with statistical arguments, putting his own interests first. Tom found not much warmth in the man, but would sooner have him as an ally than an enemy.

Tom had applied for the job, had got it without trouble, and nearly ten years ago had bought New Orchard Cottage, part eighteenth century, where he now lived. It had been in poor condition, but his own hard work and careful use of the profits from his Beechnall house had thoroughly modernised it.

Now as he listened to Elizabeth, his wife, playing the piano, he vaguely thought over his parting with Janet, the divorce, his move here. He could remember it without pain, as he could not ten years before, when he'd work from six in the morning to eleven at night, reading, writing, marking, building and repairing to diminish his agony at the loss of Janet. She had been generous to him in the financial settlement; perhaps she felt guilt. He was not sure. His shock had surprised her; she had not expected it, but he had thought that would not unduly affect her logic or her arithmetic.

He smiled to himself. This morning it seemed not to matter. He had not seen her since the divorce, and had heard nothing of her. He did not know whether she had remarried, whether she had been offered a partnership, where she now lived. Elizabeth confidently played the piano. Andante and Rondo Capriccioso by Mendelssohn. She had told him that the composer was probably still a schoolboy when he wrote the work. It pleased him. She rattled away at the rondo; he shook his head with the rhythm. He could understand this, could whistle it. When she played Ravel, as sometimes she did, Ondine from Gaspard de la Nuit, he felt baffled. The brilliance of the showering notes did not assume the shapes he demanded from music. He could not recognise a mistake from a correct note.

18

The front doorbell rang. Elizabeth stopped playing in mid-bar. He put down spray can and duster and made for the hallway.

3

Tom Tyler had not expected visitors. When he had lived in Beechnall he was, he remembered, invariably interrupted in his work during the school holidays by pedlars of window-leathers, covers for ironing-boards and gardening gloves, or by salesmen for double-glazing or conservatories, or carriers of fresh fish from Grimsby or tea-salesmen their wares vacuum-packed on the plantation, or more rarely evangelists, politicians at election times, collectors for charities. Out here at Orchard Cottage, he had been able to sit all day at his desk without a visitor of any sort. It suited him, he said. Loneliness encourages work. He did not allow self-inflicted pauses.

Today, whistling Mendelssohn's Rondo, he opened the front door, pulling back two large bolts, a chain, and finally fiddling with a lock. Nobody had been through the door this morning. In the bright air a large man, broad-shouldered in an anorak, cord-trousers and heavy boots, stood there scraping the bristles of his face with a big left hand.

'Good morning,' he said, courteously, then looked away and upwards at a bird which had begun to shout. 'My name is de la Tour. George de la Tour.'

Tom knew that. The painter from 'The Hollies', the big house. He'd seen the man about occasionally, but they had never exchanged a word.

'Come in.'

George de la Tour stepped inside. He crowded the narrow hallway. Three inches above Tyler's five feet ten, he seemed almost overpoweringly broad; the left hand still grasped the bristles. His breathing sounded heavily in the confined space.

'You were kind enough to give assistance to my housekeeper the night before last.'

'Plato overbalanced and fell.'

'So I hear.' The visitor chuckled. His voice squeaked higher than Tom expected from so large a frame. 'I was surprised that she was so perturbed. She cultivates this odd appearance, hair straight up, but she's sensible, so that I was amazed that she ventured outside. That's the last thing for a woman to do in an out-of-the way place like this. She recognised you, she says. She takes an interest in what goes on round about. Not that there is much: who's driving which tractor or what time the postman arrives.'

Tyler led de la Tour into the sitting-room, and offered coffee. The visitor spread his legs in an armchair which he dwarfed. Elizabeth in the kitchen now, a look of inquiry on her face, was led in and introduced. The painter stood, though it was something of a struggle, and breathily inclined his head as he shook her hand. Tyler backed out towards the percolator.

When he returned with the tray he found Elizabeth and the visitor talking easily. She seemed to be explaining how she would set about teaching a difficult piece to a student entered for a competition or examination. She talked with real élan, once even wagging a forefinger in emphasis. Unexpectedly vivacious, he thought. De la Tour sat straight in his chair, eyebrows raised, nodding like a Buddha.

'Are your pupils all gifted?' he inquired.

'A few, only a few,' she conceded.

Elizabeth taught four full days in the music department of a college of further education, and one whole day in a private music school. In the college the standards varied; some students were prepared for diplomas while others were drilled in simple four-part harmony, two and three part counterpoint and not too tricky ear-tests as entrance qualifications for other examinations.

'What percentage?'

'Ten, perhaps.'

'That's high,' he asked, 'isn't it?'

'It would be higher if they had been better taught.'

'Do you have private pupils? Right out here?'

'Yes. No. I hire a studio.'

As soon as he had received his coffee and refused a chocolate biscuit de la Tour asked,

'Could you teach me to play the piano?'

'Have you had any lessons? As a child?'

'No, never.'

'Have you sung in a choir?'

'At school.'

'Do you listen to CDs? Or go to concerts?'

'To some extent.'

Elizabeth paused, looked the man over.

'Why do you want to play the piano then?'

'I don't, but I just wondered if it were possible. Is it?'

'If you were keen, yes. But it's relatively slow progress that you'd make compared with a child's, I imagine. I'm speaking without my book, because I've never tried to teach anybody of your age. The one or two I've known have tried to teach themselves, but not very successfully. It would be possible, but not likely, for them to reach a high standard.' She smiled. 'I'm speaking outside my experience. Can people start to paint at your age?'

'They do. Lots of them. Classes are full of middle-aged, even ancient daubers.'

'And they don't do very well?'

'No. But they get enough satisfaction out of it to make it worthwhile. But that would be true of young students who attend art colleges. Not many will turn out as Rembrandts or Cézannes. But the stuff they paint is worth framing quite often, and hanging on walls.'

'If you had the chance to buy a very good print or a not so good original which would you buy?' Thomas Tyler joined in, obliquely, wanting his part in the discussion.

'In my own case, I don't know. I've greater access to originals than most. I can still learn from prints and photographs, but you must realise my house is full of my own paintings. Some I like; some weary me after a time. Now with your average picture-hanging householder, snobbery raises its ugly head. For some people any original is better than a print. And prints vary enormously.' He pointed to the Vermeer 'Lacemaker' on the wall. He had to turn to do so, for he had been sitting with his back to it. He shook his head.

'No good?' Tom asked.

'It's too big, and the light's wrong, the colour. You could learn a great deal from that, or get great pleasure from it, but it's not the real Vermeer.'

'Where's that?' Elizabeth asked.

'In the Louvre.'

'You greatly admire Vermeer?' Thomas.

'You can't help doing so, though he's not my kind of painter.'

22

They waited for further comment, but it did not come. The man sat, hands clasped between knees, utterly still, withdrawn, as if the simple questions asked and answered in the last few minutes had posed such difficulties for him that only silent and powerful concentration could deal with them. He brooded, eyes half closed, ignoring his hosts. When the meditation was done, he stuck out a finger towards Tyler and spoke.

'Anyhow, you did Mrs Woodcock a good turn. She was full of it when I arrived. And that's unlike her.'

'She doesn't usually say much?' Tyler helped out in the conversation.

'Oh, she can talk if she wants to. But I'd have guessed she wouldn't in this case, as she appeared to disadvantage. But she did.'

'I couldn't tell,' Tyler said, 'whether she was afraid or not. And I was surprised that she knew me. To the best of my recollection I've never seen her before in my life.'

'Once seen, never forgotten. Not you. Her. How old do you think she is?'

'In her sixties.' Tom Tyler looked to his wife for confirmation. She nodded, uncertainly.

'Fifty-one.' The painter shook his head as at his own disbelief. 'She's an oddity, but she suits me and my concerns.'

'Is she a widow?' Elizabeth asked, shyly.

'No, there's a Mr Woodcock. Still extant. He doesn't live here. He did at one time live in with us, but not at 'The Hollies'. And we've been here for four, nearly five years. He'd cleared off. He visits her, now and again. He's been back briefly a couple of times that I know of. He's a law unto himself.'

'No children?' Tyler inquired.

'A daughter. But she's grown up. She makes infrequent phone calls. She's appeared once, but I was away.' De la Tour suddenly laughed, turning towards Elizabeth. 'How did you rate her hairstyle?'

'Is it like that during the day?'

'Sometimes. She adopts that barbaric fuzzy-wuzzy just to annoy me. If I'm using her as a model I make her comb and brush it in a more orthodox way. That doesn't please her, either. "What does it matter?" she asks me. "You don't paint what you see."'

'And you answer?' Tyler asked.

23

'I just look at her. We've known each other long enough. She was a model at the Art School I taught at, oh, getting on for thirty years ago. Useful. She knows how to sit still.'

George de la Tour suddenly stood up, heaving, breathing heavily, like a minor earthquake.

'I must be on my way,' he said. 'I try to fit in with her mealtimes. It's the least I can do. You come along and visit me. Are you interested in painting?' he asked Elizabeth. 'You can have a look round my studio.'

'Do you like explaining to people what you're doing?' she asked.

'No. But I'll say a word or two to you.' He made for the door. 'For you. Thanks very much for the coffee.' He barged into the hall passage. Elizabeth did not follow. Once the door was open, he said, brazenly, 'I didn't know you were married. Nor did Ellen.'

'Ellen?'

'Ellen Woodcock.'

'It's recent,' Tom answered, as they walked down the path to the front gate. 'Last Saturday. This is our honeymoon.'

'I'll be damned.' He pushed his hat to the back of his head. 'You wouldn't want me here, now, would you?' He guffawed. 'Apologies.' He set off at an energetic, heavy pace away from New Orchard Cottage. 'I'll give you a call.' He stopped, turned round. 'Do you want to come this week?'

'Yes, if you please.'

Indoors, Elizabeth had set about Mendelssohn again.

De la Tour, as good as his word, telephoned to invite them over on Saturday afternoon, making mock apologies for interrupting their honeymoon. 'A short break from love,' he said, hoarsely, 'will do you both good.'

Mrs Woodcock met them at the door, clothed chastely in a grey dress with narrow navy piping. Her hair had been pulled back into a bun, and shone like steel in its straight neatness. She spoke politely, advised them to keep their outdoor coats on as the studio upstairs was never very warm at this time of the year.

'He won't keep you very long,' she warned. 'He doesn't go in much for explanations. You're very honoured that he's invited you at all.'

'What's he doing just now?'

'A big picture for some American millionaire. It's going to be fastened to the wall in the man's house. He sent exact measurements.'

'And?'

'You'll have to ask him. He cursed for days once he'd got the commission.'

'He's not pleased, then?'

'He never is.'

Ellen Woodcock led them upstairs, where they stopped outside the studio, all silent, attentive. The housekeeper rapped sharply with her knuckles on the door. It must have hurt her, Tyler thought. There followed a hiatus before the door was flung suddenly back.

'Come in,' the painter called, moving his massy frame backwards.

Elizabeth went first; Tom Tyler signalled for Mrs Woodcock to follow, but she shook her head, directed him through the door, and remained standing on the corridor.

'Are you coming in, or aren't you?' de la Tour rudely asked.

'You don't want me there.'

'Please yourself.'

'I shall.' At this she stepped forward, through into the studio, closing the door quietly behind her.

'February's no time for visiting studios,' de la Tour said, rubbing his hands. 'Too cold. I'm not doing anything very interesting, either.' They were now standing at an untidy desk, with two lamps switched on. George de la Tour pointed to a great white rectangle, erected and buttressed some distance away. 'That's what I've come home for,' the man said, laughing to himself.

They all stared at the rectangle, six yards by two. It had not been there the other night.

'It's a commission,' the man said. 'From some American.'

'Is it canvas?' Tyler asked.

'No. Wood. And a hell of a job we had getting it up here. He pointed at the large window. 'That's made to swing back for just such ostentatious sizes. And then it had to be made to stand steady while I paint it. Had to have a couple of carpenters in for that. They've worked for me often enough. They made the panel, in fact.' He strode across, and gave the structure a violent

25

shake, as if to fetch it collapsing down. It withstood the assault. 'And now it's primed.'

'Did you do that?' Elizabeth asked. 'For yourself?'

'I did. Double coat. Ordinary household paint. Brilliant white. That should do.'

'And what next?' Elizabeth continued.

'I'm doing sketches. Looking at photographs. I've been thinking about the thing, on and off for a month. Slow rush.' He laughed again, scattering the pile of papers on his desk. 'Sketch after sketch. Sit down,' he ordered Tyler. 'Sit still.' He picked up a pad, and set about his work with a kind of busy abstraction. It did not take long. He held it up for them.

'You've caught the likeness,' Elizabeth said.

Tyler thought his face appeared grimmer than usual, dark, heavy, ill at ease with the world.

'That's another face if I need it,' de la Tour said.

'Do the young lady,' Mrs Woodcock said, sharply. 'You know that's what you want.'

The painter bowed to Elizabeth.

'Would you like to sit?' he asked. 'It's painless. Won't take above a few minutes. Might be able to use it in the picture. You and your husband.'

Elizabeth took the chair Tom had vacated. George de la Tour crouched ready with pencil above sketch-book. They were all silent together for ten minutes as he worked, sniffing deeply, once grimacing at his model and grinding his teeth together. When he had finished he cocked his head, then laid the book on the desk. There were two sketches, one of a few lines only, the second done in more detail, but both catching a likeness, the delicacy of Elizabeth's features, the bright glance.

'Very good,' she pronounced.

'Marvellous,' Tom echoed.

De la Tour closed the book, smiling wearily. 'I can always do with more faces,' he pronounced.

'For this?' Tom pointed at the huge whiteness.

'Yes.' The painter struggled up from his chair. 'Yes. Some American millionaire got in touch with my agent. He's bought a mighty castle somewhere in the west of England. I haven't been to see it. He sent photographs of the place. And one room has classical pillars, and he wants a picture to be fixed to the end wall behind them. A classical picture. I ask you. Orpheus leads Eurydice back from Hades.'

'Interesting,' Tom murmured.

'Might be to you. Not to me. He'd seen, according to my agent, some of my portraits and two nudes I did about ten years ago, and had decided I was the man for him. I don't understand it myself. They're the last things I'd have chosen as exemplars. Still, there's no telling. He and my man, Philip Grétry, put their heads together, and came up with this idea. I didn't want to do it.'

'But you've been persuaded?' Elizabeth asked, sweetly.

'He'll do anything if the money's right,' Mrs Woodcock interrupted.

'I came here five years or so ago to get out of the race against others, to start retirement. I'd enough to live on. I was beginning to tire of critics who were writing me off as old-fashioned.'

'Are you?' Tom asked.

'No, he isn't.' The answer, sharp as vinegar, burst from Mrs Woodcock.

'Yes, if that means I've found what I have to do, what I do best, and try to do it better rather than shooting off in some other daft direction I don't believe in.' The painter looked formidable as he rose. 'Come on, let's have a look.'

De la Tour said little as they strolled round, merely pointing with a hand held palm upwards at pictures he thought needed closer attention. They paused for a long time in front of a nude, done strongly against a background of greys. A woman lay, strong legs slightly apart, as if any minute she'd bound upward with jerky energy. Her face scowled, not unbeautifully, as if to suggest that she would immediately rectify her present stillness, leap into life.

'Ellen in her youth,' the painter said, ungraciously.

Mrs Woodcock stared at the picture, with a proprietorial air, showing no embarrassment.

'He's not made me very pretty, has he?' Mrs Woodcock said. 'But he can paint.'

The woman's naked flesh glowed against the abstract shapes of the varied darknesses behind. Tyler moved close to the canvas to examine the brush strokes. The paint had not been thickly applied, but Tyler was amazed at the number of dabs, of diverse colour, the slight modifications, the irregularities, deviations that from a few steps back became living, blood-fed, human skin. He marvelled.

'A long job?' he asked.

'I'll say.' Ellen Woodcock.

'I was trying something new. It took months to get it finally right.'

'It's a miracle to me that you catch that, that body so perfectly. You feel you could touch it, that it would be warm, and then when you go up to it all it consists of is a dot or dash or two here, a dab, a blob, an interrupted stroke of paint. I don't know how you do it.'

'I had to learn my trade over a good few years.'

'And I had to lie there shivering, goose-pimples all over.'

De la Tour shook an admonitory finger, laughing now.

'It's not framed,' Elizabeth said.

'No. It's one of three, and the other two have gone, been sold. This will belong, belongs to Ellen when I snuff it. I did frame it once and hung it, but madame didn't like the flaunting of her private parts straight in the faces of visitors. So it's kept up here. That wasn't in this house.'

'My husband used to look at it,' Mrs Woodcock offered, 'and he'd say, out loud, not to himself, 'You dirty whore.' And in a way I could see what he meant.'

'He didn't like your working as a model?' Tom asked.

'He didn't mind. George did him naked twice. And once the pair of us together on a bed. He called it 'The Wedding Night'. It looked as if we were having our honeymoon in some dirty old attic or cellar. We went to a big hotel in Bournemouth. But he's now got the habit of this background. I don't know why. It's what goes on in his mind, I guess.'

De la Tour listened, a wry smile on his satisfied face, as if what she said saved him from commentary.

He marched them smartly round the rest of the pictures, saying little, not even pointing a hand.

'Ellen,' he said, when they were nearly back to his desk, 'go and put the kettle on, please, and we'll have a cup of coffee. Downstairs.' As soon as Ellen had gone, he turned to Elizabeth and muttered, 'May I make another sketch of you before we go down? Ellen'd be a bit jealous, I guess. She's odd. I suppose we all are.'

He indicated the chair, and Elizabeth took her place. De la

28

Tour began work at once, without preliminaries. Tom watched the man who hardly moved his trunk, concentrated his whole energy and strength on the movement of his rapid pencil. He pouted his lips when he had finished, and held up the sketch for his visitors.

Elizabeth nodded approval.

'Beautiful,' Tom Tyler said. 'Sums her up exactly.' He obviously struggled to find the words to express his admiration. 'The character suggested.'

'Her beauty,' the painter snapped.

The two men spoke as if Elizabeth was not there. She, embarrassed, kept her mouth shut, not looking either in the face.

De la Tour struggled to his feet, urged them downstairs, closing his door on the smell of turpentine.

'Stinks the house out if you're not careful,' he said.

'I thought you could buy an odourless variety these days,' Tom ventured.

'Why should I? I've always painted to that smell. It's part of the process.'

Mrs Woodcock burst into the drawing-room with a tray of black coffee in wide shallow cups. She inquired about cream and sugar, and having served them, suddenly asked Elizabeth,

'He made another sketch of you, didn't he?'

'Ellen, Ellen,' George de la Tour gently rebuked her.

'Yes, he did.'

'I knew he would. I knew he would.' The repeated sentence took on itself a small, savage tune, like a child's playground chant.

No more was said on the subject. They talked about the disadvantages of living in the country. Tom described a nightmare journey to school, from the previous year, driving through drifting snow, windscreen plastered.

'He did some snow paintings,' Ellen said. 'Little things.' She indicated the size. 'Sold them all in no time. Lovely, they were.'

Ellen Woodcock considered herself the painter's social equal, a wife rather than a housekeeper. She shooed away the visitors after the second cup, allowing her master to return to his sketchpad upstairs.

'What did you think, then?' Tom Tyler asked Elizabeth as they walked back by a footpath in the brightness of the February noon. He had been surprised at his wife's silence in the house. Without rudeness, she had barely said a word, though her facial expression demonstrated her lively interest.

'That was something I've never done before,' she answered. 'I've been round art galleries looking at pictures often enough. This was quite different.'

'And how did you like George? He was obviously taken with you.'

'He was quieter than I expected. Not so argumentative. I suppose he thought his pictures spoke for themselves.'

'Ellen wasn't slow in saying her piece,' Tom offered.

'No. I didn't quite make her out. She was shy in some ways and then she'd push herself forward. Is she his mistress?'

'Is? Has been? Don't know about now.'

'He made her body very attractive in that picture,' Elizabeth said. 'Any man would want her.'

They reached home, breathless, still discussing techniques of painting. Tom made his wife sit down as he threw together a salad, boiled potatoes, served all with cheese. She had tucked her legs under her on a chair as she read a pocket Jane Austen, *Emma*. He loved to see her, as it were, retiring from him, hibernating, retreating into herself, unmindful of him. He was all the time obsessed with her presence, her beauty, sexual appeal, promise. She could, it seemed, without difficulty dismiss him completely from her mind as she immersed herself in her little book. This attracted him the more; she had superior powers. He knew himself to be dependent on her, but she could abstract herself. As he laid the table he glanced at her; she looked up and smiled and became immediately absorbed again in her book.

'Not very attractive,' he said as they sat down. 'Salad's dull at this time of year.'

'Fills the inner woman,' she said, eating heartily. They decided to drive over to the supermarket that afternoon to shop together. He usually went on Friday night; it helped, he said, to wind him down, pushing his trolley and consulting his list. 'We'll stick to that,' she had agreed. 'It's no use throwing good habits overboard. You're a well organized man, Tom.'

He was never sure that she wasn't gently making fun of him. She lacked malice, but could see things straight. It would keep him up to the mark, he decided. He marvelled that such a girl could marry him, but when he said this to her she warned him that she was as full of faults as the next woman, and he'd soon find out how short she came of perfection.

They washed up together, made love, shopped at Sainsbury's and were back before it was quite dark. The cottage glowed warm and after dinner, while he did the dishes, she played the piano. This time she chose Schubert, the B flat Impromptu, which she played almost as if she were improvising it. He had, he thought, never heard more easy playing, and it suited the drawn curtains, the low lights and winter outside.

He had first heard Elizabeth nearly twelve months ago at a concert in aid of Oxfam to which he had reluctantly dragged himself, expecting little. Staff and students of the college where she taught had offered a varied programme, some of it nowhere near a professional standard. Elizabeth had played two Bach fugues from the 48 to open the programme, and in the second half Chopin nocturnes. Her unostentatious appearances, the extreme clarity of her playing, the delicate variety of her dynamics made her all too brief pieces outstanding for him. In this he was not alone; a claque of some sort in the audience applauded with strength, called for an encore after the Chopin. She came back to the stage, curtsied prettily but did not play again.

'That was very beautiful,' he said to the young woman next to him, a warm clapper, presumably a student.

'You should hear her set about Brahms or Rachmaninov. She's marvellous.'

They met next a week later at a party where he was not quite sure that the girl in the flowered frock was the soloist he had so admired. After he had established her identity, he made a point of talking to her. At first she appeared shy, taciturnly so, but after a time sat down with him and described some lessons she had received from a brilliant Russian virtuoso. Her professor at the College had arranged these for the benefit of the young man. 'You'll improve his English, and he'll show you how to play the high Romantics.'

The pianist had, in fact, spoken very fluent English, but with a thick accent. Scholarly, he would provide Elizabeth with a cup of black coffee when her hour at the Brahms' Handel Variations or the First Concerto had finished, and talk to her about his views. His chief heresy was that while Brahms was a great composer, Schumann was a genius of the highest order.

31

'Did he make a good case?' Tom Tyler had asked.

'Well, yes. As far as it's possible. And he'd jump up and illustrate on the piano. He even tried to sing.' She almost giggled. 'If you heard him play at a concert, you'd think he was self-contained; he creeps on stage, bows very stiffly and has no expression on his face. When his audience goes raving-wild he just bends over, remains down for slightly longer than usual and then stalks off the stage. But when he talked about Schumann he was excited, and threw his hands about and rolled his shoulders and spoke so fast he spluttered and stammered and used Russian expressions which he never usually did.'

'Did he convince you?'

'He made a strong case. I could understand what he was driving at. But it was like comparing Westminster Abbey with Lincoln Cathedral. I'd need to know a lot more before I'd begin to make my comparisons.'

'Was he married?'

'Yes. To an English girl. They had a son. That's why he stayed here.'

'Were his lessons worthwhile?'

'Yes. My professor was going to be away for pretty well a whole term, and so he fixed these lessons up. That surprised me. He wasn't very conscientious about substitutes in the ordinary way.'

'He must have thought highly of you.'

'To some extent. And he wanted to help Yuri. He was a vain man. There was nobody near his class, in his view.'

'Who was he?'

'Timothy Thurlough.'

'I've heard him. Very good.'

She nodded.

'The same initials as you,' she offered. 'Exactly. T.F.T. Timothy Francis Thurlough.'

'That isn't why you chose me, is it?' he asked.

'It is not. He did me well the two years I had him. As a teacher. But he wasn't my type. He was something of a lady's man, but I had no difficulties with him.'

'Did you always think of teaching or did you ever consider a career as a concert pianist?' He'd asked this of her before.

'I didn't think I'd ever make it. I did win one of the smaller competitions. And a prize or two at the college. I've still got an agent, and he gets me engagements now and then. Not very many. Five last year. It hardly seems worth his while. But he does it. And it makes me keep my practice up.'

He knew that she gave these occasional recitals, at provincial music clubs or institutions. He had no idea whether these were important to her, since she so rarely talked about herself. She was free enough with information when he asked, but did not volunteer a great deal by way of commentary. He'd learnt as much in this last week as in the few months he'd known her.

Not until he first proposed to her, six months ago, had he found out that she was recovering from a deep unhappiness. She had arrived in Beechnall four years back, and had fallen wildly in love with another musician at the college, a violinist only two or three years older than she, and married. How she could have been so foolish she could barely imagine now, but they had been irresistibly attracted, unable to keep away from each other. It had altered her life beyond account. She had taken up this position at the Cavendish College with a sense of anticlimax; it meant the end of life in London where she had just managed to make a living, but always in the expectation of some opening-up of her musical career, some opportunity as a recitalist. After three years of this, she had begun to despair, and applied for the post in Beechnall. What it meant was a solid salary, paid every month, and the college authorities had said there would be plenty of private tuition available, and even that they would free her for any recital work she was offered. The steadiness of a regular income had not, however, taken from her the dread of humdrum teaching, week after week listening to not very gifted pupils struggling with musical history or four part harmony or sonata form. And this, she feared, would be the pattern of life ahead, for years, until she married or retired or dropped out of life. Her friends affected to praise her realism; they were sorry that she would not be able to exploit her real gifts as a pianist, but said that teaching was no duller in the long run than a chain of recitals. A person, they said, might well go out of fashion as a virtuoso, and then what? Elizabeth was disappointed with herself; she could not disguise it.

In this mood of dissatisfaction she met Simon Kent. At the Christmas Concert at the end of the first term at the college they had played, impressively, Beethoven's Kreutzer Sonata.

The head of the music department, a hard-bitten little man, had stopped her in the corridor next morning to say,

'That Beethoven was magnificent. You managed to do what so far I haven't, to get Simon Kent to put his back into something.'

'Oh?'

'He's idle. Talented, but bone idle. I've never heard him play so well. He tried to keep up to your standard.'

'Thank you.'

A look of slight surprise crossed the man's face; he grunted and moved off saying no more.

Elizabeth and Simon Kent gave another recital in the new year, and became lovers. She tried to be sensible, excited and exalted as she was. At first Kent would have spent every evening of the week with her, as well as the considerable time they passed in practice together at the college. She would not allow this, in spite of his sulks. She pointed out that she must use some of her spare time to keep herself on top of her work and up to standard at the keyboard.

The affair lasted for eighteen months, and then began to decline. Mrs Kent was pregnant again, with her third child, and the head of the department was beginning to lean on Simon. He had never approved of their association, and said so to both parties. Elizabeth was furious, argued with the old man, reiterated her own point of view time and again in her head. She saw the force of the head's thesis that whatever else she did she should consider Simon's wife and children. His second line, that her lover nowhere approached her in talent or temperament or teaching ability, seemed plainly wrong. The man hated his subordinate, refused to see any good in him, wrote him off out of jealousy. To her Simon Kent outclassed her in attraction, in skill, in talent, in ideas. She might never marry him, but he had made this dead-end job as thrilling as a performance at the Proms, a call to play in Paris, or New York or Sydney. Life pulsated; she looked forward to what every day would bring, taught and practised the harder to be worthy of this unexpected bliss. When she thought about it, not often, she became convinced they would never marry; that in any case would be a come-down. What she knew, and knew for certain, was that this was a life she had never experienced before, a delight compounded of music, of physical contact and abandon, of limitless opportunity. The pair could listen to a Mozart quartet which they knew well and find it profoundly different because of their love. Heaven touched them.

When Simon began to show less interest, and he blamed the head of department who was piling extra tasks on him, she comforted herself by thinking that this was the nature of love, and lovers, that the ordinary must sometimes take preference over the ineffable. She knew her own affections were as deeply engaged, and judged his to be so. He said so often enough.

She finally realised that he had changed, when he twice let her down at practice engagements and cancelled two evening meetings by phone at the last minute. For a few weeks, she hung on to her self-delusions. Low in mind, she watched him. Charming as ever, he offered his specious explanations, and she smiled, humbly. In the end, after he failed to turn up at a concert he was supposed to be helping her to produce she faced him with his deceit.

At first he denied the charge, but as she carefully listed his truancies, dismissed his obviously feeble excuses, he suddenly changed.

'If that's the way you feel about it,' he said, bridling, 'then we'd better break off seeing each other.'

This phrase 'seeing each other' dashed her hope.

'We'd better.' She kept her lips tight as she walked out. The womens' toilets were empty and there she sat wildly sobbing. Slightly recovering, she ran along the corridor, passing two colleagues who continued their conversation, into her studio, fortunately unoccupied, locked the door and collapsed again into grief. She did not appear at lunch, but as soon as she had given her two afternoon lessons, done without overt trauma, she made immediately for home, speaking to no one.

She barely slept for the next week. She made up her face with care whenever she left home, she delivered her lessons, ate her lunchtime sandwich on her own, kept well away from her friends. She had an excuse to hand: inside the next month she had three recitals, in Manchester, Stockton-on-Tees and Tiverton and needed to practise. This was not exactly true, in that she was playing much the same programme in all three places, and was on top of it all. But she practised to give an air of credibility to her unsociable absences.

The recitals proved life-savers. Although she felt incapable

35

of doing justice either to the music or to herself, she played well. The Manchester society immediately signed her up for the next year and all three gave favourable reports. The local papers praised her. 'It is rarely that one meets so fine a sensibility with so fluent a technique.' The compliments lifted her for the moment but she soon fell back into despair. Nothing could go right; her confidence evaporated. Whenever she met friends she thought they despised her as a failure, one thrown over by a lover. She expected to do nothing right, and the depression did not lift. She would weep as she went to bed, or woke in the night, or prepared a meal, and moreover she would allow the fit of grief to overwhelm her. She would suddenly hear the howls, the groans she emitted; the noise, the intensity surprised her; the sounds burst out unchecked, ripped from deep in her belly.

To counteract this she taught, marked, practised, studied with all her strength, trying to fill in or blot out every minute. It was not easy. In private she would find her mind had switched to the shifting, grey vacuum of sorrow which seemed less her longing for Simon than the inadequacy branded by herself on herself. Simon Kent kept out of her way. Whereas she had once run across him in the college four or five times a day, now she saw him at most once or twice in the week. This she tried to dismiss as cowardice on his part, but she feared that if he made some overture of reconciliation she'd capitulate, throw herself at him again, against her deepest will. No such opportunities occurred. In public she behaved impeccably, taught lively lessons, made friendly contacts, undertook extra duties, spoke her mind in departmental meetings, though all this rather seriously, without smiles. She went to a concert or two with a young administrator in the college, but he was no Simon, and her body seemed leaden, dead. She shied away from physical contact, lived celibate.

Her grief became bearable, but not until more than a year later did she consider herself at least partially recovered. The local university had a quartet in residence, and three of its members and an internationally known double-bass player invited her out of the blue to perform the Schubert 'Trout' Quintet with them. She had played it twice at the Royal College and since, so that it took her no time to reach the standard she set herself. The leader of the ensemble, a Scot, let down by the sudden illness of his first pianist, had consulted Yuri Lermontov, who finding out the venue of the concert, had immediately recommended Elizabeth. Hugh Donald rang on Saturday morning, invited her to play it through that afternoon. The concert itself was Monday evening.

'I'll look at it this morning,' she said. 'When you've heard me you can decide if I'm up to standard.'

'It's you or nobody,' Donald said, rudely.

'And if it's not me, then what?'

'We'll play a straight quartet. We've plenty prepared. But we'd particularly like to do this.' He did not say why.

The rehearsal proved magnificent; the strength of the professional players lifted her. They said little, argued less amongst themselves than she expected, treated her as an equal, made suggestions briefly, showed their approval when she deserved it. She arranged another hour with them on Monday morning, and then on the way home realised that she was teaching. She rang the head of department, who said he'd replace her himself – it was a harmony class – and then began to enthuse, quite out of character.

'So you're playing with the Lombard Quartet at the university? So, that's it, is it? We'll have to make something of this. We'll get notices round the college first thing Monday morning. Drum an audience up. It's not every day that one of our staff is invited to play in such exalted circles.'

As good as his word, he even provided money from some fund for students who could not afford the entrance fee. Some forty from the college went, he told her afterwards. 'Quite a fan club.' Room was found for them in the enormous dining chamber of one of the halls of residence where the concert took place, but the authorities had to search the rest of the building for chairs to accommodate an ever enlarging audience.

'You're popular,' the violinist said to her. 'This is by far the biggest number we've had here. Ever, I guess, in all our times of residence here.'

In the first half Elizabeth sat at the back with Julian Dinsdale, the double-bass player, to listen to, first, the Mozart 'Hunt' and then the Beethoven Op 19, No 6. She felt both terrified, and astounded. Julian seemed non-committal, a friendly, careful young man, nodding to himself as he listened. The players up front presented powerfully inflated versions of their rehearsing selves, at ease, and if one closed one's eyes, angelic. And at the back of the stage, closed, in shadow stood her Steinway, which would be wheeled into position during the interval. As they moved out to change into their 'performing gear', the bass player's term, Dinsdale said suddenly to her, 'You surprised them, you know. Hugh told us that. Yuri Lermontov had recommended you, but you were quite different from what they'd expected.' He said no more, and she disappeared into the small closet they had given her, to wash her hands and change into the summery sky-blue gown she had bought five years ago, and which still fitted. She examined her face in the mirror, made nothing of it.

She joined the other performers in their room; they appeared relaxed. Hardly any visitors cluttered the cramped space. Hugh Donald asked how she felt, and when she answered, 'Nervous', said, 'Why, so am I. Always am.' As they walked along the corridor to the hall, Elizabeth did not tremble, but caught her breath as she was ushered on to the platform to a burst of applause. She bowed, fiddled with her piano stool, pressed the sustaining pedal. There seemed to be a slight commotion amongst the all-highest in the middle of the front row; one of the men was standing, stooping over a lady, and all were laughing, rather loud. Dinsdale had told her that they were not only to be patronised, his word, by the Vice-Chancellor and his lady, but by the Chancellor himself, a Duke, no less.

'Give us an A, please,' the violist said. 'We might just as well play at the same pitch as not.' Elizabeth recognised his kindness.

Once they had begun, Elizabeth's fear left her; she knew she played well, matched these professionals in expertise. Dinsdale turned his head away from the audience to droop an eyelid at her after the first movement. When they concluded the work, the applause seemed beyond all reason as they lined up to bow. She stood between Hugh Donald, the leader, and the violist, who held their instruments and bows in the right hand in exactly the same way. They signalled her to lead them from the stage; for some moments they stood in the narrow corridor; they could hear the applause crackling outside.

'Good,' Hugh told the world, then turning to Elizabeth. 'Beautiful. A beautiful performance. Superb.' The others silently manifested their agreement. Dinsdale, the only one with hands free, fondled the crook of her arm very briefly, decorously.

'Well, we'd better get back and let them have another look at us,' Hugh ordered. Elizabeth had the impression that the instruction was for her benefit; he would just have thumbed his professional colleagues on. 'You'll be able to see this time if you recognise anybody you know in the audience. They advanced; she occupied the same position as before; they bowed; clapping increased. The Duke was talking to a young woman two seats on as he brought his hands politely together forward and to the right of his trunk. Elizabeth's pupils would be hidden out on the back rows. The players bowed again, filed out. This time they took the extra few steps to the men's changing room. They put down their instruments, wiped their hands on large handkerchiefs. The applause did not diminish.

'It's up again,' Hugh told Elizabeth.

'Are we going to play again?' Dinsdale asked.

'Sounds like it,' the 'cellist said, not displeased.

'What?'

'Do you think you can manage the air and variations again?' Hugh asked Elizabeth. She nodded. Fear struck again, but bearably. 'Right, let's get it over,' then to Elizabeth, 'They love us. No doubt about it.'

They trooped out; people gathered in the corridor now who themselves broke into smiling applause. The swelling reception in the hall made it plain what the audience wanted.

'Right,' Hugh said, nodding the others to their seats. He remained standing, and in his most precise, pedantic Doric announced, 'We'll play the penultimate movement for you again.' The sentence was rapturously received. 'Let's tune,' he whispered.

Once more they excelled; not a hitch. These men, these associates needed no stimulus to touch the highest of standards. Elizabeth herself now seemed beyond feeling, even of exhilaration. Her fingers obeyed her, took the trills and turns with élan without her conscious will; in her favourite variation she rippled above the cello and the contra-bass but with no glory to herself as if it were natural for her to move with such limpid, swift clarity. At the reception afterwards the Vice-Chancellor said it had lifted him out of his grey life of committees and decisions and planning and money. 'I wanted to laugh, if you know what I mean, without making a sound, out of high spirits. It's what I felt sometimes as a child, and all too rarely since.'

That seemed right to Elizabeth, exactly as she or God or Schubert had intended. Pure, graceful hilarity both limited and extended by delight. She knew how much had depended on her fellow players, their accuracy, beauty of tone, the steady dance of their rhythm underneath her flying, air-skimming beauty. The Vice-Chancellor, a young man, already knighted, passed on; the Duke shook her hand; neither knew what to say.

From this night she dated her recovery.

After the encore, as they stood acknowledging applause she noticed that here and there people stood, as at a political conference, to emphasise their pleasure. The largest group, some two or three rows, were at the back to her right. They must be the Cavendish party. She squinnied to see them better, made out in the middle of the front rank, hands held high to clap, Simon Kent, leading their approval. She felt no pleasure. He towered over his pupils, his movements larger than theirs, his long hands prominent. Elizabeth bowed with the rest, knowing the worth of this evening's performance.

None of the Cavendish people had been invited to the short reception. The one or two university students present seemed much at home amongst the exalted company. The professor of music congratulated her, said she must come next season to play for them again. He would phone her; he took her number into a notebook. He asked if there was anything she would like to play. Offhand she mentioned the Brahms-Handel Variations, that would keep her in practice, and he said it fitted his plans perfectly. An old lady, not recognising her, asked her if she was on the staff of the university or a student.

'No,' Elizabeth replied, 'neither.'

'How do you come to be here then?' she was asked brightly.

The group of younger people with her tittered. One took the old lady's arm.

'This is Elizabeth Stanton, Aunt, who's just played "The Trout".' The woman seemed in no way abashed, might even have been delighted by her error. 'I didn't recognise you. Oh, my eyes. My eyes. You look so much smaller. Than you did up there. You might be one of us.'

'One of the human race,' a man said. They all laughed sedately.

Next morning at the college the head of department swept her in for coffee with the principal. This had never happened before.

40

The principal apologised that she had not been able to attend the previous evening. 'I understand from Derek that I missed something.' They praised her; this young woman had done something they would never do, and they realised it. Elizabeth felt empty, as if they spoke of some third party.

At the end of the week she saw Simon Kent approaching along the corridor. He greeted her with a deep, ironic bow which he held. She wished him 'good morning' and walked briskly past, leaving him bent. She dared not look back to see how he took the rebuff, even feared a hand dropping heavily on her shoulder to drag her towards him. At the staircase, where she turned, she glanced back, but he had gone. She felt a twinge of triumph; she had put him in his place. As she walked upwards to her class, she reproached herself, thinking she might have been more magnanimous.

Six months later she had first spoken to Thomas Tyler at a party. He had impressed her at once as a serious man, though he looked younger than his years. They had married inside thirteen months. He had somehow convinced her that she did right, though she did not immediately sell her flat.

4

On Monday morning Elizabeth looked round the house before she left for work. Her husband had set energetically off soon after eight o'clock, but her first class was not until ten. She crept round the upstairs rooms, checking that the windows had been locked. The third bedroom was now her husband's study, and as she looked it over she smiled.

His desk, like the rest of the room, was utterly tidy. He had an out-tray and an in-, a large wastepaper basket to hand, now quite empty. The books which lined the walls had been divided by subject matter, and stood in strictly alphabetical order within each category. On the two small bare stretches of wall hung two pictures, prints, framed in fumed oak, both of woodland and water, rather abstract in treatment, but immediately attractive if subdued, the reflections catching and holding the stillness of the trees.

'They were wedding presents,' Thomas had told her, 'at my first marriage.' When she had made no comment, he'd said, guardedly, 'Shall I get rid of them?'

'Do you like them?' Elizabeth had asked.

'Yes.'

'Keep them then.'

He had cleared his throat, rather relieved. She admired these diffident moods; she'd already admitted to him. They made him seem older, his real age. 'You should grow a smart, little moustache,' she said. 'Like an army officer.'

'Not a beard?'

'You're not rugged enough.'

Elizabeth moved round the other windows. In the main bedroom Tom had provided a wardrobe, a chest of drawers and a cabinet in her half of the room. Her side was, she'd carefully seen to it, as neat as his. He had made the bed, not she, and the coverlet was squared, smooth, straight. When she asked him if he'd served an apprenticeship as a hotel chambermaid, he'd smiled, not minding her chaffing. The windows were spotless;

42

perhaps he had specially cleaned them for the honeymoon. She could imagine his careful preparations. Not only was she to be welcomed as mistress of the cottage, but provided with a faultless home. She wondered what he'd be like at work, if he'd be down on the subordinates who did not come up to expectation or quick to set them right with examples of his own work. A younger colleague, not knowing who she was had praised her then fiancé.

'He knows what he wants, and what he wants is reasonable.'

'Always?'

'Nearly always. And he knows how to bring it off. He carries the Head.'

She had been surprised to hear this, as Tom had always spoken well of his headmaster. When she'd raised the matter, he'd crinkled the corners of his eyes and answered,

'I've seen worse.'

Now she checked the ground floor, locked the door and set out on this cold February morning for the first working day of her married life. Her car flashed by 'The Hollies'; no one appeared on the drive or at the gate; not that she expected anybody. She looked forward to this journey into the city, especially at this empty end of the road. The fields and hedges lay dark either side of her; downstairs windows were still lighted in some houses; the sky stretched relentlessly grey. To look forward to her return already slightly amused her, as if her life had so soon altered focus. Back at the college she observed no change. Colleagues had taken a week's holiday, but had done nothing extraordinary with it. 'I don't want to go away at this time of the year,' one woman had said grimly. 'I haven't the energy.' 'Not even to somewhere warm?' 'No. What I do is to indulge myself. One morning, not half an hour after James had gone to work I was sitting there with a gin and tonic and a newspaper.' One of her quietest colleagues had been to stay the week with her mother in Warrington but had lasted there only two days. Nobody wanted exotic journeys for this short week in poorish weather; it was a change from teaching, but barely more interesting.

Elizabeth walked the same corridors, smelt the same disinfectant, spoke to the caretaker, found her students sad as always on Monday morning, but could not suppress her excitement at what she had accomplished in those last nine days. The wedding had been arranged so quickly, with so little trouble. She had acquired a new name, a new husband, a new home, totally different expectations. From now on she would appear on the college prospectus as Elizabeth Stanton (Mrs Tyler). In eight months' time she'd be thirty years of age and her husband already fifty. He made love like a young man. Simon Kent had performed in the manner of a virtuoso, but, as it were, serving to demonstrate his skill and charm; both were great, but she felt sometimes called on to applaud him. Tom took her as one who was granted a rare privilege. He was not inexperienced, but rested after their sex like a man beatified. Trying to put this into words for herself (she couldn't quite say why it was necessary), she thought he must feel much as those men who once frequented temple prostitutes in oriental countries, bodies relieved, but souls dancing, released as the result of passion.

Lessons passed much as usual. Lunch provided trivial small-talk. Nobody questioned her closely. They all knew she had married; they had contributed generously to the cheque which lay unspent in her bank, but beyond 'It all went well?' or 'How's rural life?' little information was sought. They knew, she guessed, that they'd waste their time to do anything else. None of them had met Tom more than casually. No one had remarked on her marrying a man twenty years older than she was, a rather well dressed fogey, an academic or one with pretensions in that field, who did not shriek with laughter at some faint stroke of verbal wit or some unpopular authoritarian's downfall. She had thought that Tom would have got on well with her Head of Music, and on the one social occasion Tom had visited the college, a departmental party, the two men had sat apart and talked for perhaps twenty minutes, to the amusement of her younger colleagues.

'Derek's giving him a right going-over,' one ventured.

'Do you think he'll approve?' another asked.

'What if he doesn't?'

Elizabeth had watched the two together. A mere four or five years separated them in age, but Tom looked young enough to be Derek Duggan's son. Both wore suits, unusual enough at these informal get-togethers, but Tom's seemed smart, well-cut whereas Derek's had the air of being much worn. 'If you took his jacket off and shook it,' one of the

44

irreverent younger men had said, 'you wouldn't half see the chalk fly.'

She had asked Tom how he had liked Derek.

'Not my sort,' he'd answered at once. 'Very straight with you. That's the advantage, I guess.'

'But?' she teased him.

'He seems quite content to live inside the limits of his department.'

'Is that bad?'

'No. On the contrary, There are too many amateurs and fly-by-nights in education today, even in my subject. And I'm not talking only about the ignoramuses, those who know nothing and won't be bothered to learn. But I'd have thought, and I'm speaking without my book, that with music it was different.'

'Why?'

'It's like literature. You're introducing students to master-pieces.'

'Yes, but in examinations they have to answer boring history questions, and do ear-tests and analysis of sonata form and the rest. It's like your subject. We're so busy drilling the basics into them, making sure that they know something that they can build on, that we tend to ignore the high points. If we asked some examination candidate to compare and contrast, let's say, Purcell's Golden Sonata with Beethoven's Spring or Kreutzer should we expect them to write anything that would convince the reader that these were works of the highest order? I doubt it. Ask 'em how long, how many movements, in what keys and you're getting somewhere.'

'Um.' His lip drooped. 'Your Duggan certainly seemed concerned only with the nuts and bolts. Everyday humdrum.'

'Like any teacher. Get the classes started on time, make sure you know who's there and who isn't, cover the syllabus not half of it, see to it that your pupils know what sort of answer is expected of them.' She hummed to herself. 'And I sometimes hope that they'll commit the great works they're studying to memory. That's the beauty, the expectation of it all. Some will; some won't.'

'He spoke very highly of you.'

'Good,' she said, with irony. 'I tighten the nuts up properly?'

'He said you were very gifted, and he hoped that Cavendish College wouldn't knock the talent and spirit out of you. He told me all about the 'Trout' Quintet you did with the Lombard. You played them off the stage, he said.'

'No. They're an extraordinary group. I'm nowhere near their class.'

'That's not Duggan's view.'

At one end of New Orchard Cottage a former owner had transformed a long outbuilding into a further sitting-room, and Tom had had this cleared and decorated for his wife. Her Steinway, her library, one of her most comfortable chairs, a Bösendorfer upright, her music centre and disc cupboards were moved in.

'This is your kingdom,' he'd said, gruffly, sounding uncertain.

'Won't you be allowed in, then?'

'No,' he answered. 'Not unless you invite me. That's why I've left the old carpets and curtains. You can change them, when you're used to the place.'

She kissed him, thanked him prettily enough and suddenly found herself overwhelmed with tears. He appeared startled, even affronted, shyly put his arms round her.

'What's wrong?' he had asked. 'What is it?'

'I don't know. You're so good to me.' Putting forward these two inadequate sentences released more tears. His sweater grew wet where she rested her head. 'I don't deserve it.'

They kissed, then made love on one of the old carpets. He suggested early in the encounter that they should go up to the comfort of the bedroom.

'You stop where you are,' she said fiercely, boring down on him. Tears still marked her intense face. 'None of your middle-aged foibles.' She pulled his hair, and they passed beyond coherent words.

With the post-coital coffee she asked again about the Bösendorfer.

'I just don't know. My grandmother acquired it somehow. She used to play quite a bit, I believe.'

'Did you never hear her?'

'No. We visited her in Hampstead, but never for long. Never overnight. So what with talking and eating the piano was never touched.'

'Not even by you?'

'No. Gran kept it locked. And I soon learnt that she wasn't keen on little finger-marks on the case.'

46

'Oh, dear.' Elizabeth acted mock-dismay.

Thomas has asked her advice, and had brought in her tuner to set the instrument to rights. She liked the round, mellow tone, and often played Schubert or brilliant Scarlatti on it.

'Your Gran knew how to buy a good piano,' she had said.

'My Gran knew a lot of things.'

This evening she put her car into the double garage, glancing at her watch. Five-thirty. Only five minutes behind time. She'd left her husband a note. From the kitchen came a delicious smell of cooking.

'Curry,' she said, pushing in. She put her bags to the ground. Tom came over to kiss her. They hugged.

'On the table at six,' he said. 'Good day?' He had already laid their places. She went upstairs. He'd already made it clear that he did not like either help or hindrance as he was cooking.

When they sat down, (he had served both the food and wine), he took his first mouthful and asked, 'Too hot?'

'No. Delicious.' They ate on, very contented.

'I've two pieces of news for you,' he said. 'First, George de la Tour rang, oh, forty minutes ago to ask if he could have a couple of hours of your time. He wants to do more drawings of you. In fact, he has it in mind to make you his Eurydice. He's been working on those sketches he did of you.'

'When?'

'As soon as possible. This Saturday or Sunday. He said something about profiles. It won't take him long.' Tom waited for her. 'What do you think?'

'I suppose so. I'm not madly enthusiastic.'

'Why not?'

'I don't like sitting still. And I wasn't altogether impressed by de la Tour.'

'Were you not? He's made a considerable name. Anyhow, think about it and then let him know. If you don't want to, I'll tell him.'

'I'll see.'

They returned to their eating, apparently at one. After a time she asked,

'What was the other piece of news?'

He put down his knife and fork, straightened his head.

'I'm going to act as headmaster in the summer term.'

'Great,' she said. 'Why is that?'

47

'Stephen Miles has been given one of these schoolmaster fellowships in the summer term. I didn't think they handed them out at that time of the year. But you never know with these places. They're a law unto themselves. But I thought what with Finals and May Balls and so on he wouldn't find enough to do.'

'Perhaps that's what he wants. An extra holiday.'

'Perhaps so.'

After a time of silent mastication, she asked,

'And how do you feel about it all?'

'Oh, I shall try one or two of my theories out.'

'Such as?'

'I think all headmasters and mistresses and principals should teach. So I shall keep my GCSE and A level History sets. And I shall issue instructions that I am not to be fetched out of the classroom during those periods.'

'And?'

'I want to see if my classes do as well. I shall have more time for marking, for certain.'

'I thought heads were up to their eyes in paper-work.'

'I don't believe it. They have deputies and heads of departments to take some of that off their hands. Of course some are energetic and like to fill their time in with bits of research. That's what Miles is going to do in Cambridge. Write a little book, drawing it all together.'

'Will it be valuable?'

'Not it. He'd have done better to teach science, his chemistry. But he wasn't keen; you have to work in a disciplined way. And I don't suppose that he'd like his efforts at pedagogy compared with those of his subordinates.'

'Wouldn't he do well?'

'Oh, Miles is no fool. He's clever. But there's no great advantage to be earned by teaching well. They don't draw up government league tables of teachers' results.'

'Could they?'

'They could. Heads of departments very carefully allocate examination forms out amongst their staff. As at your place, I guess. Except my sorts of school before this one have been used to entering pupils for important public exams for years, and were up to all the tricks. That was their strength, that and outside activities: games and societies.'

48

'I can see you're going to take all this seriously.'

'What other way is there?'

'You could just have an easy term.'

'I don't think I'd like that.'

'It won't be putting ideas into your head, will it?' she asked.

'Such as?'

'You might like it, and start applying for headships.'

'I'm too old. No one would appoint a man of fifty to a first headship.'

'Why not?'

'They want the young and dynamic. The innovators. The men of the future. And, moreover, these days heads have to do all sorts of jobs they never met before. They have to organize,' his voice expressed scorn, 'the finances of the place. They have to be well versed in public relations. Not easy, or so accepted wisdom has it, for old men, set in their ways.'

Elizabeth could see that her husband was excited, and encouraged him to talk. He had ideas, there was no doubt of that, and he'd need to examine them. She could be useful to him; a sympathetic face sometimes does as much good as a probing mind, especially to a man who is expert already. Still talking, they finished the wine, washed up, stood in the warmth.

'Are you practising tonight?' he asked.

'I did an hour or so in college today. I worked really hard. But yes, another hour won't do me any harm. I'm just keeping my fingers in trim. I've nothing else of importance to do.'

'May I come and listen? An exceptional treat?'

'Surely.'

Thomas poured himself a further glass of wine, loosened his collar a button, and settled in the armchair in her practice-room. It was comfortable in the place, almost hot, and she had only a single lamp on by the piano.

'What shall it be?' she asked, old fashioned in word and curtsey.

'Would a Chopin nocturne or two be out of place?'

She played three, nominating the keys, the first two in G minor, with a muttered opus number, 37, for the second, and then for the third E flat, 'your favourite'. As she finished this, she dropped her hands, waiting perhaps for a comment. When he said nothing, she glanced in his direction, and slipped briskly

49

into a Domenico Scarlatti sonata, following it with another, and then another all brilliantly played.

'Wonderful,' he said. 'This is marriage.' She had turned on her stool, and sat facing him hands between knees surprised at his last sentence. 'Would it be too banal to ask you to play that E flat Nocturne again? I'm afraid my taste is not very advanced.'

She consented.

'Why do you like it so much?' she asked. 'Do you know?'

'It makes me feel seventeen again. All my pianist friends used to play it. I imagine broken clouds blown across the face of the moon. I was unhappy, or perhaps dissatisfied then. Now when I look back those days seem marvellous to me. I felt capable of anything, and somehow I have forgotten now all the irksome discomforts and obstacles that I know existed. I heard a woman pianist play it. We were invited to a concert at the girls' school. Our sister school. The headmistress didn't want us there, great clumping, sex-mad oafs. But she let us in for the odd afternoon concert. I've forgotten the pianist's name. She wasn't very well known, but she played really well. And this nocturne was one of the things she gave us.'

'Why did it seem so good?'

'The place, the time, the opposite sex. It arranged,' Tom coughed on his word, 'my longings into an order, a perfect order.'

She thought about that, congratulated him on its expression. She'd married an unusual man.

'Have you any photographs of you at that age?' she asked.

'There are one or two about. Not many. We didn't use the camera nearly as much as we do now. There's one of me as a member of a cross-country team.'

'Were you a good runner?'

'Moderate. Nothing out of the ordinary. Just good enough to scrape into the team.'

'Did you like it?'

'Not really. I wasn't prepared to practise hard enough. I'd other more important things to do.'

'Such as?'

'Reading. Thinking. Day-dreaming.'

Again she felt surprise. She looked on her husband as a practical man, who'd been so from his youth up. She played

50

him Beethoven's Pathétique Sonata, which she was teaching to two examination pupils at her Friday school. He thanked her, congratulated her, insisted on pouring her a glass of wine, but it came again as a small shock to her to realise that her husband did not know this work. He would have been as taken aback if she had confessed that she'd never heard of King John, or Richard the Third or Queen Anne. Persons with these gaps in their knowledge would be only half educated. She said nothing. She had been brought up amongst people whose main talents were musical. Elizabeth felt a slight qualm that her husband, a good man, an educator, something of a scholar should have reached the age of almost fifty without having heard Beethoven's C minor, Op 13.

He inquired again about de la Tour's proposal to sketch her. She asked Tom to telephone, to arrange two hours on Saturday morning next, here at New Orchard Cottage. She felt unsure about all this: how she was to behave, how long she had to hold her breath and sit unmoving, whether she was allowed to talk. The painter arrived ten minutes late, to Tom's annoyance, but refused cups of coffee, said he'd like to start. She posed for him in an upright chair in the light of a south window, and he took his sketch book from a bag.

'Will you want a desk or table?' Tom asked.

'No thanks. Knee will do.'

Tom left; he was busy in his study with some paperwork from school. De la Tour seemed in no hurry to start, but sat looking, weighing her up.

'I shall have to stare at you,' he said. 'I hope you don't mind.'

'I like it,' she mocked.

Once he began to sketch, he worked hard, indefatiguably, occasionally sighing or breathing heavily, shifting heavily on his hams so that the chair creaked. After he'd done a drawing or two, he moved her and began again. He did not talk at all, until he had changed her position, again, when he began to hum, no tune that she could recognise, quietly but with energy. She was impressed by his concentration; his eyebrows dodged up and down as he frowned and once he opened his mouth and squared it, holding it stiffly open, baring his teeth. Clearly he had no idea of the exhibition he was making of himself. The end of the pencil compelled his attention. His eyes as he stared at her were red-rimmed, slightly swollen, ugly.

'Relax now,' he ordered. 'Have a breather.'

'Do I do it properly? Sit still, I mean.'

'Perfectly. I'm pretty quick. I couldn't keep still myself for above a few minutes, so I get on with it.' He had put his book and pencils to the ground. 'When we start again I'd like to do you walking or standing. Do you mind?'

'No. I go into a sort of trance while I'm sitting. I think about things.'

'Such as?'

'The lessons I have to teach.'

'The dinners you have to cook?'

'No. Tom usually decides on that. He enjoys organising, and cooking. We don't have dinner here every night of the week.'

'Do you like teaching?' he asked.

'Sometimes. I need the money. Don't you?'

'I don't dislike it. I go up to London one evening and one day every week, Wednesday night and Thursday to give classes. I tell myself that I can learn myself from the exercises I set the students, and I suppose to some extent I can, but then I think to myself that if at my age I can't learn sufficiently from my own performances then there's something radically wrong with me.'

By this time she was standing, and when he needed to adjust her position slightly he'd do it by saying what he wanted and then touching her with his fore-finger end. The touch seemed asexual as if he straightened a pile of books. She felt slightly disappointed; she had expected to be avoiding slight fingering of the breast or buttocks at least. He only shifted an elbow forward, asked her to incline her head, prim as a hairdresser. She had seen, quite recently, two of his nudes featured in a Sunday magazine, and though she judged them superb, they seemed the work of a lecher who dominated women and revelled in it.

'That'll do for this morning, thank you,' he said.

'May I have a look?'

He passed his sketches over willingly, but stood at a distance as she examined them. She admired the skill which suggested her features with a few lines only. Where he had drawn more thoroughly, had shaded in her face, her head took on the solidity of sculpture. That he could make so little do so much was a great

52

gift, she considered. In the first of the sketches of her standing he had drawn her in the clothes she wore, and then secondly in a thin silk shift which revealed the figure beneath. He had used the same change of clothing in the two drawings of her walking. In these she seemed to be stepping out, forward, upwards, on the way to light.

'Marvellous,' she said.

'Useful,' he answered. 'I hope.'

'How long will the panel take you?' she asked.

'Two or three weeks. I shan't hang about. I give it my full attention when I'm at it, but there's another picture I'd like to finish. Or to be truthful, that'll turn out to be two or three shots at the same thing.'

'You know that without actually trying?'

'I know, yes. They'll all be different. I want to try one or two things.'

'And what's the subject matter? Or is it a secret?'

'No, it's a cliché. A nude, from the rear, bending over to look into a bathroom mirror.'

'Have you done your preparation?'

'Yes. It's Ellen again. Ellen Woodcock. I did preliminary drawings last summer. She has a beautiful body still. You wouldn't think so under those tablecloths and rummage-sale overcoats she wears. She doesn't like stripping off in the winter.'

'All three will be oil on canvas, I take it?'

'They will.'

George de la Tour had sat down again, an elbow by his sketchbook on the table. He seemed in no hurry, ready to talk.

'Have you plans for these new pictures?'

'I have. I've a small exhibition at the Walker Gallery in London, and I've promised one for a six months' loan in York, then Leeds, then Bradford.'

'Will there be any advantage in that? To you?' Elizabeth asked.

'I hope it will get me some publicity. The stylish magazines might take it up. Both here and in the USA.'

Elizabeth frowned and spoke slowly.

'It must be very satisfying to be as famous as all that.'

De la Tour screwed up his face, horribly self-deprecating.

'That's not the way I see it. It's true I make enough money

to live on, and save even. My needs aren't great. But the sort of patron like James Hayman Muller, the man who's commissioned the Orpheus panel, is getting rarer.'

'Because of economics?'

'No. Because they like pictures different from mine. I'm considered old-fashioned, if I'm considered at all. I don't get half the mentions in the critics' columns that I had twenty years ago. They, the critics, are young men with their way to make, and they think that all that can be usefully said about my painting has been said by their predecessors.'

'They're wrong?'

'I think so. But then I would.'

'Do they know anything about it?' Elizabeth asked.

'That's difficult to answer. They've studied the subject, completed their degrees in Fine Art or something of the sort, and some of them have even done training in art schools. And, of course, in the course of their profession they've looked at a great many paintings. And read a fair amount, not counting each other.'

'So?'

'They deal in words. It's not the same as paint or pencil. When I'm working I'm trying out this technique or that. Making my way. Expanding or contracting my methods. Some critics understand this. Sometimes. And they try then to tie this up with narrative elements and the like. Some of them rattle on all the time about the subject matter. They'll be able to do that with this Orpheus panel. As they couldn't if I were an abstract painter.'

'What would they write about then?'

'Shapes and colours and spaces and tones and variations.'

'Which they'd also talk about if they were dealing with a picture which told a story?'

'They'd say so.' Again he pulled his sour face. 'Some of the best ones do.'

'Can you learn anything from them?'

'For myself, no. Not much. Though one can learn if you're that sort of person from anywhere, anybody; by watching, let's say, the merest beginner scratching about.'

'And you're not.'

'Let's put it like this. I'm a conservative. I'm not on the lookout all the time for something blazingly new or different.

I've learnt to do something, to put paint on in certain ways, and that's complicated enough for me. I believe, or hope, that inside my limits I am always going to surprise, delight or disturb.' He stroked his face tentatively, as if he realised that he was not explaining himself as clearly as he might. 'You're a musician. Take your J. S. Bach. The contemporary young men looked on him as old-fashioned, a fuddy-duddy. He'd write a fugue, or a canon, a thousand times better than ever they could, but they didn't much care for such worn-out, unpopular forms. Music had transcended such stuff. But now, nearly two hundred and fifty years on we can see how great Bach's achievement was. The young bloods were right in their time; of course they were. But now they're as out of date as old Bach is. Their forms have disappeared, or are as useless to moderns as crab canons. So. What do we conclude? That I'm getting old. And I don't like it. And I'm going out of fashion. And I don't like that, either.'

'Have you ever written art criticism?' she asked.

'From time to time, but it's not my forte. I'm as full of prejudices as the rest of them.'

He threw his arms out, a histrionic gesture, large, comical in itself, before laughing.

'Here endeth the lesson,' he said. 'Give your husband a call, will you? I must be on my way.'

5

Elizabeth's agent wrote to ask if she could take a fortnight off from Cavendish College in November to play a series of concerts with the Lombard Quartet in Durham, Newcastle and Scotland. They had failed to agree dates with John Dutton, the pianist, and she was now premier second choice. They'd play 'The Trout' at least twice and the Brahms Piano Quintet, Op 34. She consulted her husband and her head of department. Part of the tour fell in the college's half-term break, and if she could rearrange her private Friday lessons all would be well. Derek Duggan seemed genuinely prepared to put himself and departmental arrangements out to allow her to accept these engagements. She borrowed a miniature score copy of the Quintet from the college library, ordered a copy for herself which the man at the music-shop said he'd obtain for her in a hurry. Derek Duggan turned up the next day with a full-sized score.

'Did you have this at home?' she asked, surprised.

'No.'

'Then how did you . . .'

'I have my methods.' He walked away laughing, this imp of an organist. He soon put it about Cavendish College that she was to do a tour round English and Scottish universities with the Lombard. The professor at the university in Beechnall sent her an old tape one of his students had made of her Schubert performance there. It delighted her.

Her husband, pleased beyond measure, prepared himself to take over his school in the summer term.

'Are you excited?' Elizabeth asked. 'Or apprehensive?'

'No. Not really. Neither. I shan't be able to do anything out of the way. Quite a bit of the time will be taken up with A levels and GCSEs as well as school examinations. Their dates are fixed, and the public examination candidates won't be back except for one day to hand in textbooks. I've consulted the examinations-king, and we've drawn up a timetable for the school exams, as late as we dare. That's upset a few who say they aren't used to marking in such a desperate hurry and that they won't have time to go over the corrected papers properly, blah, blah, blah.'

'Is there any truth in this?'

'Yes. An element. They don't like change. And they like to complain, to let me know they're still about. So that I won't take advantage of my undeserved status.'

'Is it important?'

'Not to me. Schools are full of petty squabbles. People think they aren't appreciated, are being disparaged, not treated according to their worth. And this place is no different, except that it's pretty large so the noise of battle's spread round several different common-rooms. That could be bad if dissension or discontent were serious, but they aren't.'

'You sound pretty confident.'

'I shall only teach my exam forms for their last few weeks. Otherwise I shall be hanging about waiting for things to happen. Signing bits of paper.'

'And Mr Miles?'

'He's not with us except in physical person. His spirit's already in Cambridge. But the school secretary's excellent, so that all seems at peace.'

'I sometimes wonder,' Elizabeth answered, 'what you really think of that school of yours.'

'Ah. You have me there. You really do. It passes muster. Let's put it like that. It's catchment area is mainly rural so that the pupils are more amenable than townees; the exam results are passable, but we all seemed becalmed. I don't know.'

'I hear all sorts of stories of village children acting like yobboes or taking drugs.'

'A few. Possibly. Not ours. Or not many.'

They talked to and at each other in this way often, at meals, in the car on the way to the supermarket or a concert. This was a daily bonus, spending time at table and sink, no more than an hour at most, which they both enjoyed. They'd then disappear to their own work. Later, one weekend Elizabeth spent a couple of hours at a cricket match at Tom's school during his period in charge, when he felt he ought to make an official appearance, though Miles never did, but she found herself quite lost. She had no grasp of the game; the male teachers appeared to be playing

57

against the senior boys, but the teams were distant white figures to her, running or dawdling in the sunshine. She was introduced to members of staff, their wives, governors, parents, one or two boys. Eyes brightened, but they were too many to remember. One or two boys showed admiration, and one, a curly-haired boy with a red face, even attempted mildly flirtatious remarks. Old Tyler's choice of a wife clearly met the approval of the younger people. Elizabeth herself felt at a loss. She ought to have studied her rôle, but Tom had said nothing of that in their conversations. Phyllis Miles appeared but rarely; Tom had never considered his wife's part in the hierarchy of schoolmastery. It was as well, she concluded, but made no complaints.

In late March she had a play through at home of the Brahms' Quintet with the Lombard who were giving a recital in Newark. They called in for Sunday lunch, Tom doing the cooking, and then spent an hour and a half in the music room with her before tea and the drive to Chester. They expressed satisfaction with her performance, made suggestions; the leader marked her score, rather diffidently.

'If these don't fit in with your ideas, ignore them,' he said. 'They are only hints.'

They had a cup of tea, delicious sandwiches, large slices of fruit cake, and then, replete, surprisingly asked permission to rehearse Shostakovitch 8.

'It'll save us time, later on. And this room's ideal. We don't have to work too hard.' They talked little during rehearsal, but, she decided, each learnt from the playing of the others. They knew each other so well, that they could imitate phrasing or even atmosphere without words. If they did speak it would be one of them saying, 'Can we have that again? I got it round my neck', and giving the number of the bar. Now and then the leader asked them to repeat a passage, and twice the 'cello made suggestions, barely audible, to the viola, once demonstrating on his instrument. The others watched, listening, fully aware, saying nothing. When they had finished, they packed away their instruments, made their thanks and were out of the house, suitably muffled, in ten minutes.

Elizabeth not only felt intense excitement but was moved that her husband seemed equally elated.

'Not many people can claim that they've had the Lombard

Quartet giving them a private performance this weekend,' he had said.

'Do you think our luck has changed since we married?' she asked, kissing him.

'I hope so. Why?'

'You're going to act as headmaster, and the Lombard have taken me up again. They said they would a year or so ago, and nothing happened, but now they're doing so.'

'I think that if nothing had altered in our work, and we were just struggling along as usual, I'd still say I was very lucky. I did not anticipate I'd be so different. I didn't expect you to accept my proposal for one thing.' She laughed at him. 'No, I'm being honest. I thought I'd be hanging on somewhere in the skirts of your presence, if I can use this improper metaphor, glad to see you smile or acknowledge me now and then.'

'And here we are cooped up together in this out-of-the-way cottage.' She hugged him, kissed him, laughing. 'Each other's. You're not frightened, are you?'

'I can hardly keep my hands off you,' he said.

'Don't then.'

'I don't mean now, at this minute. All the time.'

'It'll pass,' she answered lightly. 'You'll grow out of it.'

Tom became suddenly grave.

'When you were playing that Brahms this afternoon you were a quite different person. I didn't belong there. You were elsewhere. It was Brahms that mattered.'

'I knew you were listening. I played the better because of it.'

'I don't think so,' he answered. 'You know I'm no judge of music.'

'You're argumentative.'

'I like to see things as they are.'

They stood apart from each other for a short period. The log fire he had lit blazed up in the grate.

'At my time of life you don't expect . . . no, you're not on the look-out for much. I'd settled. I had a job I quite liked. I was getting on with my little textbook on Edward III. I'm not saying I'd put all thoughts of marriage out of my head. I hadn't. But I imagined it as a sensible arrangement, oh, good, yes, but comfortable, humdrum.'

'Would that suit you better?'

'No. In no way. But I just did not envisage that somebody like you, young and right out of my class, would ever consider me as a husband.'

'You're a romantic,' she said.

'Who wouldn't be?'

'And as to "out of your class", well, you'll soon learn. I've all sorts of bad habits you'll have to put up with. Or wean me from. And I've already seen one or two matters with you, my man, that I shall have to change.'

By this time she was sitting on his knee, and love-making had begun.

They lay naked in the heat of the replenished fire, sipping whisky, in no way considering the week ahead.

A fortnight later Ellen Woodcock invited them over to 'The Hollies' to view George's panel 'Orpheus and Eurydice'. He was away, she said, in Italy for a month, but had given her instructions to contact them. They fixed the first day of his holiday, the third of Elizabeth's for the visit.

The Tylers intended to walk, but it was raining hard when they were ready for setting off.

'It's the car,' Tom said. 'So you have another quarter of an hour.'

They parked on the rough verge outside 'The Hollies'; Mrs Woodcock met them at the door. Her appearance surprised them; she wore a long, silver-grey gown, cut deeply away by the breasts; her hair had been disciplined to a shining surface. She greeted them friendly but unsmiling. The hall was dark, and smelt slightly of damp.

'Can I get you a drink, or will you go straight up?' she asked.

'We've just had one, thank you. We mustn't waste too much of your time,' Elizabeth said.

'Right. Stairs.'

Ellen Woodcock lifted the skirts of her dress and led the visitors upwards. She seemed to be wearing ballet shoes. Moving with long steps, energetic but awkward, she chuntered out loud but unintelligibly to herself. When she reached the small passage outside the studio, she stopped and said, as if justifying herself, with stark clarity,

'It's not very warm in there. I've kept the stove burning, but it's a big room to heat.' She flung the door open so that

it crashed into the wall. 'Let's have light.' She ran her hand
flat down the six switches. 'There.' Now she led them forward.
'I'm to do three things,' she said. 'Or so the lord and master
instructed me. First: to show you Orpheus.'

The painted couple still climbed, but had almost reached the
top of a rocky, uneven path and above them through a gash, a
gully one could see a torn oval of storm-dark skies. The rocks
rose jagged, black and wet, yet lit with the red of sunset or
fire. Both figures marched strongly on. Orpheus, in front, had
a fixed position of the head, under stress, but determined not
to look back. The fingers round his lyre pressed into the frame
as though all his trials could be resolved by the firm grip on
the instrument which had won him his heart's desire. One could
read the strain in the muscles of his neck as he looked towards
the sky. Somehow, Elizabeth felt, the painter had suggested that
the musician wanted to look back not to feast his eyes on his
beloved, but to make sure she walked safely in this dangerous
place. His legs moved confidently, but he feared for her perhaps
or for his own strength of will.

Behind him Eurydice stepped, and without striding easily kept
up with her husband on this wild path. Immediately recognisable
as Elizabeth she had something of the almost inhuman, divine
blandness, blessedness of the Madonnas of the great Flemish
masters, Jan Van Eyck or Hans Memling. Her husband had
served her well, rescued her, and she would follow in perfect
obedience and confidence. The dark clefts in the rocks close by,
the distant precipices, the mountains gothic with horror meant
nothing to her; she did not see them. She concentrated on the
back, and neck of the steadily advancing figure of her husband.
They had not much further to go before they emerged into the
upper air. In the next few minutes Orpheus would turn and the
solid, beautiful, dependable form of his wife would melt and
shred back to Proserpine's unreal realm. But at this moment
success seemed assured.

The whole panel appeared alive. The humans marched on,
step after strong step, but the mountains, peaks and depths round
them were not static, writhed, as if the landscape were in the grip
of some earthquake, no natural convulsion but one of evil intent
to force, tempt, throw this beautiful couple from their almost
achieved happiness. The oval of sky above offered no welcome;
black clouds raced, lightning flickered; Eurydice would never

breathe the freshness of the upper world under that disordered heaven. He, shocked beyond reason by his foolishness, would reach it, and the lyre he clutched and his voice would change, subvert nature so that trees would uproot themselves and follow his beauty of sound; the wild beasts would doff their ferocity and weep great human, humane tears at the sorrow of song until the musician himself would die, torn into pieces by the wild women.

'Good, isn't it?' Ellen remarked, flatly. Her voice jerked Elizabeth back to a cold Spring morning in green England, a place of trees and streams, but also factories and hospitals, an incongruous mixture of sharp purity and gross pollution.

'Utterly striking,' Tom said.

'The colour is so marvellous, and varied,' Elizabeth added, uncertain what to say.

'It's a masterpiece,' he said.

'Is Mr de la Tour pleased?' Elizabeth asked. She could barely tear her eyes from the panel, discovering every second some new powerful detail.

'Well,' Mrs Woodcock drew the syllable out into dubiety. 'You know him. He's never satisfied.'

'Eurydice's very like you,' Tom murmured. 'And yet it's not. It's angelic.' He did not falter over the word.

'That's him,' Ellen Woodcock said. 'If he painted you as the devil, you'd be devilish, but you'd still recognise yourself. Now, number two.' She led them over towards an easel, the back of which they could see. 'I don't think he's finished with this yet.'

'Is he always altering?' Tom asked.

'He would be if he had time. But he has such a number of commissions that he's hardly able to keep up with them. "Ellen," he says to me, when he's particularly cheerful, "when I get thoroughly out of fashion, I shall have the time to finish my pictures off properly."'

'Do you think that's right?' Tom asked.

'I don't know. I'm no expert. I think he can do as much in a day as most of 'em in a fortnight.'

They stood in a small line on the other side of the easel.

'It's nothing like as big as Orpheus,' Mrs Woodcock told them. They could see that. The painting was perhaps thirty inches by two feet. A naked woman seen from the back bent

62

over a sink to stare into a looking-glass. A curtained window to her right and on the same wall as the mirror glimmered with subdued light through its gauzy drapes as if to lessen the impact of the arched body. The reflection of the model's face shone dim but vital.

'Do you recognise that?' Mrs Woodcock asked.

'It's you,' Elizabeth answered.

'It is.'

'You're beautiful.'

'A bit broader in the beam than I like. He's done three versions. The other two he's lent out, though they're nothing like dry. The galleries know that. They'll know how to handle them.'

'Is this the best?' Elizabeth asked.

'I don't know. I think perhaps it is. It's the biggest. He said the shapes were interesting. I don't think he meant me, but the floor, the bit of carpet, that wall and skirting-board, the wall above the mirror.' Ellen pointed with her finger, not directly, drawing curved shapes in the air at each mention.

'Are you pleased with this?' Tom asked.

'Pleased? It's nothing to do with me. I'm a model, the model. If I wanted to get clean I'd use the shower or the bath. He thinks he's paying homage, he says, to Degas.'

'He admires Degas?' Tom, the schoolmaster.

'Admires? I don't know. He says he got one or two things right, if that's the same thing.' She giggled curiously, a clucking sound. 'You don't hear him praising anybody very much. He tells me, "They aren't doing what I'm doing, and that's the end of it. I don't bother whether they do it better than I do. You wouldn't compare vaccuuming a room with darning a sock, would you?" He says odd things. I told him, "You don't darn socks these days." But that's him.'

'What does it feel like to be part of a picture?' Tom asked.

'You should ask your wife.' Ellen pointed towards the panel.

'It's new to her.'

Ellen shrugged.

'Now, number three,' she said, and pulled open, not without difficulty, the top left hand drawer of the paint-stained desk, and extracted a brown-paper rectangle. 'There,' she announced. 'Number three. The best of all.'

63

The parcel was secured by a small piece of masking tape.

'Break it. Open it,' Ellen ordered.

Elizabeth did as she was told. Inside the brown paper, carefully wrapped in white, backed by but not fastened to a piece of card lay a page of de la Tour's sketch-book, one of the pencil drawings he'd done of Elizabeth, signed and dated.

'He wanted you to have that one,' Ellen said. 'I wrapped it up for you.' It was one of the more delicate attempts, with few lines and little shading, and yet the artist had caught not only her likeness, but the set of her head.

'It's beautiful,' Elizabeth whispered.

'Very good,' Tom muttered. 'Very good.'

Her shoulders, just showing, appeared to be naked.

'What do *you* think?' Ellen asked Tom.

'Very good,' he murmured again, as if displeased.

Elizabeth felt pleasure flush her face. She wanted to open the drawing again and study it, but Ellen had refolded the packet, and resealed it with the original tape. He had not inscribed the picture to her, merely signed it in the bottom right-hand corner with his initials. G de la T. To date the month he had used Roman figures.

Ellen shooed them from the room, and when they reached the hall said she must dismiss them at once, since she had a bus to catch.

'Can I give you a lift anywhere?' Tom asked.

'No, thanks. I meet my friends on this bus.'

'Where do you catch it?' Elizabeth wanted to know.

'At the crossroads.' Ellen pointed.

'It was raining quite hard,' Tom argued.

'I'm not sugar. I shan't melt.'

She dragged on a raincoat with a hood, changed shoes, hitched up her skirts and picked up two shopping-bags already standing prepared, banged both outer doors behind her, and set off at speed round the bend of the drive, shouting back, 'See that the gates are shut, will you?' As they drove into the road, then briefly parked for Tom to leap out and deal with the gates they could see Ellen advancing down the dip towards her stop. She had pulled on a wide-brimmed felt hat over her hood.

'The witch,' Tom said.

'I hope she doesn't have to wait too long for the bus in this rain.'

Back at home Elizabeth unwrapped her parcel on the sitting-room table. She had protected it from the rain. Tom hovered by her, and this slightly annoyed her so that she took her time over the job, unfastening each layer and folding that carefully before attending to the next. The drawing now lay revealed. Both looked at it. Elizabeth was surprised that she resented her husband's presence. She ought to share her pleasure with him.

'Let's have some light,' Tom said, breaking away. 'It's a dark morning.'

He switched on the newly installed candelabra; she walked to the window.

The drawing trembled in her hand; the artist had made her look not straight at him, but slightly away, giving her a kind of shrewd shyness. Her hair had been sketched in more detail than she remembered, and her eyes, darkly wide, had been drawn like nose, cheeks and forehead with the plainest economy of line. The neck, slightly shaded, stretched beautiful beyond reason, and her shoulders, represented by two unlifted pencil strokes seemed naked, though it must have been a product of the imagination. De la Tour had indicated no background, no wall or shadow, had drawn straight on to the ivory paper. The figure represented seemed to her the result of a clear appraisal and an immediate translation into lines, without corrections or second thoughts. Yet about it there was no sense of hurry; confidence reigned, both that of the woman's beautiful face and the immediacy of the artist's realization. Elizabeth held her breath, but not from choice.

Tom had now walked across, and stood at her elbow.

'What do you think?' he asked.

She could not speak.

'It's marvellous,' he said, helping her out, as if he understood her silence. 'He's very talented. It amazes me,' he waved an instructive hand, 'that he can make so little do so much.'

She murmured agreement; he waited for more.

'Do you like it?' he asked in the end.

Elizabeth burst into tears, though she could not say why. Suddenly she knew herself overwhelmed with a surge of pride, pleasure, surprise all commingled with annoyance at her husband's banal attempts to make her talk. She could not account for it; no words she could find could describe the uprush that had shaken her heart, dashed tears down her face.

65

Almost immediately she was herself again and in control. She dabbed at her eyes with a paper handkerchief, handed the drawing over to Tom so that he could have a closer reappraisal, stood back from the window and from herself. Her husband was singing; he often did, practising for the school choir. His voice, a pleasant baritone, was nothing out of the ordinary, but now it rang with the harmonics of happiness.

'My spirit sang all day. Oh, my joy.'

She looked at him, and laughed, out of pure pleasure.

'Gerald Finzi,' he said.

'The words, I mean.'

'I think it's Robert Bridges, but I'm not sure.' He looked hard again at the drawing, and then, first clearing his throat quoted, '"It is that your perfection set me free".' He spoke drily like a schoolmaster.

'Say that again,' she ordered. He did so. She waited, and not vainly, for a further explanation.

'It's a poem by John Wain,' he said. 'I used to like it. "Apology for Understatement". I hadn't thought about it for years, and suddenly I remembered that line.' He also recalled, but did not mention, that he had once quoted the line, in a letter, to Janet, his first wife, before they were married. 'It's the drawing.' He handed it back.

The moment passed, and soon they discussed the framing and mounting. She favoured a kind of brown wood, plainish, with a gold inner rim, and a widish mount, four inches, five below. They talked of preferences rather quietly, and then she ceded to him the making of the choice; he'd get it done, take it in Monday, to a place not far from the school.

'Put it away somewhere safe,' she said.

'I'll lock it up. We mustn't lose that. You'll write to him, will you?'

'Yes.' She laughed at her schoolmaster.

A week later the picture hung above the mantelshelf in the sitting-room, framed exactly as she had ordered.

'They've fixed the drawing in some way,' he had told her. 'I wasn't sure, but the man in the shop advised it. He said pencil marks disappear, and he also said I should photograph it, or he'd have it done for me.'

'And did he?'

'Yes, I've brought my six copies home, though I'm going to keep one at school. On my desk.'

'Mr Miles never went in for such eccentricities?'

'Not he.'

'How many children have the Mileses got?'

'Five. All close together. The last three at the university.'

'Poor Mrs Miles.'

'We rarely see her at any sort of function.'

'She's been too busy,' Elizabeth guessed, 'and now she's grown out of the habit.' She laughed. 'Do you think we should start a family?'

'It depends on you. I'd give you a year or two more before you began now that you're beginning to make headway with your recitals.'

'But if my career as a soloist really took off, then we'd never have children.'

'I don't know about that.' He stroked his chin. 'They're more likely to let you loose a few months if you're really well known.'

'I shall never be in that class,' Elizabeth answered. 'So we can forget it. What about you?'

'I've been thinking about it. I keep doing so.'

'And what do you conclude?' she asked.

'As usual. I'm too old. When a child of mine reaches the age of Stephen Miles's youngest, I shall be seventy.'

'But you're young for your years. And energetic with it.'

Tom Tyler backed away from the drawing and then took three large, determined steps towards it.

'When I first realised I was in love with you, and considered proposing marriage, this used to bother me.'

'But not for long,' she mocked.

'No. I was by no means sure that you'd accept me.'

'So you began early on a long campaign?'

He shook his head, and stood legs apart. He did not know how to answer her teasing, but she guessed that had she been a subordinate, a teacher on his staff, he'd have frowned, set his shoulders, put a stop to nonsense at once. She liked him the more, this vulnerable efficient man.

'You make your age an excuse for everything. Too old to be a headmaster, a father. What next? A husband?'

He wagged a finger at de la Tour's drawing.

67

'Too old to be the husband of anyone as beautiful as that.'

'That's only a likeness.'

They had discussed this difference of age many times, before and after marriage. It had become a set-piece, sometimes without much attempt at variation, and almost always initiated by Tom. Clearly it was important to him to let his wife see that he had seriously pondered the matter. She rarely let it trouble her. If they had a child, or children, in a year or two (and she saw this as a possibility in that she did not imagine her career as a solo pianist would prosper to such an extent that it would put an end to thoughts of family) then he'd have to learn to manage. Many fathers did. Genetically-based disorders were more likely in older men, but they'd have to risk that. And if he died, she'd have to struggle on with the upkeep of the children; there were hundreds of young women, teenagers many of them, bringing up children without the help of fathers or grandparents or anybody except the grudging state.

'Poor old man,' she said. 'You'll do.'

She was never sure that he felt any better for these passages of discussion, but did not shy away from them.

'Will you write to de la Tour to thank him?' Tom asked.

'I've already done so.'

'Where?'

'"The Hollies". I don't know his Italian address.'

'Good, good,' he said, the schoolmaster again, pleased with his pupil. 'I don't suppose you've heard from him.'

'No. Neither from him nor from Ellen Woodcock. I wrote to them both.' She grinned at him. 'Just to make sure.'

6

During the Easter holiday they had a weekend in Paris, travelling by train. Again her husband's enthusiasm for Euro-Star or Le Shuttle surprised her.

'I'd love to drive that,' he said. 'Think of the power and the speed.'

'You've never grown up.'

'I know. And in some ways that's a serious criticism.'

They wore themselves out in the sunshine, dashing from this place to that, marching round the great galleries of the Louvre, loitering in the Tuileries, with ice-cream, eating ravenously at night, running up and down steps at their hotel, on the métro, up the steep streets to the Sacré Coeur. Outside the church, sheltering in the portico from a shower, an old lady addressed them. She seemed to be one of a party, but had determined on her own way. She walked straight up to the Tylers as if she knew them well and announced, 'It's forty-nine years since I was here last.' She spoke in a loud voice, admiral on the quarter-deck. 'I was twenty-two. Now I'm seventy-one the day after tomorrow.'

The old woman turned about in the wind to look over the city.

'We were just married. The war wasn't long over.' She pointed, rather wildly so that Elizabeth had little idea of either place or district. 'We ate somewhere over there. Lamb, cheese and pancakes. I stuffed myself. And wine.' The Tylers mimed interest. 'It was beautiful. Wine. And a big meal. Not like England. This was a fling before we emigrated and settled down.' Suddenly she frowned as if she couldn't quite remember some detail. 'I don't know why I'm telling you all this. But it was so beautiful, so memorable.'

'Is your husband with you now?' Tom asked.

'He died two years ago. We lived in South Africa. He was a mining engineer. And I came back in January of this year to live in England for good. And I thought I'd slip over to Paris while I was able. It was this time of year. Easter. But that's a movable feast. Forty-nine years.'

'Has it changed much?' Elizabeth asked.

'I don't think so, though everybody says it has. Perhaps I don't recall very clearly. I went in here.' She pointed to the door of the church. 'It was the same. Dark and crowds of people. They have candles now. I can't remember candles then.'

'Perhaps they were in short supply.'

'Perhaps.' She shook her head. 'This is a very old building.'

'No,' Tom said. 'Not really.'

Elizabeth looked at the faded eyes behind the fancy spectacles. When the old woman was last here Tom was a baby in nappies. She glanced at his smart suit. Impossible to imagine. His legs would be sturdy, the infant's expression serious.

'Oh, isn't it? I thought it was.'

Tom said no more; he had made the necessary correction and that would have to do. At that moment the rain stopped and the sun came out, quick and amateurish as a lighting change in a school play. Though they could see the showers, grey sheets, in the distance, streaks of blue began to shred the clouds then dominate the sky.

'Paris in the Spring,' Tom said to the old lady, who did not hear him. She tottered away towards the rest of her party. The Tylers descended to the Seine, to sail and sightsee, hand in hand. They discussed their outings and rencontres.

'All clichés, don't you think?' Tom ventured.

'Yes.'

'But. New to us. That's a thing history has taught me. You come across what seems an utterly expected event when it's reduced to a sentence, but look further and it blossoms. It's complicated, like all human affairs, bears looking at.'

'So we're not wasting our time?' she asked.

'I'm not,' he said. 'You must speak for yourself.'

She kissed him. He seemed more satisfactory by the minute. Even when he had drunk too much, there was an air of rational control about him. He became larger than life, more hungry for love, but with both feet to earth, realising that tomorrow or next week his living had to be earned.

At the beginning of the new term, when he'd taken over as acting headmaster, his father wrote to say he'd like to call in on them. He was visiting an old friend in Kent, and thought it a good opportunity to see them; he suggested he'd arrive Friday evening and leave after lunch on Sunday. 'I hope this won't inconvenience you,' he wrote, 'but it seems the most sensible way of paying my respects to your wife.' He had not attended their wedding, claiming in excuse that he had been 'off colour' and did not like travelling in winter. He hoped they'd be good enough to send him a carefully marked map.

'Is this typical?' Elizabeth asked.

'Yes. He makes his mind up about small details in a hurry. This visit to Henry Fisher in Kent will have been arranged for months, but the call on us will have shot suddenly into his head.'

'Does he really want to see us?'

'You never know with him. Yes, he'll be pleased to look us over. He won't interfere, just make suggestions. He never quite knows how to occupy himself. My mother used to look after all the holidays, and outings. He travelled about the world on business, but that was all arranged for him.'

Victor Tyler had been an engineer, and had spent considerable time in the United Arab Emirates where he'd made money and built factories, bridges, roads, railways to some effect. He was sensible, had collected an excellent small team of colleagues and had made a considerable reputation, so that he was able to retire in some style to the Hampstead house, in which his wife prepared to play hostess to her friends. Janet, Tom's first wife, had been considerably impressed by their home and hospitality. He telephoned that he'd have a pub lunch en route, and arrive at two or thereabouts. Tom would not be home until after five, but Elizabeth rearranged her Friday lessons so that she'd be there to meet him. She spent spare time making preparations for their evening meal.

Her father-in-law arrived nearly an hour later than she expected, parking his brand-new Rover in the drive in such a way that Tom would not be able to get his car into the garage. He was smartly dressed, and, to her surprise, taller than his son. He accepted a cup of tea, and stalked rudely about the sitting-room, closely examining walls, furniture, fittings, pictures. He paused before the drawing of Elizabeth.

'That's good,' he pronounced. 'Who did it?'

'George de la Tour.'

'No. I've not heard of him. Is he well-known? Or local?'

He sat down to listen to her information, nodding. He seemed less at ease than her husband would have been.

'Well,' he said, 'this is the first time we've met. I couldn't get down for your wedding. I don't like travelling in mid-winter. His first marriage was in summer. And I wasn't well that time. I honestly don't know whether it's real illness or hypochondria. When you get to my age, and I was eighty last birthday, you don't know whether you're ill or just deceiving yourself. Betty, my wife, Elizabeth, the same name as yours, odd that, wouldn't have any of it. If she wanted me to drive her somewhere, and I said I wasn't up to it, she'd just tell me to pull myself together.'

'And did you?'

'Yes. Usually. I was younger then. She's been dead nine years now; soon be ten.'

'You miss her?'

'Yes, that's right. I do. She was the one who organized things. I spent a good part of my working life abroad. Mostly in the UAE, but in South America, Australia and one spell in the States. She knew her way around here.'

'Did your wife live abroad with you?'

Victor looked surprised, as if he was unused to questioning.

'Some of the time, yes. Not always. These Middle East Muslim countries are no place for a European woman, even with the best of air-conditioning. The social life didn't suit her. I'm not surprised. And we lost our oldest boy, Alfred, abroad in a swimming accident. He was a year or so older than Thomas. Seven years old. I didn't think Betty would recover. Tom was two or three at the time. We had just the two boys.'

Victor sucked in his lips, as if in anger, and drummed hard on the arm of his chair with the fingers of his right hand.

'She never forgave herself. Not that it was her fault, but she was there. Saw it happen. It meant she mollycoddled Tom. We sent him away to school, Rugby, but she liked to be at home for the summer holiday. He'd fly out at Christmas if it could be arranged. And Easter. But she insisted on being at home in summer. That's when she bought the Hampstead house from a cousin. With her own money. It proved a very good investment, when I came to sell it. But that wasn't the idea in the first place; it was to see something of Tom.' Victor looked across at Elizabeth. 'You're a lot younger than he is.

72

You must be. You look it. Janet, his first wife, was older than he was.'

'Do you see her still?'

'No. Didn't see much of her when they were married. When she came to work in London, she used to call in on us. Betty got on well with her. They were birds of a feather.'

'And you didn't?' Elizabeth asked.

'I wouldn't say that. She went out of her way to be pleasant to me. But it became clear that she was thinking of giving Tom up. Don't ask me why. Perhaps she didn't like the idea of living apart from him. But it was her choice in the first place. Betty and I lived apart for long spells. If that was part of the job, you accepted it. Tom was willing enough as a husband. He'd drive up to London, any and every time she wanted it. Perhaps she grew out of him. Betty didn't like it. She said so.' Victor Tyler suddenly jerked his head upwards. 'I oughtn't to be talking to you like this on my first visit. About his ex-wife. It's not tactful. Do you mind?'

'I quite like learning more about Tom.'

'Does he talk about her much? About Janet?'

'Not really. He's said things from time to time.'

'It hit him hard. He was getting on for thirty when he married. It lasted eight years from wedding day to decree nisi. And that's eleven – twelve – years ago. He didn't say much to me. And his mother died two years later. You knew that?'

'I knew that.'

'And he bought this place, and enlarged it. His mother left him money. He used some of it on improvements. But it didn't bring us any closer together. We'd phone once or twice a year, if one or the other wanted something. If I were in the vicinity I'd call in. But, well, we were our own men, finding our own way, such as it was.'

Elizabeth lowered her head to show she had heard. She could make little of her father-in-law's intentions, indeed whether he had any. He talked of his son as if of a third person who had no close connection with him, or her. He was trying, she could see, to be pleasant, but did not realise that the impression he made on her was unfavourable. He talked as if he had answers to every problem, as if there were no difficulties he could not master, see his way round. His voice had the same clipped certainty that she had noted in her husband's public pronouncements. Perhaps he was nervous, or used to issuing orders, or since his wife's death unused to easy conversation with equals.

In one awkward silence Elizabeth asked,

'Is Tom more like you or his mother?'

'Ah. You have me there. I've never considered it, really. In looks, no. He's not much like either. His brother was very like Betty. In his ways, I suppose he takes after his mother. She came from an artistic family. Her mother was a painter; she used to go off to Cornwall. She introduced me to the Lake District. Tom had her piano. Has he still got it? That's why he took to the arts side.'

'Would he have made a good engineer?'

'I guess so. You have to know how to handle people. On the site.'

'Is that hard?'

He seemed to detect no irony, and boasted modestly. Later, to her surprise, he asked her to play the piano for him. He commented favourably on the size and comfort of her music room.

'We have to try to keep the temperature and humidity level for the pianos,' she said.

She asked him what he would like her to play.

'Oh, I'm no musician. Something not too long and with a tune in it.'

She rippled through a Chopin waltz. He listened, still standing.

'Who wrote that?' he asked, briskly, as if perhaps she didn't know.

'Chopin.'

'And what's it called?'

'Just "Waltz". Opus 64, No 2.

'Brahms wrote waltzes, didn't he?'

'Yes.'

'Could you play one for me?'

She did the B major, the first of Op 39. The sounds of the piano clanged grandly about the room, a tempo giusto.

'I like that,' he said. 'Would you do it again?' She did so. 'That's what I'd call music. It has, as we used to say in the forces, "bags of swank". Very good.'

He asked about Betty's mother's piano, listened to her play a very short Chopin prelude on it, and then said, sternly,

'Nothing like as good as your grand.'

'It's different, certainly.'

He looked at her suspiciously.

Elizabeth smiling said she must go and see to the evening meal. He asked after the expected time of Tom's arrival, though she had already informed him of this.

'Where would you like to sit?' she asked. 'Dining-room? Sitting-room? Or in here?'

'Somewhere out of the way, your way.'

'I shall be clattering about in the kitchen. You'll find books in here. I can't let you have today's paper. We don't get one delivered right out here. Tom collects it on his way to school. Would you like a cup of tea?'

'Dear lady, I am used to looking after myself. I can occupy my leisure. I might just wander about, if you don't mind. Poke my nose into this or that. Or take a turn or two around your garden.'

Victor was still in the music room when Tom returned at about five-thirty. His father claimed jovially that his armchair had proved too comfortable and had induced an hour's excellent sleep 'It's a life-saver for old men', he told his daughter-in-law, who brought in a tea-tray for the pair.

As she worked in kitchen and dining-room she could hear the two men talking. There were few silences, to judge by the test-pauses she made by the door, and the conversation was shared equally, equitably between the two. She was pleased. Tom would get such information as he wanted from his father, and the old man enjoyed company. Three quarters of an hour on their own could do nothing but good.

Over dinner both seemed in excellent spirits, and made sure that they did not exclude her from their exchanges. Victor did not eat very heartily for a big man, so that his son chaffed him, but without rancour on either side. After the old man had gone to bed early, Elizabeth and Tom settled to exchange confidences.

'He's going straight after lunch tomorrow. He's calling on an old friend in London.'

'Why's that?'

'Last minute decision. He tries to cram in as much as possible. I used to think at the time that he daren't stop anywhere too long in case he found he wasn't enjoying himself.'

'He didn't seem difficult to entertain. Not awkward.'

'Well, he liked you for a start. He's fond of women, but

they have to be up to a certain standard. You went beyond it.'

'Standard?'

'Good to look at, for a start. And then not contradicting him too often. But within reason. He'll tell you he likes a woman who knows her mind; but she mustn't argue with him about things he's expert on.'

'Such as engineering?'

'Yes. Janet used to argue with him about, oh, science, pollution, medicine. He didn't like it.'

'Who was right?'

'God knows.'

'But you get on well enough with him?' she ventured.

'We don't meet often enough to quarrel.'

'That wouldn't stop you if you disliked one another.'

'No. But we've always hit it off pretty well. When I was young, he was abroad, and so only saw him for a few weeks at most in a year. My mother was responsible for me. He'd talk to me, ask questions about school, explain how he was building this bridge or that road, but in a dry way. I don't know quite how I saw it in those days. Perhaps I thought all fathers were like him. Oh, he was friendly enough. But he treated me as if I were a junior member of his firm. He didn't show much affection that I remember.'

'Did he to your mother?' Elizabeth asked.

'No. Not when I was about. But I don't suppose she minded. When they lost Alfred, and I wasn't very old, they tried for another child, but my mother miscarried. I didn't learn about that until much later.'

'Was he upset when she died?'

'In his understated way, I suppose he was. That was only ten years ago; he'd been retired for some time. And he grew, or had grown, to dislike change. He sold the Hampstead house. It made him a mint of money. I have some of the things from it here. Grandmamma's piano, the four-poster bed, the dining-room furniture. But he hung on to the flat they had in Kendal, which they kept for holidays. He used it more than she did, though she loved the Lake District, had spent a lot of time there with her mother as a child.'

'Is he happy?' she pressed.

'Contented is perhaps a better word. He's not ill; he's found

76

plenty of things he can do, and that suffices.' Tom rubbed his left hand up and down his cheek, quite hard, whitening the skin. 'Do you know, when I come to think about him, I don't know him very well. We've grown apart. We don't make much contact these days. Haven't done so since my mother died. There's not much affection, feeling there between us. There never was, really. I liked him. He gave me presents and sometimes told me interesting things. But there wasn't anything that could be called love. We were perhaps both deficient in some way.'

'And when you see him now?'

'He's an interesting old chap. I wondered how he'd like you. He's pleased with you, for sure, so perhaps we'll see more of him. I guess our attitude is quite common these days. People look on aged parents as on neighbours or colleagues. We ought to love them, but we don't know them very well. We know infinitely more about the people we work with. At one time we'd have thought this was wrong or unnatural. It's our sort of society. I see it at the school. The parents don't seem to worry themselves about their children. Or a goodish proportion of them. They leave it to us.'

'Hasn't this always been so? Your parents sent you away to boarding-school?'

'Perhaps it's a misinterpretation on my part. Parents such as mine sent their offspring away because they thought that it was money well spent, that the teaching, and the sports training and the moral grounding were good enough to fit us for the life they approved. I don't suppose my father bothered whether I was religious or not, except in the most limited sense. He never went to church, except for weddings or funerals. But he put me, or my mother did, into the hands of tutors who knew what was what. With our children, there's quite a sizeable proportion of parents who don't know what they want from us. Oh, they know a bit about GCSEs, and like to think their children will do well, but that's our job, not theirs. They don't nag their children about not doing homework, or looking smart, or being on time, or acting politely. That's my duty, they think. I'm paid for it.'

'You sound down-in-the-mouth,' she said. 'Acting as head-master doesn't suit you.'

'It's not that. It's meeting my father that's made me think about these things. And perhaps I'm exaggerating. Many parents do worry about the progress of the family. But I can't help feeling the number is getting smaller. And it's spread out through the social classes.'

'And can you do anything about it?'

'I'm by no means sure.' He coughed. 'My first task is to see that the pupils at Albert Ball know what their duties and allowed practices or liberties are inside the school. I want them to understand what my expectations are, what we'll put up with and what we won't. That doesn't mean they'll always come up to scratch; there'll invariably be some delinquents or bolshies, for this reason or that.'

'Did Stephen do this?'

'Yes. But I'm trying to tighten things up.'

'In one term?'

'Oh, I know it's a tall order. But it's worth a try.'

'What sort of thing are you thinking of?'

'I'll give you one small example. Litter. Everything is wrapped these days, and youngsters take a sweet-paper off and drop it without a thought. I want them to consider what they're doing, why it's unacceptable, and what are the advantages to them of clearing it up. We've laid on a scheme.'

'Is it working?'

'I think it is. Early days yet. But they're getting the hang of it.'

He outlined the practice, and mentioned other areas he intended to improve.

'Nothing too much,' he said. 'But on the other hand I must do something, make something happen.'

'Would you sooner be chasing these youngsters up than writing about Edward III?' she asked.

His head jerked up, and was lowered. He rested chin in his left hand frowningly.

'I think,' he answered slowly, 'that I can do both. I've even a bit more free time, I guess, for private reading and writing.' He lifted his head again. 'Which do you consider more important?'

Elizabeth looked puzzled, so that he began to explain.

'Which is time better spent?' he asked, earnestly. 'To improve the behaviour of a thousand or so schoolchildren or to write a small book that will be useful to a few hundred sixth-formers or university students with exams to pass?'

78

'I just couldn't say. It would depend which one you were better at. If you were more successful at history than headmastering, then it would be sensible to stick to Edward the Third.'

'You suspect that I can't manage both?'

'I suspect nothing of the kind. You are capable of both.'

He rewarded her with a swift smile, showing his teeth, quite altering the shape of his face.

'It does me good to talk to you,' he said. 'You flatter me.'

'I wouldn't marry anybody, you know.'

They went up to bed happy, holding hands like schoolchildren. He wondered what his father would think if he had seen them.

Next morning at breakfast, father Victor talked expansively, full of hearty life. Again he did not eat a great deal, but gave the impression of one presiding over a great feast.

'You're very comfortable here,' he told his son. 'But it looks better now there are women's touches.'

'Such as?'

'The picture of her ladyship over the mantelpiece. The alteration of those prints. And that mirror.'

'I didn't think you'd notice.'

The old man roared with laughter. He rapped the table top with his knuckles.

'Do you think I should sell my London house?' he asked Elizabeth.

'I didn't know you had one,' Tom answered for her. 'I thought you'd sold my mother's old place.'

'So I did. This is another.'

'Whereabouts?'

'Hampstead again. Not so grand as the other, but infinitely nicer.'

'You must be a millionaire,' Tom said, jocularly enough. 'Two houses in Hampstead.'

'Well, yes. I've spent some of it.' The old man matched his son in joviality. 'What shall I do with the money? That's if I do sell it. It makes a nice little income. Enough for me to live on, in my quiet way, even with all the expenses. If I sell it I'll get six or seven hundred thousand at least, but what good is that? What shall I invest in?'

'Pictures,' Tom said, pointing sagely at the drawing of Elizabeth.

'I'd need advice. Do you know I never bought a picture in my whole life. Your mother inherited quite a few, some of her mother's and her friends'. I often looked at them, with pleasure even, but if I ever went to a gallery or an antique dealer's with your mother, I'd no idea what to buy.'

'Didn't my mother even try to explain?'

'No. She knew my limitations. She never mentioned art to me. Nor music. And yet we got married, and stayed married. Forty-one years. Till she died.'

'And both as happy as the day's long,' Tom gibed.

'Well. Your mother was a remarkable woman. She saw the sort of nomadic life, if that's the word, I had to lead, and she geared her own to it. She came out to live with me from time to time; she brought Tom up, and his elder brother Alfred until he died. She suffered miscarriages trying to replace him. It wasn't easy. I knew that. But she hung on, put up with the setbacks and filled her life. She enjoyed reading as I never did; she attended classes. She'd learnt ancient Greek at school. I remember her reciting me a poem one morning over breakfast. 'The moon is down and the Pleiades.' By Sappho. Very short. I don't know why it stuck. I guess she didn't do it often.'

'Did she teach you poems?' Elizabeth asked Tom.

'Yes. Not that one. English poems. She liked to recite.'

'She liked the sound of her own voice,' Victor said. 'It was a good one, I'll give her that.' He coughed, cleared his throat with such vigour that his cheeks reddened. 'She was like her mother. And I guess Tom takes after her. Within prescribed limits, she knew her mind.'

'What does that mean?' Tom inquired.

'She knew her place in society; she knew what was expected of her as a woman, and a wife, and a mother. But she made space for herself, and filled it as she wished. I did my job, and any spare time I used up, enjoyed myself, but never like your mother. Any one occupation was as good as another. I played tennis, and badminton, and cricket and football and rugby, when people asked me, I went drinking and dancing, and walking and climbing and a bit of exploring, but always at the invitation of others. I suppose I wanted to show them I could do it as well as they could, if not better.'

'But when you were left on your own?' Elizabeth asked. 'It must have happened.'

80

'You'd be surprised. But a glass of whisky would do. And I could sleep well, even when I was young. I worked hard, in places where it took it out of you physically, and so I could drop off, if things were going well, even in adverse conditions. But my leisure was haphazard. It's only recently I've been thinking about this. Your mother seemed to have organized her spare time. Used it.'

'Wasn't the difference that she looked for cultural pursuits, and you for physical?' Tom asked.

'Yes, but she chose to do this or that. I'd turn out for the cricket team, or join somebody jogging or playing squash. One was as good as another.'

'Then you must have been pretty gifted at all of them,' Elizabeth argued.

'I could hold my end up. Yes. But now they seem young men's occupations. I played cricket into my fifties, and still have a whack at a few holes of golf or old men's tennis. But the time will shortly come when I shall be reduced to walking a few yards down the road to the pub. There are dozens of my age who aren't capable of that.'

'Are you a regular at the local, then?' Tom asked.

'I have my lunch there four times a week, and the other three I'll walk out for a drink at night.'

'Is the company good?'

'Not particularly. One or two interesting people. But like me, getting deaf or garrulous. Your mother would occupy herself with Mozart or Keats.'

'And that's better?'

'I can't help thinking so. Pehaps because I never had them. I don't know whether they make life any better for old people. Your mother was only just sixty-six when she died, and still pretty active. But you can carry Beethoven and Shakespeare about in your head when your legs have gone. That is, unless you're gaga.'

'The value of culture,' said Tom, judicially sarcastic.

His father frowned, cast about in his mind.

'I don't know,' Victor finally ground out. 'I've known some learned old men who were pretty miserable. Old age is nothing to boast about.'

'All passion spent?' Tom inquired. His father ignored him.

'I don't know if anything can make up to you for growing

old. When you're younger there's always something ahead to look forward to. Now if you feel a bit off one morning you wonder if that's the beginning of the end, the first faint sign of terminal illness. That's so for everybody, I guess, who's kept his wits about him.' He pulled his lower lip back from his teeth, in what might have been rage. 'But I can't help thinking that those like your mother are better off, when they're finally cooped up in their rooms and can't get out on their own, if they can take their pleasure from a book or a CD.'

'You can read Wisden, can't you? Or your technical journals?'

'I'm not there yet, so I don't know. I hope you're right, but I doubt it. When I look back on my life, I suppose I can count myself successful. I worked hard. I was lucky enough to do quite a bit in these oil-rich countries and so made a fair amount of money. I enjoyed good health, got on well with people, had a high old time, but didn't unduly waste my money. I had setbacks, like everybody else, disappointment now and then. But I could take you to places all over the world and point to bridges and roads and say, with a fair amount of truth, "That's where it is, and how it is, because of me."' He nodded brightly. 'Of course, Alfred died, but I was away at the time. And that was typical. Anything important in the family line was handled or decided by Betty, not me. She knew what I would want, I guess, but she had to make her own mind up. And that suited her.'

Victor smiled at Elizabeth.

'There am I, carting on. You don't want to hear all this stuff about old age and its aches and pains, do you? You'll come to it soon enough.'

'It's interesting,' Elizabeth answered, seriously.

'Is it? I'm glad. You'd soon get fed up with my grousing. But I've enjoyed every minute of it here. I wish now I was staying longer, but I have made other arrangements and can't change 'em now. Though Dick Hyndman whom I'm calling on in London would be only too delighted to be rid of my company. After the first hour.'

'You can always come again,' Tom said. 'You don't live a thousand miles away, and the civil engineers have knocked up some pretty fast roads between them.'

'It wasn't,' Victor said, 'that I was unsure of my reception. Tom's got a pretty smooth public manner, whatever his private thoughts. But I didn't know how you'd receive me. I'm not everybody's cup of tea.'

'Come again and stay longer.' Elizabeth spoke with warmth. 'In the holidays when we have a bit of time to spend on you.'

'I might take you up on that.'

Later in the morning Victor brusquely asked Elizabeth to play the piano for him again.

'What would you like this time?' she asked.

'That Brahms waltz. I was really taken with that.'

She rode through it with élan. He demanded it again. She repeated it with gorgeous panache. His face glowed. He sat upright with a young man's strength.

'Is there another as good as that?' he asked.

'The A flat's very well known.'

She played it through, dancing.

'I know that,' he said. 'I've heard it. I think Betty used to like it.' He whistled the first line to prove his credentials. 'Just one more good one. Have you a favourite?'

This time she gave him the C sharp major. He grinned and nodded as if he wasn't altogether convinced, nor exactly sure whether Brahms could entertain him longer. She closed the piano-lid. He nodded his agreement to that.

'Thank you,' he said. 'Wonderful. Tom's a lucky man.' Victor withdrew to the window, and stood with his back to her. 'Don't let me delay you, Elizabeth. I'm sure you've plenty of jobs. Betty was always pleased when guests kept themselves out of her way in the morning.'

He asked permission to make a couple of phone calls, and she left him to it. Soon after midday they went out to lunch, which the father-in-law insisted on buying.

'Least I can do,' he said.

'We're both working, you know,' Tom told him.

'And I'm a rentier, with not much to spend it on.'

They took a turn round the garden, now full of flowers, and then Victor announced that his bags were packed, and he was ready to go. Elizabeth kissed him and he hugged her briefly before shaking hands curtly with his son. He waved militarily and was gone.

'My word,' Tom said later, 'you please the old man. I've never known him so civilized. He's usually arguing about something. Or pointing out this fault or that drawback.'

'Do you know,' she answered, 'he'd folded up his sheets and duvet at the end of his bed?'

'Good for him. I wouldn't have thought that was very like him. Did he say anything about it?'

'Not a word.'

Some three weeks later, an oil painting was delivered to Tom Tyler at school. The day before, he and Elizabeth had received a letter from Victor thanking them for their hospitality and saying that he was sending them a picture for the cottage but addressed to the Albert Ball Comprehensive. He wanted somebody there to receive it, so it was no use posting it to New Orchard because there was nobody at home most of the time. 'It will be pretty solidly packed, in a wooden crate, but I don't want Tom to open it until he's back at home, and Elizabeth is there with him. It will just about go into the back of Tom's car. It's by Grandma Blane-Porson, Tom's grandmother, and will suit Elizabeth's music room to a T. Tell me if you like it.'

The crate was certainly substantial, and they broke into it outside the garage doors. They took the first look at the painting in the evening light al fresco. Tom propped it against the garage, and they stood back. The canvas was perhaps two feet by two and a half and portrayed a kind of jester in black and white motley with a dark, wide-brimmed hat from which sprang a golden feather. The figure, they could not see whether it was male or female, made a high step from the floor with the athletic right leg while both arms were thrown upward, fingers curled. The clown stood out from a background of dark, abstract shapes, a wild, youthful personification of energy against the dim variations of sombre neutrality behind.

'What do you think?' Tom asked.

'I like it.' She examined it again. 'Very good. Have you never seen it before?'

'No. Or not that I recall. But we don't know what he's got tucked away. That second house in London. You'd have thought I'd have heard of it, wouldn't you?'

'It must be recent, do you think?'

'He hadn't got it when I lived at home, for sure. Perhaps it was a bequest.'

'From his parents?'

'No. They both died while I was young. I don't remember them at all.'

84

Tom carried the painting into the music room, where they discussed positions and then hung the picture in a darkish corner.

'It could do with one of those small lamps above it,' she said. 'But no, that would spoil it. It suits the place as it is.'

He switched all the lights on.

'What about that, then?'

'Good. It's all good.' She kissed her husband. 'This is a real present. If only your father knew how much this has pleased me.'

'Write and tell him.'

'I will. And you?'

'I like it. A great deal. And even more when I see it brings you so much pleasure. Well done, Father.'

7

Elizabeth wrote almost immediately thanking Victor. When she attempted to show her enthusiasm, she judged the result to be gushing, girlish. She decided against altering her first draft, showed it to Tom who instantly approved. It took her father-in-law a fortnight to reply, a stilted letter which showed him in as much difficulty as she over tone. She immediately sent him a photograph of the music room, with the picture in place, and invited him to visit them during their summer vacation.

One evening a day or two later she arrived home expecting to start preparations for the evening meal, but found her husband at work in the kitchen.

'What's happened?' she asked. 'Has somebody blown the school up?'

'Not quite. They cancelled the choir practice. And there is another bit of news. But I'll tell you when we're eating.'

This was unlike him, but she fell in with his mood, and when he refused her offer of help, retired to the music room to mark and practise. She heard nothing of his efforts in the kitchen, though the meal was at least half an hour later than she expected.

He had taken trouble with the pork-steaks; the potatoes were roasted goldenly crisp. Three sorts of vegetables appeared, and apple sauce. He served white wine; she did not much like red.

'My, my,' she said. 'You've excelled yourself.'

'I wanted something to do,' he answered.

'I can always find something for you,' she said.

He smiled appreciatively, and began to eat. After a time, he put down his knife and fork.

'The headmaster called in today,' he said.

'Stephen Miles? I thought he was at Cambridge?'

'He walked in unannounced with the chairman of the governors.' Tom paused, obviously expecting a question. As none came, he continued. 'He's not coming back.'

'Why's that?'

'He's sixty. I didn't know. I thought he was younger. He'll be able to draw his pension. And they've offered him some sort of advisory or administrative job in Cambridge. I don't think it's connected with the university. It's one or a group of these language schools, I gather.' Tom chewed his lip, then returned to his plate. After an interval he began again. 'The governors are not sure that they'll be able to appoint a new head by September. By the time they've drawn up and published the advertisement, it's possible that an existing head of a school won't be able to work out his notice with his present authority. They, therefore, want to be sure that I'll be willing to continue in my acting post until the New Year.'

'And if you wouldn't?'

'I am willing.'

Tom settled back again to his dinner, helping himself to more vegetables, gravy, apple sauce. 'I'm enjoying this,' he said. Elizabeth watched him, interpreting his hearty appetite as an answer to the unexpected challenge. She congratulated him again on the excellence of his cooking. Not until he had cleared his plate did he speak. He'd do this as he wanted.

'Both of them pressed me to apply for the headship.'

'And will you?'

'Ah, that's it, isn't it?' Tom massaged his chin vigorously. 'Stephen and Williamson, the chairman of the governors, had discussed the retirement earlier in the year, before he went off to Cambridge. Not a word in my direction. They can't promise me the job. They will have to advertise. Stephen said they won't officially consult him, but he's made his views known to James Williamson and to Roy Green, the deputy chairman. All three are agreed that they want me. At least according to him.'

'But they haven't seen anybody else.'

'As I pointed out. Stephen said I had the right sort of background in schools that did well in the examination tables. That I was scholarly in myself, a very unusual thing amongst schoolmasters these days. That I knew the school well, and that I'd shown how to handle pupils, staff, parents.'

'And will you apply?'

He leaned back in his chair. By this time Elizabeth, who ate much more slowly than her husband, had cleared her plate.

'I'm consulting you,' he said, 'for a start.'

'My views don't carry much weight.'

'You may think not. But you may have very strong feelings about it.'

'Why should I?' she asked.

'Well, you may suspect that it will take up more of my time, that I shall have less to spend on you or the home.'

'That's one of the risks of promotion. You don't object when I have to go away from home to give a recital.'

'You don't do it often enough to upset the present balance. If it were two or three times a week, I might feel different about it. It can be important. My first wife, Janet, was an ambitious woman. She spent a great deal of her spare time on her law cases. But I was busy; we had no children to consider, so it worked out satisfactorily. When she decided to transfer to London, a move much to her advantage, I must say, I thought and I suppose she did, that our marriage was strong enough to stand up against the changes.' He drew in a heavy breath. 'But it wasn't. I was contented enough. It had its drawbacks. I had to clean the house and cook at weekends at home. We couldn't go regularly to concerts or the theatre together. I used to drive up to London twice a month at least at the weekend. She hardly ever came down to see me. Perhaps that should have made it plain to me that she considered the marriage over and done right from the time of her change of job. She wouldn't have gone otherwise. She made a lot more money here in Beechnall than ever I did. But I had no such suspicions. She wanted to get on, and I wanted that for her, too.' He held up a hand as if to stop any objection she might raise. 'I did say, I must confess, that I wouldn't move unless it was to a job as interesting and fulfilling as the one I had here. I don't know why I said that. Asserting my independence, perhaps. So it's possible it was my fault as much as hers.' He laughed ruefully. 'I don't know. When she finally divorced me, I threw up my job, and took over as deputy at the Albert Ball, which was nothing like as suitable. My pay was slightly higher, but the pupils were nowhere near as good.' Now he puffed out his lips, dismissing his own arguments. 'That's why I'm consulting you.' Fiercely. 'Now.'

'If you want it, go for it,' she said, at once.

'I'm not sure.'

'That's up to you. What I'm impressing on you is that if it means you spend less time here and with me, then you can disregard that. I shall be sorry, but I can put up with it.'

'You sound pretty certain.'

'I don't want you failing to try for something you want on my account.'

'Isn't marriage more important than work?'

'I doubt it. In the long run. The first depends on the second, doesn't it? It'll vary from person to person and from time to time. I can see that your fear that Janet's reaction, work, promotion, status all rated above love and marriage, is typical. And you do right to be suspicious. But I'm telling you to get on with your application. You say you're not sure, but I think you want the job; you're confident you can handle it.'

'Suppose I apply, and don't get it.'

'You'll have to learn to live with your disappointment. It might even be good for your character.'

They went over the same ground for the next week, and then he applied. She posted off his letters to his professor, now retired but still lively, to the High Master of Beechnall Grammar, to Stephen Miles asking them to act as referees. She saw to it that his application form was neatly completed on his word processor and then delivered, by her own hand, to the private address of James Williamson, chairman of the governors.

'Why do they want so many copies?' she asked. The school had demanded twelve.

'Saves them money. It's dead easy on our machine.'

'Will the education committee have any say?'

'I guess they'll have a representative on the interviewing board. Perhaps even two.'

'Do you know any of them?'

'Not really. Vaguely. I've met them.'

'Will they be in your favour?'

'I don't see why they should; and they may have preconceived principles that one doesn't appoint from within except in unusual circumstances. I just don't know.'

She made herself responsible for the typing of the paragraphs he had to submit explaining his views of a headmaster's rôle, of the place of a comprehensive such as the Captain Albert Ball in a rural society, of his ambitions for the school, of the changes necessary in education countrywide. Tom had written plainly and shortly, had not attempted to argue any case at length. The effect of this brevity was impressive; here stood a man who knew his mind, decent, liberal, prepared here and there to cede a point, but standing by principles derived from his urgent wish to improve the standards of education at all levels. In some way she could not quite understand his statements made without ostentation seemed to brook no argument.

After the application had been submitted, he spoke about it to her. Occasionally he told her what the chairman of governors had reported to him about the other applicants. A short list, very strong according to Williamson, had been drawn up and the final interviews had been fixed Monday and Tuesday, May 29th, 30th.

The strong figure of his introductory paragraphs had now disappeared, and he often muttered to her that he didn't know whether he had done right by applying. The tenor of his present views was that he had gone wrong in the first place by leaving his job as Head of History at Beechnall Grammar. There he knew his place exactly; he coached clever boys into the best universities; he built up his department from pupils he'd known since they were eleven. He knew how to beat off the challenges of the senior disciplines, classics and modern languages and the sciences, to encourage the brightest students into his department. His results were excellent. There were few social difficulties: pupils were there on scholarships or because their parents thought it worth their money to send the children to the school. Many of his old pupils had already made something of a name in the wider world. Moreover, he had had time to continue his own research. He had done badly, in the emotional turbulence of his divorce, to throw over so suitable, admirable a post.

'But all that was twelve years ago,' she argued.

'They don't change in fundamentals; not in that sort of school.'

'They must keep up with the times.'

'Yes, but they take advantage of all the changes. They know their way about.'

'Besides you have at least another ten years to do. Some sort of major change is probably good for you. You've done well enough at the Albert Ball. They wouldn't be encouraging you to apply if you hadn't impressed them.'

'I'm not so sure Williamson is quite as enthusiastic now that he's seen something of the qualifications of the other candidates.

'That may be so. But I wouldn't concern myself, if I were you.'

'Why not?'

'It's quite possible that he doesn't know his mind, one way or the other. I think the best thing is for you to appear to him to be above the conflict.'

He laughed, and flinched. She had never seen him so concerned or nervous. He might, from the sight of his twitching, be about to commit a crime. Elizabeth took his arm and they stood stock-still together, man and wife, by the kitchen sink.

A week before the interview Tom's father rang. Elizabeth was out.

'Have you heard,' Victor asked his son, 'anything about Janet recently?'

'No.'

'Has she been ill at all?'

'Since the divorce settlement was agreed, I've heard nothing either from her or her solicitors. We've made no contact. Not Christmas cards. No. Nothing.'

'Reginald Martin rang me from London last night, and said that her death had been reported. He'd seen it both in one of the nationals, the *Telegraph*, he thought, and one of the local Kent papers. A month or two ago.'

'Did it say what she died of?'

'No. Not as far as he could remember. He hadn't paid much attention at the time because he thought we'd know all about it. He was at your wedding, if you remember. She kept her maiden name for business purposes, and Foulkes was also his mother's name. That's why he remembered it. He knew you had been divorced.'

Tom was glad that he was sitting down. The news of Janet's death silenced and unnerved him. Breathing only with difficulty, he listened to his father's chatter. Reggie had just mentioned Janet's death amongst other bits and pieces, and Victor had had to press him for further information.

'He's no idea. I know he thought I'd have heard, but you'd think he might have cut the announcement out, just in case. The man's stupid.'

'It was just a notice, was it?' Tom managed. 'Did he mention who'd inserted it?'

'No, he didn't.'

'I wondered if she'd married again?'

'He didn't say. It took me all my time to drag this bit out of him.'

His father went on to more interesting subjects. He seemed in excellent spirits, quipping, darting from topic to topic. His son answered or questioned with miserable brevity.

'Are you all right?' Victor asked, in the end.

'Yes, thank you.'

'And Elizabeth? Is she in?'

'Yes, she's fine. She's out this afternoon at rehearsals.'

'Pity. I'd have liked a word with her.'

Tom spent ten minutes slumped in his chair, desperately attempting to account to himself for his weakness. He had been married eight years to Janet; they had lived, slept, planned, holidayed together. He recalled their first meeting, and his realization two months later that this clever, attractive, ambitious lawyer was in love with him. It had not seemed possible. His mother had taken at once to Janet; the two would talk at length, trot off together to exhibitions or open days at gardens or concerts. Both adored Wagner. Tom had chosen wisely; his mother knew it. He remembered the wedding in Yorkshire where Janet's father, already a widower, was a general practitioner. Betty cut a striking figure, made up for the absence, the loss of the bride's mother. She was stately, but not patronising, setting everybody at a decorous ease, adding what Tom could only, vulgarly, describe as 'class'. Janet, in bridal white, had seemed unlike herself, subdued, as if dressed for a part in a play. The veil, the train, the silk and laces, bouquet, the three bridesmaids seemed to have left her shy, subdued, unusually short of words. Tom had been surprised; he had expected her to look different, as she had, and magnificently, but this diffidence, this assumption of maidenhood, (she was not a virgin,) transformed her at once into a new sort of woman, and lifted the day's proceedings as it were, beyond mere human activity. When one of his mother's cousins, a Blair-Porson, had described the day as 'divine', he had concluded that what to her, he supposed, was a cliché, somehow exactly described this new Janet and this unique day. It had all been remarkable, beyond his expectation.

It had ended in tears. He had been batting, as the old head of history at Beechnall Grammar used to grouse, out of his league. But it had lasted six good years before she had left for London.

And now she was dead. Her mother had died early, with a cancer, and perhaps Janet had inherited some fatal genetic defect. She had always appeared strong, not only mentally but physically. She would have been fifty-two when she died. Had she been in hospital, or in a hospice after a long period of suffering? He had no idea, and he only tortured himself with these conjectures. Her death might be the result of an accident? Or suicide? He did not think that likely.

He leapt from his chair, and wandered about the house, angrily now. Janet Foulkes, whatever her faults, however much hurt she had inflicted on him, ought to be alive at this minute, pursuing her energetic way. What right had she to disappear, to be removed? The universe without her was incomplete. He had ranged the whole house twice, dizzy with uncouth thought, and now he made for the long garden path, the signs of Spring, these trees and shrubs which Janet had never seen, and yet had been chosen and positioned by the man she had so largely shaped. He groaned out loud. Fast walking eased him temporarily.

By the time he had prepared the evening meal, he had become calmer, though stabs of memory wounded still. He concentrated on his cookery; usually he was directed by interest, but now he followed instructions, or made his own tentative, slight alterations, as if a moment's inattention might ruin the meal.

At five, Elizabeth appeared exactly on time. She made a point of completing her rehearsals exactly as she appointed. People arrived when she said or went unattended. It meant cutting and slashing, harsh words, tears as well as praise, but she claimed that she could teach her students no more valuable lesson.

'Amateur music's like amateur drama, only half-time work if you aren't careful. They should come prepared, and they don't. You tear a strip off them. You know you could make an improvement by, let's say, another run-through, but you don't allow it because it will keep somebody else waiting. You cut them off in full flight, thank them, and call the next in. God, I have to harden my heart or I'd be there all night. I try to be efficient and set them a good example. If an hour is all you've got for practice then you have to fill it, really use it. And that's for the individual on her own. When you're preparing a concert, you've a dozen or a hundred preparing to go at their own slipshod pace, and your job is to train them to work properly. Only those who are prepared to exert themselves efficiently like this will get anywhere.'

'Aren't there some people so talented they don't need . . .'

'No,' she had interrupted him, 'there aren't. Not within my orbit. There may be one or two geniuses, but they never come to me for lessons. And even they, I guess, would profit from an efficient, well-planned régime.'

'But sometimes,' Tom had argued, 'with the best will in the world, one is interrupted; something unavoidable happens which makes your scheduled practice impossible.'

'Then you fill in what you have left. And the more disciplined you are the better you employ the few minutes you can have. We're all idle; we'd all step aside to do something that's momentarily attractive; we'd all sooner dodge dull work.'

Her voice had a powerful energy about it that seemed in itself creative. He wondered if this line would recommend itself to his interviewing panel. It reflected his own views, though he had reservations. He remembered his friend Jocelyn Browne at Oxford who had worked from six in the morning until ten at night, with breaks only for meals, and a short one-hour walk if the weather was fine in the afternoon. That effort, and an admirable memory, had achieved its objective, a congratulatory first in History. Browne doubtless with some of the topics knew more than his examiners, but on the few occasions he and Tom Tyler had talked together he seemed to his friend to be lacking in understanding. It had been difficult enough at the time for Tom to formulate his criticisms exactly. He thought perhaps that it originated in his envy of Browne's assiduity, application and the consequent accumulation of knowledge. History, Tom tried to tell himself, was more than a mere acquisition of facts and theories and their rearrangement into intelligible patterns. It should make the psychology of mankind, and the organization of its societies, the relationships between people, or peoples, the breakdowns, wars, alliances, forms of family life as well as nationhood, the religious ideals, even the clothes they wore interestingly alive, and if not altogether explicable, humankind was too complex for that, too many contradictions and mysteries abounded, at least bright with pointers, indicators to further study or understanding. Browne had been more like a machine, replete with facts or correlations or conjectures; one pressed the robotic button, and out came an answer with dozens of supporting illustrations, and because the man was clever enough, expressed with clarity, even energetic charm, but not somehow quite credible; Tom had felt that had this wealth of knowledge been applied to some modern problem not yet solved Browne's answer would be as likely to be wrong as right.

Jocelyn Browne had done well; for fifteen years now he had been a full professor, in two English and one American universities, and had within the past year been appointed to a chair in Oxford. Married, with a family, he appeared on television, and radio, blinded opponents with his wealth of knowledge, corrected them, and all with a quiet air of authority, in beautifully shaped complex sentences, yet still giving his old fellow-student the impression that human life was a game of chess, God knows complicated enough, but based on a few easily-grasped rules.

This was jealousy on his part, Tom decided. Browne had done, to perfection, what he had set out to do. They had last met at a conference only a year before, and Browne had seemed glad to greet him, treated him with respect, even as an equal. 'We got our degrees at the same place in the same year,' he'd introduced Tom thus to another professor. He'd praised an article of Tom's he'd read and remembered on East Midland priests at the time of Richard II. 'We could do with more work like that,' he'd said. 'It's a grim slog chasing up information, but if it's done thoroughly, as yours was, it really is valuable.'

Elizabeth appeared ready for the evening meal. He'd cooked a steak and kidney pie. As they had a moment before he served he said,

'My father phoned today. With bad news.'

'What's that? Is he ill?'

'No. Janet has died.'

'Janet?' The name did not appear to mean much.

'Janet, my ex-wife.' He intervened quickly.

'Oh. Has she been ill?'

'I don't know. My father had his information from a friend, who'd only given it half his attention. He'd seen it in the papers.' Tom explained about the name Foulkes as he served the meat pie steaming straight from its dish.

'That looks delicious,' she said, helping herself to vegetables and gravy. Then, diffidently, 'I'm sorry about Janet.' She began to eat, with enjoyment.

95

'I'm sorry,' he said, 'that I didn't know at the time.'

'Would you have gone to the funeral?'

'Probably not. But I could have given it a little thought.'

Tom looked serious, deeply engaged. She wondered whether he was recalling the years of marriage to Janet, or if superstitiously he saw this as a bad omen for the imminent interview. Elizabeth waited for him to talk, to explain but he did not. Dinner on Saturday evening was usually a feast, slow because of the constant interchange of ideas, the wines, the laughter, the sharp criticism they hurled at colleagues or politicians or artists, the events of the week now they had the time to spend describing them.

This meal stretched barren. They spoke, but no topic of conversation lasted above a few minutes. Janet's death loomed between them. Elizabeth had no idea what Janet had looked like; he must have photographs of her somewhere about the house, but she had never once seen them. The snippets of information he offered were short and added up to nothing like a clear tale. She was glad that Janet had never lived in, or left her mark on, this house, though she guessed that some of the furniture, pictures, ornaments must have survived from the first marriage. Once when they were driving in Beechnall he had pointed out the house where he and Janet had lived, but it was all over in a second and he had spoken as normally as he would if he had been speaking of one of the places where he had had digs before he had married.

They washed up together, but said little. Later he had said he'd go up to his study.

'I must get one or two thoughts on paper ready for Monday.'

'Good idea,' she'd answered.

Their love-making was perfunctory, and on Sunday morning he'd retired again to 'sort himself out'. They'd arranged to have lunch at The Mitre early, but the journey there and back, and the meal were quiet affairs. She fearfully watched him trying to act with his normal weekend joviality, to raise matters interesting to her, but he did badly. His mind flitted elsewhere; he had no heart for his own subjects.

After they returned he went out to toil in the garden. He wanted no assistance.

'You've plenty to work at,' he said. 'It might do me good out there in the fresh air.' He did not sound optimistic.

From time to time during the afternoon she slipped upstairs from the music room to spy on him. She caught glimpses of him, back bent, hard at work; at other times he was hidden presumably at the far end of his plot. Between half past three and four she ventured out to ask if he wanted a drink. Great white cumulus clouds sailed; the sun struck hot on the back. She found him weeding well away from the house.

'Hello,' he said. 'I've neglected this corner of the vineyard.'

He looked more cheerful. He sweated; there was dirt in his fingernails and a smear of soil across his left cheek; he had scratched his hair untidy and revealed the incipient bald patch. He grinned, more himself.

'Do you want me to come in?' he asked.

'No. I'll bring it out. Whatever "it" is.'

'A big mug of tea.'

'A dirty big mug of tea,' she said, encouraged.

'Exactly.'

She stood with him as he held his drink, fingers round the mug, handle ignored. His arms, thick with fair hair, seemed powerful. He looked formidable, as if his nervousness had evaporated when he had put off his suit and donned gardening clothes.

'What about supper?' she asked.

'Salad,' he said, 'but uncomplicated. No fancy work.'

'Fish?' she inquired. 'Sardines? Pilchards? Tinned salmon?'

'Fine. Spruce my brains up for tomorrow, eh?'

He was himself. As he sipped the hot tea, he explained his plans for this distant part of the garden.

'Ah, next year,' he said, 'you won't recognise it.'

In the morning he went off cheerfully enough. He wore a beautifully white shirt; that, he joked, should guarantee him the job. He wasn't quite sure of the time of his interview; he guessed it would be in the afternoon. The committee treated him as moveable; he'd appear at their convenience. He'd also have the job of welcoming his rivals, though not showing them round the school. The chairman and vice-chairman would do that. 'Williamson will have a field-day,' he said. 'Two, in fact.' The interviews would conclude some time Tuesday morning, and they'd announce the decision in the afternoon. 'Williamson will prolong the proceedings if he can. He's sensible in most things, but he does love the trappings of power.' The chairman,

97

to add complications, feared his deputy, a barrister, and the representative of the education committee, new on the scene, a Dr Richmond, was reported as a formidable personality.

They arrived back home almost together; Elizabeth had just emptied her case when she heard her husband come in. She did not rush out to greet him; he would not want that, however well or badly it had gone, and in any case the decision wouldn't be made until the next day. She waited a moment or two, straightening her belongings in the music-room, before she pushed open the door.

'Hello,' she called. 'Went the day well?'

Tom was sitting in a high Windsor chair, one he had never used before. He looked up.

'They haven't called me in yet.'

'Why not?'

'The man from Worcester couldn't make it tomorrow, and rang Williamson during the weekend and they arranged to see him this afternoon.'

'Was he any good?'

'One of the stronger candidates, Williamson said. He's already a headmaster.'

'Did he impress you?'

'I hardly met him. He seemed presentable. Didn't throw his weight about. Very modest. Not wasting his high eloquence on me.'

'If he had any,' she said. 'What's his subject?'

'A historian, I think.'

'So when do you appear?'

'I'm last. They've done four today. They started very late for some reason or another. It was nearly eleven-thirty. And they dragged the first one out. The others were more reasonable, just above half an hour each. I'm the final one. That would be sensible, Williamson said. Then we can compare the incumbent with the rest. "You're the sitting tenant," he'd already told me. It also means they can call me in at any time. If the other chap's late. He's due at ten. Williamson's having a high old time. "We'll do this. We can easily rearrange that. No problem." He's loving it.'

'You sound as if you don't like him much.'

'He's all right. Well intentioned. It's just gone to his head, but that will pass.'

'And what were the other candidates like?'

'Decent. All a bit younger than I am. Well-dressed, well-spoken, not saying much. One did just mutter that they had asked awkward questions at the interview. Richmond, the education committee man, was the worst.'

'Now you sit there and I'll knock supper together,' Elizabeth said.

'You won't. It's my day.'

'But . . .'

'But nothing. One of my famed omelettes. It'll give me something to do.'

Both were busy that evening with their work, but they spoke now and again, as paths crossed. They took a nightcap together just before they went up to bed. Tom seemed especially cheerful, saying he had made a very good start on some figures of absence in the school. 'It's an investigation into truancy.'

'Is it bad in your school?'

'No. We have rather less than most, I guess. Much less than city comprehensives.'

'Inner city, is that?' she asked.

'No. I don't think so. Any city comprehensive.'

Next morning he was up first, and brought her a cup of tea. He laid the breakfast table.

'Let's see. Tuesday's an easy day for you, isn't it?'

'My easiest.'

'Good, good.'

He left earlier than the previous morning, with a clean shirt, a different but still sober tie, his black shoes newly shined.

'You show 'em,' she said. She touched the arm of his charcoal-grey suit. 'I'll be back first.'

She was on the lookout when he returned that evening, carefully observing him as he moved from the garage to the front door. She could not tell from his walk, the set of his shoulders, the way he carried his briefcase how he had done in the interview.

When he let himself in, she ran into the hall and kissed him. He patted her absently on the back.

'They've offered me the job,' he said.

She kissed him again, hugging him, then danced him into the living-room. He watched her antics soberly.

'A congratulatory sherry?' she asked.

99

'If you'd like it.'

When she returned, he had sat down again in the Windsor chair with his briefcase propped against his legs. He remained so still that he might have been asleep upright with his eyes open. He smiled, and as they played with their drinks described the interview. He'd gone in at about 2.15 p.m. It had lasted just under half an hour, and had been easy and friendly. They'd dashed through his CV, asked about discipline, wondered whether the school's examination results could be improved. The man from the education committee had demanded whether the school was sufficiently protected against intruders, both during the day and in the hours of darkness. They had touched on the carrying of knives, on bullying, on drugs, on punishment. They had ended with suggested improvements. He'd told them what he thought, but his answers could not have been news to them, for all these topics were raised frequently at governors' meetings. He thought they'd had enough; he was the sixth candidate. They seemed jaded, even sleepy, and made no great show of arguing with him. At three-thirty Williamson and Green, his deputy, had come into the office to offer him the post.

'Unanimous,' Williamson had purred. 'You were head and shoulders above the rest.'

He had thanked them, and the vice-chairman had immediately left, saying the decision had been easy. Williamson then sent out for a cup of tea, and described how Robin Richmond, from the education committee, had queried their cheerful unanimity about the selection, but he'd soon been put in his place by Roy Green. 'I wouldn't like to get across him in court,' Williamson had said. The chairman had hung on for half an hour, sipping his tea, angling for thanks from the new appointee and for compliments on his sagacity.

'Are you glad?' Elizabeth asked.

'I suppose so. I'm not sure. I think it's what I want.'

'That's not like you.'

'I don't like change.'

'Even for the better?'

'I'm never sure that it is.'

Later he asked her to play the piano to him. She performed in high spirits, Bach to Shostakovitch, but at his request finished with the Chopin E flat Nocturne. She sat on his knee. Four times they were interrupted by phone calls congratulating him on his promotion. He looked glummer, shaking his head, but he kept the telephone in its cradle.

8

In the next week or two Tom Tyler settled into his work, as his wife continued to question him.

'Are you making changes already?' Elizabeth asked.

'No. I'm working on just as if Stephen were coming back in September. I shall start soon on next year's timetable. I've asked heads of departments to let me know of any changes they might want. They won't come up with much out of the ordinary, but I don't expect them to. We're a very big school, and we can't rush pupils from campus to campus. But I've given them a chance to say their piece before they make their claims.'

'Will there be many staff changes?'

'Not so far.'

'Are there some you'd like to get rid of?'

'Yes. Two especially.' He pulled a face. 'No, don't ask me to tell you who they are. I shall have a word with them.'

'Are they capable of improvement?'

'I doubt it.'

'Does that worry you?'

'I'd like it to alter, but it won't. All educational institutions are like that. There are lame ducks and people with chips on their shoulder, cripples of the system. Neither of my two is very influential. And we'll use them to the best of their ability.' He cleared his throat. She thought he was glad to have to put into words the difficulties he faced to someone sympathetic who would, moreover, make no attempt to suggest solutions. 'When I was preparing for the interview,' he told her, 'I came up with new schemes. But they were just words, ideas. That was important. Now I have to see how I can fit into these schemes the staff and pupils who are there, in the place.'

'Difficult?'

'It's all difficult. People's minds have to be changed. You have to know who to persuade and who to coerce.'

'And how about Edward the Third?'

'I've put him aside while all this was going on. I'm reading again.'

Elizabeth judged him to be happy but unwilling to admit it too openly.

About this time a musician, a clarinettist telephoned her unexpectedly asking if she would join him and his wife, a viola player, in a performance of the Mozart 'Kegelstatt' Trio. Both were former members of the BBC Symphony Orchestra, but had come to Beechnall two years before so that the husband could join his father's business which was beginning to expand very promisingly. He hadn't been sorry to drop the life of an orchestral player, and his wife now had a job as a peripatetic string teacher. 'It pleased me and Agnes, at the time, and my father,' and now he had taken to the new life, his father was in plastics; he was just beginning to look round. Out of the blue, they, or he, had been invited to give a performance in the summer, he named a date in June, at Leicester House, the home of Lord Longborough, of some suitable classical work. Elizabeth's name had come immediately to their minds because they had heard her 'Trout' with the Lombard.

'There'll be two performances, on consecutive nights, both for charity in the hall of Leicester House.' The man, who gave his name as Smithson, spoke like a businessman. They know how to entertain; she'd enjoy every minute, or if she felt like it she could arrive ten minutes before the performance and then walk straight out afterwards. 'The only thing that remains is to let you hear us, to judge if we're anywhere near your standard.' He made suggestions of a venue for the audition: at her college, at one of the music studios in town, or at his father's house about two miles from the city centre. She chose the latter, on a Tuesday at lunchtime. That was her easiest day and she could give them an hour or two without trouble.

The run-through was a success. The Smithsons were professionals, and had practised the music. She had not played the trio before, surprisingly, but the three quickly knuckled down to combining their skills and ideas. Mrs Smithson, she used her maiden name Agnes Woolf professionally, was an outstanding player and a personality. If she made a suggestion, invariably with modesty, she'd illustrate with a bar or two on her modern viola, and almost always convincingly. 'She plays for the composer,' her husband had said when Agnes was out of

103

the room. 'I just show off.' Edward Smithson seemed cheerful, outgoing, careful but optimistic. 'I don't know whether anything will come of this,' he said. 'I mean of a more permanent nature. I doubt it. I don't want to go back to orchestral playing or teaching. But Agnes has revelled in it. What we're doing this morning is as good as a win on the lottery to her. I came back here to Beechnall, because my father was expanding and he needed me. I'd worked for him before in holidays, so it wasn't altogether the culture shock you might imagine, and now I find I prefer my life in plastics. I make more money and meet more people. Suits me altogether better. But Agnes followed me down here. She teaches, but that's nothing. She'll build up a clientele of pupils, I expect. But she's a performer. That's why I made a move to do this E flat trio for Lady Longborough's party. She doesn't know a trio from a kick in the teeth, and I wouldn't bet much that her friends are any the wiser. But I coaxed, and she was willing in the end. But it's for Agnes. She's joined a couple of orchestras here, and she's tried to get a string quartet together, but playing for weeks on end with amateurs isn't exactly her style. She's no snob. It's not that. But to do this skittle-alley properly will be a great treat for her. I don't know if she really wanted to give her job up and come here, but she followed me. We've no children. She could have stayed in London. But she didn't. Like a good wife she trotted behind me to Beechnall. And this is the reward she gets. The first of many. So I hope you'll do it with us.'

Agnes crept back into the room, looking them over suspiciously. Smithson had changed his tune since the first phone call. Agnes originally had been glad to come north; now she was unsettled. A stout woman, with fair hair and Wagnerian braids, she stared at them with colourless, narrowed eyes, knowing quite well they'd been discussing her. She spoke in a musical, Home Counties voice, her wide mouth anxiously smiling. She had about her a Slavonic air, with her high cheek-bones and strong arms.

'We'll need to rehearse,' Elizabeth said.

'I am away all of next week and the week following,' Smithson said. Both he and his wife drew back, as if they'd be dismissed, Elizabeth thought; she felt uncertain.

'Can you drive?' she asked Agnes.

'Yes.'

'Perhaps you'd like to have a run-through with me one evening. Not the Kegelstatt, but your own stuff.'

Both man and wife smiled, broadly. 'Love comforteth,' Elizabeth remembered as she saw them, 'like sunshine after rain.' She had accepted them with the right words. Briskly she laid down her terms, places and times. Agnes chose a date.

'I'll come to you,' she said.

'It's rather a long way out.'

'That doesn't matter. It will be such a joy.'

Elizabeth, prosaic still, drew a map for her.

She told her husband about the arrangement.

'I shall free myself so I can listen in,' he said. He'd do no such thing, she was sure.

'She's a very good player. First desk of the BBC Symphony's viola section. And she seemed very grateful. I don't think she's managed the sort of playing she wants since she's been up here.'

'Why did she come? Couldn't she have stayed in London?'

Elizabeth listened, baffled. Had he forgotten his own first marriage, or did he think now that would have been wrecked in any case even if he had thrown up his job to join his wife in the capital?

'I don't know the details,' she answered flatly enough. 'They didn't say much about it. She perhaps thought her place was with her husband.'

'He's not had second thoughts?'

'No. My impression was that his father had been at him for quite a long time to throw up his instrument and join the firm. They're expanding, apparently, doing very well, and so it was a good time to get the son permanently in. And I also got the impression that his life as an orchestral player was beginning to pall on him.'

'But it's a very good orchestra, isn't it?'

'Yes, yes. But they have to travel around, and work in the evenings.'

'If he's in a prospering business, he'll work long hours. And probably have to traipse about the country. Are there no children?'

'No.'

'That's one important consideration out of the way.' Tom frowned. 'All very interesting.'

'I hope so.'

'You're not taking too much on yourself, are you?'

'I don't think so. The keyword today is "challenge". I expect you used it in your interview.'

'I did not.'

'Perhaps that's why you got the job. No, but every time anyone's asked why he or she's done something, up comes "challenge". Something that will put you to the test, that you're not quite sure you can bring off successfully.'

'But these things you'll play with the Smithsons, you'll manage perfectly well. You know that. They're not out of the way in terms of difficulty. Or are they?'

'No, but they're pieces I wouldn't otherwise look at. And if Agnes Smithson is as accomplished as I think she is, then it'll do me a power of good to learn what she thinks, and how to play with her.'

'But you'd be taking on new works, wouldn't you, even if you were left on your own.'

'Yes. I hope so. But playing with somebody really talented helps me along. You'd be surprised. That's why the Lombard excursions are so good for me.'

Tom nodded slowly, solemnly, in the style of a headmaster, an acknowledged wise man, an elder of the people. She giggled.

'Good, good,' he said. 'I'm glad. Marriage to me isn't making you middle-aged.'

'Was it likely?' Elizabeth asked.

'I'm well into it,' he said, 'and you might fall into the habit of trotting alongside me, rather than blazing off on your own.'

'Mightn't you chase off after me?'

'I hope I do, impossible as it is.'

As they sat together at breakfast on the next Saturday morning they heard a knock on the front door. They invariably enjoyed the more leisurely first meal on Saturdays, where they read their post, toyed with the newspaper, and talked with an energy sometimes missing after a long day's slog so that they resented interruptions.

'I'll go,' Elizabeth volunteered. 'You rest your aged legs.'

Ellen Woodcock stood at the door. She looked quite presentable, with no great eccentricities of dress; her hair had been carefully brushed, but her face appeared lined, careworn.

106

'I hope I'm not disturbing you,' she began. 'But George asked me to call.'

Elizabeth led her in, settled her at the table with a large cup of coffee. She refused toast, saying she had not long finished breakfast. She offered a remark or two to Tom, and then burrowed into her shopping bag, making a performance of it.

'Another present from the lord and master.' She presented a small, neat parcel to Elizabeth. 'He sent it back from Italy, with strict instructions how and where to have it framed.'

Elizabeth broke the framer's masking tape and unwrapped the parcel, to reveal a small pencil drawing of Eurydice walking, head back, in flowing, diaphanous robes which blew out behind her in a furious gust of wind from upper earth. This, to the best of her memory, had not been made from life, but must have been worked up from his other drawings. Economical in line, rather delicate, it had yet the strength of steel. Eurydice pressed saintly upwards, following the husband just outside the limits of the picture. 'To Elizabeth from G. de la Tour in admiration'; he had written the inscription in tiny letters. One could imagine Eurydice's snatching in a mouthful of air in anticipation of her final rough steps into the full light of the fields and rocks above.

'It's beautiful,' she said, and passed it to Tom, who stared hard at the picture.

'Very good,' he pronounced in the end, but without marked enthusiasm.

'It's marvellous,' Elizabeth contradicted.

Ellen Woodcock concentrated on her wide breakfast cup.

'You must have made an impression,' she said. 'He doesn't usually bother with sketches. Just keeps them in a folder, and puts that somewhere so that it gets lost and I get the blame. But not this. He gave the exact number of the framing material and the width of the mount. He's pretty careful about what's used to frame big pictures, but with this. Well. Perhaps he thinks you've brought him luck.'

'In what way?'

'He's sold the last version of the nude in the bathroom. You saw the ones, or two of them, he did here, but he had a further, enormous, glossier dash at it in Italy, so he said, and he's sold it for half a million dollars.'

'Who to?'

'An American. Some friend of James H. Muller, the man who commissioned the Orpheus picture. George was surprised. He said in a note that he seemed to be exploding back into fashion.'

'Does he write often?' Tom asked. 'From Italy?'

'No. He doesn't. Mainly instructions on things he wants done, or finding, or seeing to. But he put this news in so it shows he must have been excited. His agent had just concluded the deal. The Getty Museum wanted it. Whether they were bidding against one another I don't know. "Not bad for a month's work," George said. That's like him. Always talking about money.'

'Is he short, then?' Tom asked.

'I shouldn't think so. Not now, anyway. He lives in a right shack in Italy. That won't cost him much.'

'Did you know he was going to have another shot at the picture?'

'I'd no idea. He doesn't tell me what he's going to do, never mind write it down. He must have had his sketches with him, though I don't even know about that. He's a very good memory. Visual memory, he calls it.'

'He wouldn't use another model out there?' Tom asked, tactlessly.

'He might. To sharpen his ideas up. Or just because he fancied another woman about the place. I don't put that past him. He's got somebody else out there, I'll guarantee that.'

'How do you know?' Tom, again.

'I recognise the signs. I've been with him long enough. He's handsome. Attractive to most women. And he knows it.'

'I'll brew some more coffee,' Tom said. The two did not dissuade him. Outside they could hear him singing, 'And many the handsome of face, and the handsome of heart'.

Ellen Woodcock sat glumly, nursing chin and cheek in her left hand.

'I don't think he'll come back,' she said.

Elizabeth could barely keep her eyes off the drawing as it lay on the table in front of her. She touched it from time to time with her finger-ends.

'To "The Hollies", do you mean?'

'Yes. He's not said so. But now he's got this money, he'll buy a house in Italy to live in. His present place is fine to paint in, but he likes his comfort; if he can get it cheap enough. And

108

since he's sold these two big pictures, he'll be on easy street. He'll sell up here, as soon as he can.'

'He likes Italy?'

'Yes. Especially the light. Good for seeing, he says.'

'And he'll expect you to go out and join him?'

'That's what I'm not sure about.' Tears began to run down the stony face. So far not a tremor affected her voice. 'He hasn't made any arrangements. That's like him. Nothing definite for long enough, and then, slap-bang, in the hands of the house agents in minutes.'

'Would you like to live in Italy?'

'I've been with him once or twice. It was too hot for me in summer, though he didn't seem to care. But I don't know.' Now Ellen's voice broke. 'It's quite likely he's got some Italian woman to look after him. He keeps me here to see to the house. I've been with him for twenty-four years now. My husband lived with us for a start. He left in the end. He was always dodging off somewhere, and then he'd come back when he was short of cash.' Her speech had steadied itself to a controlled monotone. 'I stuck with George, because it seemed safer. Clark, Archie, that's my husband, hadn't any ideas except to racket around, and enjoy himself, and throw all his money away. They weren't alike except in one thing. They were both selfish. Archie was idle, whereas George worked away at his painting and drawing. He had to go and teach quite a bit, especially at first. But he grafted. Neither of them considered me. I had to wait on their beck and call.'

Ellen drained the dregs of her cup.

'Tom'll be back in a tick with some more,' Elizabeth said.

'I don't want to talk in front of him. I can tell you. Your husband seems nice, but I don't think men understand.' She mopped the tears from her face. 'George was wild when he was young. Shouted round the house. Came home drunk. He'd got rid of his wife, or she'd left him. He didn't say much about it, except to call her filthy names.'

'Does he support her?'

'I don't think so. She married again. She took some of his pictures.'

'As part of the divorce settlement?'

'I've no idea. I only know what I do because he complained

109

that she'd sloped off with two of the best pictures he'd ever painted.'

'What were they?'

'No. You have me there. If he told me I've forgotten. It's gone.'

'Did he ever paint her, his wife?' Elizabeth asked.

'Not that I know of. I wouldn't have recognised her, anyway, unless he'd pointed it out. And you don't have long conversations with him. He tells you bits and pieces amongst other things, like getting a plumber in or what he fancies for dinner.'

'I don't know where my husband is. I should think he's growing the coffee never mind grinding it. Why did Mr de la Tour move here? Has he connections? I mean, did he grow up here?'

'Not as far as I know. He used to stay up here with a man who lived in Worksop. Some well-to-do businessman who bought a picture or two when George was younger. And he got to know the place. And at the time he bought this house, he'd made a bit of money, and he thought you could paint anywhere.'

'Was he still teaching?'

'Yes. He didn't like to lose his London connections altogether.'

'And was it successful? Moving up here?'

'Yes. It was quiet. He spent some money on the house, getting it in good order. And there was plenty of room. A bigger studio than he'd ever had. He said he'd have to pay a fortune for anything that size in London. And it doesn't take long to get on to the M1. Once or twice he even set off early in the morning of the day he was teaching and managed it in time.'

'So he's happy here? Or content?'

'He's been here long enough. He's got so many pictures and things here, I didn't think he'd move. You never know with him. He's restless. He'd go away, and stay away longer than he'd said. And he doesn't always take the necessary financial precautions. It left me in difficulties, because I'm not rolling in money. But I'd tell him. And he'd cough up. There were never any mortgages to pay. He'd bought it outright, and had it done up.' Ellen glanced towards the door, but Tom made no appearance. 'George knows the value of money. His family wasn't without it. But he'd not throw it about, except the one or two times he'd had a rush of blood.'

110

'And was there a cause?'

'Mostly women. But money does make a difference. He's coined a great deal in these last few months. Ridiculous amounts. For some reason he's taking off in both America and Japan. His agent came up here and arranged to shift quite a lot of canvasses away with him. George grumbled. "Who'd want those old daubs?" he'd ask. But the agent seemed absolutely confident that he could do well with them. "I shan't flood the market," Mr Auger said. "When you're making money, so am I." He's an American. At least he sounds like it. And if there's all this cash flying about then it's likely he might consider settling in Italy.'

'He's not teaching now?'

'He's got a half year off. A sabbatical. They didn't want to let him have it, but they want him back, so they had to give in. "Don't know why, Ell," he said. "The bloke who's taken over is miles better than I am. He's a proper teacher." But that's typical. If anybody said the man was a better painter, George'd go mad.'

'What will happen now?'

'I don't know.'

'When he's sold this house, will he take you to Italy?'

'I doubt it. Once this house has gone I've outlived my usefulness.'

The door opened and Tom entered.

'Sorry I'm so late.' He put the tray of coffee on the table. 'Had a bit of a flood outside the kitchen window. Took a bit longer than I expected.'

'Is George good at D.I.Y.?' Elizabeth asked.

'When he wants to be. He says he hasn't the time. I think he quite likes knocking nails in and hammering and sawing, but not when he wants to paint. When he hadn't much money, he'd do repairs for himself. Very neatly.'

Ellen Woodcock gulped down her second cup of coffee, and left. Elizabeth accompanied her to the gate. Ellen thrust her shoulders back, put on a brave face.

'You're lucky,' she said, clipped the gate smartly to, and almost like a man, she walked down the road with a straight back.

9

Elizabeth and Tom discussed Ellen Woodcock's predicament all that weekend.

The husband seemed most interested in de la Tour's character, and whether the painter would be prepared to throw his housekeeper out on the streets unprovided for. Elizabeth wondered about practicalities. If it happened, and she could easily visualize it, she tried to think what Ellen could do. George, up to the eyes in some new scheme, or dazzled by his recent acquisition of wealth, could issue orders for the sale of 'The Hollies', and completely ignore Ellen's deserving.

'She'd get something as his common-law wife these days,' Tom suggested. 'I'll ask my solicitor about it. Or if it happens. I don't think he'd just leave her penniless. He's some generous urges. Look at the two pictures he's presented to you.'

Elizabeth grimaced at that.

'For some reason he found pleasure in giving me those. But if there was none, I could see he'd do nothing.'

Elizabeth did not exactly agree with her own argument. George de la Tour led an unusual life and this might lead to bizarre behaviour. She realized that she, why she did not know, had cast him in this extreme rôle. She and Tom took great pleasure in dissecting the man's character, though both had precious few facts on which to base their conclusions. Tom laughed at her vehemence, told her to wait and see. As he talked, she noticed his image of de la Tour grew more and more like him, a man of reason and justice. She accused her husband of being afraid of feminism, and he said he'd been avoiding the word all day. The argument drew her close to loss of temper, but he stood back from it all.

'You don't care,' she accused.

'I can see,' he answered, 'that you feel it deeply. But you ought to admit we're arguing about a hypothetical case. He's not done anything yet.'

'She thinks he will.'

'She may be wrong. I don't know enough about either of them. Your sympathy may be misleading you.'

'By the time it happens you'll say it's too late for us to do anything.'

'I don't think we can do anything in any case.'

'So she can walk the streets of London with no money? What chance has she of employment at her age? I guess she won't have any qualifications. And it'll take six months to get a testimonial out of George. And, then, God knows what he'll say.'

As they argued her ill-temper faded. He saw her point of view, but emphasized that neither knew much about de la Tour or Ellen. His gentle 'Let's not jump the gun' did not appear as a shrugging away of responsibility. She saw that he'd be good at his job as headmaster, in that he'd let people speak their mind, making it clear to them that he had grasped what they were driving at, and thus reducing the emotional temperature. Her pleasure that he understood her fears, her anger even, and approved of her spirit grew the greater because he managed to reassure her that if he could take any steps to right the situation he would do so. He did not step aside from the trouble in order to avoid action, but to see it more clearly. She kissed the top of his head, where the hair was just beginning to thin, and he looked up in surprise, delight.

In the next few weeks Elizabeth 'phoned Ellen Woodcock, asked her over for supper one weekend, and called in at The Hollies by invitation one Sunday morning. She was not altogether pleased; work was piling, term grew more hectic and the recital with the Smithsons was next week. Tom was away on a conference called by the Secretary of State and would not be back until Monday evening. Though she begrudged the hour at The Hollies', felt she could spend it better at practice in preparation for the arrival of the Smithsons that afternoon, she was curious.

The morning sun shone; light winds jostled the leaves. Elizabeth walked, and as she progressed further her spirits rose. She should be out on her feet more often. Hardly a car passed. She had to step aside into the cow-parsley on the verge only once. The driver, giving her a wide berth, still courteously acknowledged her precaution.

The gate of 'The Hollies' had been recently painted, and the gravel drive was in good order. Money had been spent on the place, whatever de la Tour's future plans. Outside paint-work gleamed. Elizabeth touched the bell. Ellen immediately appeared; she had been waiting.

'Would you like to look at the garden first?' Mrs Wood-cock asked.

'Right.'

They passed through the kitchen, large as a slaughterhouse, and out. From the terrace, the garden looked extraordinarily tidy in the morning sun. It consisted of shrubs, or large clumps, daphne, deutzia and an unpruned buddleia, hebe, cistus, with hedges high banks of cotoneaster salicifolia, bridal-wreath, high-reaching shrub-roses. Even the flowering plants stood tall, tree-paeonies, Californian poppies; while above these rose in scattered, pleasant order trees: cherry, Japanese crab, rhus, amalanchiers, apples, pears, fir-trees, a great forty-foot holly, two silver birches. The effect was of one of economy, patches of green resting the gaze, making no violent demands against the blue sky.

'Who does the garden?' Elizabeth asked.

'I do. This side, anyway. We have a man who grows the vegetables. He feeds us and takes what he wants and sells the rest. You can't see it from here behind that wall.'

'Wall?'

'It's covered with ivy. Behind my shed.' She smiled, well satisfied. 'He's got a smallholding over there just the other side of the lane, and he uses ours as an extension. It's to his advantage, as well as mine.'

'And you do this garden?'

Ellen explained that she had been in charge of horticulture since George first employed her, in the other two houses. She had known nothing about it, and her husband had been next door to useless. But she'd bought a book or two, and taken advice from neighbouring gardeners. 'They love to tell you and provide you with plants and seeds.' When George had moved here she had decided that she would use shrubs and trees and ground cover, St John's Wort and periwinkle, to save her back. 'I'm getting on now. Well, I was forty-odd then and this was the biggest house we'd lived in, and I knew he wouldn't pay for either cleaning women or a gardener so that I'd have to do it all myself. So I made him buy the things I wanted. He was fairly flush then. And I've gradually worked on it. It's not the blaze of

114

colour you'd get if I'd set out for a cottage-garden style, but I can manage this, and shall be able to do so for years, dependent on him, of course. And I'm not sure that I don't prefer it now.'

This summer morning, Elizabeth decided, there was much to be said for the choice. It seemed sober, but the variety was wide, and across the paths the scent of the buddleia alternifolia spread deliciously. As they strolled Ellen Woodcock named the plants and trees, occasionally with a garnish of botanical Latin, and seemed a different woman, calm, doing what she did well, at peace with herself. No eccentricity displayed itself; her plain dress would have suited dozens of middle-aged housewives in the county. One could see her beauty, now that George de la Tour had drawn the attention, but it was reduced, faded to the kitchen-level, that of saucepan or duster.

Ellen led Elizabeth indoors and to one of the sitting-rooms where they sat at a wide, round table to drink coffee and eat home-made currant biscuits. Ellen inquired about Elizabeth's engagements, and Tom's work in her best social style. She seemed a different woman, certain of her place in society.

'You can see that we've spent money on the house? He wrote and asked what needed doing, and told me to get an estimate. Then he sent a cheque, told me to bank it and make a bit of interest before I paid the decorator.'

'That's good.'

'I was suspicious,' Ellen admitted. 'I asked myself why he wanted the place doing up, and I decided it was to sell it.'

'Do you still think that?'

'There's been another development.' She sat straight, like a family lawyer. 'He's arranged that the bank should put a certain sum into my account every month. This surprised me. He's not a direct debit man at all. Pay up at the last minute's his line. But I suppose it's all this money he's made recently. He can afford to pay me to keep the house in order. I tell you another thing. If he had asked me the sum he should pay, I'd have named something a lot lower than the amount he fixed on. That's what makes me think he's rolling in it.'

'But it looks as if he intends to hang on to the house.'

'Yes. I'd say so. But you never know with him. He's likely to change his mind. He can stop the order to the bank. And he'd do it, if he felt like it, without saying a word to me.'

'You don't seem to trust him.'

'Trust?' She spat the word in disgust. 'He pleases himself. In every way. I was his mistress, but I expect you gathered that. Even when my husband lived in the house.'

'Did he know?'

'He's not daft. And he knew what I was like. But he never said anything. Not a word. And he used to be very jealous when we were first married. He didn't like the idea of me sitting for George. Nude. He cried about it once. "That dirty bastard's red eyes staring up you," he said. But then it eased off. I suppose he thought that's where our living came from. And don't imagine it was against my will, because it wasn't. George was full of life, and talk, and he knew how to make a woman feel like a woman. No. I suppose I was as bad as he was, once we'd started.'

'But it's over now?'

'Well, yes. And no. He had me a time or two when he was doing those bathroom mirror pictures. He never said much. Just got hold of me. He hadn't had a woman for a time, I reckon.'

'And you didn't mind?'

'Didn't make much difference, really. I've always had a soft spot for him. He had me more than once when my husband was actually in the house. That made it more exciting, I suppose. I was all for the thrills. I didn't owe my husband anything; he got more out of me than I out of him. I used to wonder what he'd say if he knew what George was doing to me, while he lounged about with his paper or his beer. Probably he did know, and didn't care. He wasn't mad keen on women, though he'd had plenty in his time. Sex came fairly low on his list.' Ellen grinned a wicked grimace. 'You don't think it's right, saying it all out frank like this, do you?'

Ellen waited for an answer, but her guest smiled vaguely, as if she had not exactly heard the question.

'You're young. And you haven't been married long,' she continued. 'And you respect your husband. He seems a serious man. I always thought that when I used to see him about. A suit man who polished his shoes. Not like George or my husband. If you paint you need overalls or something because you'll splash it all about. And up at his college in London George used to wear one of those long, linen or cotton coats, brown, not a doctor's white one, the sort greengrocers used to wear, so it didn't matter much what he'd got on underneath. And he needs to deal with the ordinary public. Archie, that's what we called him, his real

116

name's Clark, mixes with con-men and petty criminals, dodgers like himself, and George meets with rich collectors and gallery owners, eccentric people used to their own way.'

'I was surprised when I found Tom was fond of me,' Elizabeth said, naively.

'And marriage hasn't spoilt it? Not so far?'

'No. We're both doing quite well with our jobs, and I guess if you're pleased with yourself you aren't so likely to be quarrelling with your partner.'

'Partner? Aren't you married then?'

'Yes. We are. I'm his second wife. He divorced his first, and she died quite recently.'

'Did you ever meet her?'

'No. She was a solicitor in London.'

Ellen pulled a curious face as if this was a barely believable occupation. A tribal chief in Malawi or an exorcist in Zaire would be as acceptable. Her expression was both comical and revealing. She was not displeased with the turn of events, and so could enjoy this conversation with a neighbour she barely knew.

'And the sex?' she asked. 'Is that all right?'

'Good.'

'Hmm. There are some people you can't imagine stripping off and getting down to it.'

'You mean Tom, my husband?'

'Not particularly. No, not really. I hadn't thought of him in that way, I must confess, but that wasn't what I meant.' Ellen cackled; then frowned. There was something vulgarly straightforward about the woman. 'I can usually tell by looking who'd suit me. Not always. There was one old man used to visit the house in London. I won't tell you his name. He was a painter. You'd have heard of him. And he couldn't keep his hands from up my skirts. And he'd expose himself to me. About the house.'

'And were you . . . ? What did you think?'

'Think? I got used to it soon enough. He looked old to me then, but he'd have been about my age now. But he'd got this thin silvery hair and straggly beard. He had it away with me a time or two. But I was just beginning at that time to feel strongly about George. Romantically, you know. Marrying and living happily ever after. Not that that lasted long. I couldn't get rid of Archie. And George wasn't the sort to be making long-term commitments. So my life has been pretty mixed up.'

'But you've always lived with Mr de la Tour?'

'Yes. Since I was twenty-six or thereabouts. That's nearly half my life. Nothing else turned up. Nothing spectacular, anyway. And there was always some excitement about when George was at home. Even when he was working. And he did work. I think I've told you before that if he's got anywhere it's because he's put his back into it. He'd be sketching or painting all day. "You can't expect something for nothing, Nell," he'd say. "Or I can't, though some of 'em manage it." Even when money was short and he couldn't afford paint or new brushes, he'd still go on. "I'd sooner give up whisky," he'd say, "than paint." Though he always managed to find money for a drink from somewhere. He's not nearly as bad today. Doesn't go out to pubs and clubs. But he's been ill. A heart attack. And some internal operations. That's all slowed him down a bit. That's why he chooses to live in Italy in the winter. "I can breathe there, Nellie," he says, "without coughing my lungs up." Well, it's all one. He's still energetic.'

'Do you regret having stayed with him?' Elizabeth asked, to keep Ellen talking.

'Regret? No, I don't think so. What else could I have done? Got a job in a factory, or scrubbing floors, or on the game? No. And I've had time to read. There have always been books about. I don't know how much George reads, but he approved of books, and bought 'em when he could, and some of his friends presented him with signed copies. I had time to go through them. It was a struggle at the start. They didn't teach the likes of me to read whole books. You felt fed up after about a page. I had to make myself sit down for an hour or two, and stick at it. And then I got to like it. And I joined the library in London. I took quite a few books on gardening out from there. But it's mostly novels now. Sometimes George asks me about what I've read, and suggests a name or two his London friends have said.'

'Does he read them?' Elizabeth asked.

'I don't think so. He might dip into this or that. And he'll pull my leg. "You'll be reading Aristotle next," he'd say, "*The Nicomachean Ethics*." I don't know how you spell that, but I've always remembered it. It's got a ring about it.'

'I've never heard of it.'

118

'Oh, I thought you or your husband might have a copy at home.'

'I'll ask Tom. Would you like to borrow it if we have?'

'If it's not too long.'

'Has George read it?'

'He didn't say so. He had a good, old-fashioned education, he says. Latin and Greek and all that. He reckons he's forgotten it all, but it did him good while he was about it.' Ellen squawked with a kind of laughter. 'I don't always make him out. Not that he talks to me a great deal these days. He used to, more, when I was younger, but I'm like a piece of the furniture to him now.' She grinned. 'That's life.'

Elizabeth did not stay much longer. Ellen Woodcock seemed cheerful, and settled. She did mention a week or two out in Italy visiting George. 'He rang me up about a week or two ago. Surprised me. And I don't know if he was serious. I never do these days. Ten years back, I'd got the hang of him, I thought. It was before we came here, but after Archie had flitted.'

Walking back Elizabeth puzzled over Ellen Woodcock. The longer she had talked, the more cheerful the woman had seemed. She had spoken frankly, but without tact, considering neither her present guest nor her absent employer. Perhaps she liked to confide, to let her tongue wag in the right company. Her last words had been,

'There's only one thing makes any difference today.'

'What's that?'

'Oh, money.'

'Not good health? Or love? Interesting work?' Elizabeth queried, half jokingly.

'No. Money, money, money.'

That evening Tom rang from his conference, and announced his time of arrival on Monday evening. He wasn't much enjoying himself. Not five minutes later Ellen Woodcock telephoned.

'It just crossed my mind,' she opened. 'It's just about the longest day, and I shall go at midnight to the churchyard.'

'Why?'

'To walk about among the graves. It's an annual visit. No, more times than that.'

Elizabeth said nothing.

'I go about midnight and walk for perhaps half an hour.'

119

'Why do you do it?'

'You think I'm mad, don't you?'

'I don't understand you, certainly. Have you relatives or friends buried there?'

'No. It's nothing to do with that. I just walk about, and look about. The weather's warm at this time of the year, and sometimes it's not even dark. Tomorrow will be full moon, anyway.'

'I can see it's the best time to do it.'

'Yes?'

'But why do you go? Is it a kind of ceremony?' She could be frank.

'No. A sort of little adventure. It's something different.' Mrs Woodcock waited for further comment from Elizabeth, but received none. 'I thought you might like a walk around. But you don't. So forget it.'

Elizabeth smiled grimly into the silent phone. What would a headmaster's wife be doing, traipsing about a churchyard at midnight? She was tempted. Not that she expected to see anything extraordinary, but she wondered what lay behind this visit of Ellen's. And why had she invited her?

'Would you like me to come with you?'

'I beg your pardon.' Ellen's mind had obviously been elsewhere. Elizabeth repeated her question. 'Yes, please. That would be great.' She sounded schoolgirlish. They arranged to meet at eleven-thirty.

Elizabeth, feeling foolish, drove down to 'The Hollies'. She did not dare to walk there in the dark. The clouds were widely broken over a full moon. Intermittent shadows stretched black. Ellen had left the gate open for her.

'Would you like a drink before we go? Hot? Or alcoholic?'

'No, thanks.'

Ellen had dressed in what looked like a long, pale nightgown, and over this she pulled on a bright red coat as she talked.

'Shall I need a torch?' she asked.

'No, it's bright moonlight.'

They went out, along the white, shadow-barred road towards the village. Their footsteps clacked on the tarmacadam as they made speed downhill. The church, both knew, was situated perhaps a hundred yards back from the road and was reached by a small lane, wide enough for an undertaker's vehicles, leading to a gravelled circle in front of the lych-gate. This, they found, was locked.

'I wonder why they bother,' Ellen muttered. She had said almost nothing on their way here. 'It's easy enough to get in.' She moved to the right, touching Elizabeth's arm, gently urging her on. Perhaps forty yards along the churchyard was a kind of stone stile through the wall. They negotiated this without difficulty.

'It's very narrow,' Elizabeth said. 'The villagers must all have been thin when they made it.'

'I can barely get my bum through these days. I shall have to start slimming.'

'Do you come here in the daytime?'

'Yes. When I want a walk.'

They pushed along a narrow path through longish grass. There seemed few graves, or none, in this part of the yard.

'Didn't they bury them here?' Elizabeth asked.

'I think the early ones are here. I'm not sure. They didn't have monuments, or if they did, they've all disappeared. There wouldn't be many living in the village.'

'When was the church built?'

'I went to a lecture on it. About 1250, the nave. The chancel's older. 1200 perhaps. You can't see it from here. That's the choir bit on the end.'

'Have you been inside?' Elizabeth asked.

'Several times. For this and that. They keep it locked.'

The two spoke in whispers. Ellen marched in front, her arms swinging. They had now reached the church and turned right, then left again to the south porch. On this side were graves, flat boxes, ancient and moss covered. Elizabeth stopped once to try to make out a date. Sixteen hundred and something. The moon emerged, lit a standing stone up against the church wall. Arthur Horton, A.M., Rector of this parish. Wispy cloud temporarily douted the moon. Ellen had not stopped, but was now beyond the chancel walking eastwards. Elizabeth hurried to catch her. Ellen paused to look back.

'This is my favourite part,' Ellen confided.

Here the monuments were Victorian, but in better order, though Elizabeth did not much admire the lettering.

'This one I like.' Ellen pointed to a plain stone, rather low among the crosses. '"Ellen Annie Hoskin 1855–1901, wife of

121

John Hoskin of Silverstone".' That was the next village. John had no dates, was presumably buried elsewhere. Perhaps he had married again and the second wife had insisted on a new grave in which she too could be interred in her turn.

'Why do you like it?' Elizabeth asked.

'Same name.' That seemed little enough.

'Do you know anything about her?'

'Who?'

'Mrs Hoskin?'

'No. Nothing.'

'Where's Mr Hoskin? John?'

Ellen shook her head. The question had apparently not occurred to her. Elizabeth crouched down to see a short text near the ground, partially obscured by green mould. The moonlight suddenly brightened. 'Into Thy Hands', she made out. There was something curt, uncommunicative about this stone: no exact day of the month; no adjectives – beloved wife; no periphrasis – 'departed this life'. Space below the name was unfilled: empty for her death or that of children, if such existed. They'd be dead, now, for a certainty.

'When I first came here,' Ellen said, 'I was younger than she was. Just. Now I'm older. I don't feel old, but I've had longer than she had.'

'Is that what attracted you,' Elizabeth queried, 'that she had your name and was about your age?'

'No, I don't think so.' Ellen stood, staring upwards. She brought her head down to look at the still kneeling Elizabeth. 'I got into the habit of touching it for luck.'

'But why this one?'

'I don't know. It doesn't much matter which, does it? I don't suppose it brings me luck, anyway. It's near the path. But I always do touch it. You perhaps aren't superstitious. I am. And I need luck. You don't, I expect. You can make your own.'

'Oh,' Elizabeth said, taking a step back after she had stood, dusting her knees. 'It's a beautiful night. Balmy.'

'Like us.' Ellen laughed, idiotically harsh at her feeble word-play. She whirled her frock ends. 'I've another favourite.' She marched on, until she stood by a tall monument, like a miniature cathedral tower. As one approached one saw it as more of an elaborate canopy with gothic pillars, and from the path side, though it stood slightly at an angle to the other graves which themselves were not in straight lines, one could make out a standing figure; they had to step off the path, over three yards of shaven grass, to reach the tomb. No other part of the graveyard had been mown. Elizabeth peered at the inscription, but its position and the darkly hidden moon made it unreadable.

'"Sir Joseph Wainwright Thorpe, Bart, 1857–1931",' Ellen intoned, and then in a different voice, '"Harriet Adelaide, wife of the above, 1875–1961." Now I know who they were. He was a solicitor and landowner in a big way in Beechnall, and he was born in this village, the only famous man to grow up here. He gave money for the restoration of the church, though he was a Wesleyan. His wife wanted him buried in the village. They came to an agreement to have the grave looked after. In perpetuity.' Ellen grinned at the phrase, at its pretentious use by her. She'd had it from somebody else. 'George knew his grandson. He was well-to-do. Lived in Fairstone Hall. He bought a picture or two. He was in property.'

'Do you touch this for luck?' Elizabeth asked. The figure under the canopy appeared to be an angel, wings folded, pointing down at a book, the pages of which seemed blank in the darkness.

'No. I just slap it. With my hand. Always in the same place.' She demonstrated. 'He didn't want luck. We came down here with the grandson. It wasn't the first time I'd seen it. Creeping round churchyards wasn't exactly my cup of tea, then. But. Not now really, either. The grandson, Sir Wesley Thorpe, threw his weight about. He was dressed up in his tweed jacket and riding breeches and carried a switch, though he came in his Roller. He insisted on going down to see his grandfather's grave. Just to see they were keeping their side of the bargain.'

'And were they?'

'Yes, the grass was cut and there wasn't any rubbish, for once, at the bottom of the monument. If it hadn't been right he'd have thrashed the vicar, George said.'

'Would he?'

'I don't suppose so. That was George's exaggeration. He'd have kicked up a stink. I went down with them. He was very polite to me, and had praised my coffee and scones. George wasn't sure where the grave was. "You can't miss it," I said. But Sir Wesley said he'd be obliged if I went with them. He spoke in a very loud voice as if he was telling the whole world about it.'

'Did he say anything about his grandfather?'

'Just that he was a crafty old operator. That was the word. He and George went up to the studio, but he didn't buy anything, though he inquired how much George wanted for an ornate frame, a huge thing. "More valuable to me than to you," George said. "You know my own business better than I do, do you?" Sir Wes asked him. But George didn't sell it to him. He's another awkward one.'

'Did he use it?'

'No. It's still up there covered in dust and muck. And he wasn't exactly flush at the time. But he wanted to assert himself. That's the expression he always used when he talked about his painting.' Ellen moved back a step or two along the path, drawing the red coat round her tighter. 'It's not creepy at all here, is it?' she asked. 'It's like a family gathering except nobody's saying anything. Let's get back, shall we?'

They walked, without hurry, past the shadow of the church to the stile and out to the road. There it seemed colder and they increased their pace. Elizabeth had her work cut out to keep up with the older woman so that when they arrived at 'The Hollies' she glowed warm.

'Just a quick cup of something before you go,' Ellen ordered. They left the hall and found their way along a short corridor into a cramped kitchen, suitable for a small cottage.

'My den,' Ellen said. 'Where I can get away from it all.'

She made instant coffee, pouring out with a rapidity as if she had several hundred to serve. The room seemed bare, with rough walls; the curtains over the one window were summery. Elizabeth sipped in comfort, beginning to feel tired for the first time.

'I'm not mad, you know,' Ellen offered.

'I never thought so.'

'Not going out in the middle of the night to traipse round graveyards?'

'I joined you,' Elizabeth said.

'That was just curiosity, wasn't it, to see what I was up to?'

'I suppose so, though I haven't found out.'

'I don't know that I have myself. It's partly superstition, but it's something to do. That's a big part. I'm never sure what I'm up to exactly. I clean, and decorate, and work in the garden when the weather's suitable, but it doesn't add

124

up to much. I want George here to shout at me, and ask me where I've put this and that, and to compliment me on a meal I've served up. I'm only half there when I'm on my own. I guess a good many married people couldn't say that.'

They fell into an awkward silence as if Ellen feared she'd said too much, and was thus despised by her companion. Elizabeth wondered what she was about sitting here in the small hours. She put down her cup, clattering.

'I'll have to be away now,' she said, 'to sleep. Otherwise I shall be only half alive tomorrow, and I've no end to do.' She stood.

Ellen made no attempt to detain her, but led her out to the hall.

'It's cooling off,' Ellen said. 'Thanks for coming with me.' She put out her arms, and pulled Elizabeth into her. She planted a kiss, heavily on Elizabeth's mouth, then repeated it twice, holding the other close into her.

They walked out through the porch.

'Thank you again,' Ellen said. She seemed serious, weighed down, perhaps expecting some crushing rejoinder.

Elizabeth pulled the keys from her pocket, and dipped quickly into the car. She reversed and turned, but stopped by the gate to wave to Ellen who stood in white in the middle of her drive behind her. As she drove the few hundred yards along the road, she became bemused. The kisses were fierce, desperate, and she was sure that the other woman wore nothing under the nightgown.

The whole episode evaded explanation.

Soberly but at speed Elizabeth drove home and into the garage, made sure that the whole house was safely locked up, and threw herself into bed. She could not sleep; she did not know excitement, but lay dully puzzled staring past the undrawn curtains into the dappled blue of the sky over the row of lime trees.

The whole episode seemed both humdrum and yet entrancing. A middle-aged woman had led her round the graves, touching one stone, haphazardly chosen in the past, and had repeated by heart the inscription on the largest monument. Ellen had no earlier connection with this county, had arrived here on the whim of her employer, and now had contrived from these pieces of older, staider England a magic, a ritual to bring her luck. Did she believe this? Had she made it up merely to add entertainment to her friend's evening? Ellen had become a mystery.

10

Tom Tyler arrived back from his conference about seven-thirty on Monday evening. He seemed cheerful; the conference had improved by the minute throughout Sunday and by three o'clock on Monday afternoon had edged somewhere near everyday life. He sat down immediately to enjoy the meal she had prepared.

Once they had finished eating and had cleared the table he took to his armchair and began to read his post. Elizabeth stacked the dish-washer, straightened the kitchen, and laid the table for next morning's breakfast, before joining him. He sat, with legs crossed, the opened letters neatly stacked on the small table. He was not reading, but stared upwards at the ceiling, hands crossed on his midriff.

'Would you like a drink?' she asked. 'Whisky? G & T? Before I take my weight off my feet?' They had not drunk wine with the meal.

'No, thanks. Unless you want something.' She shook her head. 'Sit down, then. I'd like your advice.'

She took the chair opposite, and waited. He was in no hurry.

'I've had a letter,' he said in the end. 'From Janet Foulkes's solicitors. My first wife's. They traced me to this address through Beechnall Grammar School. She died, as you know.' He began to cough, histrionically, clutching his ribs. Elizabeth had never seen him so afflicted. When the bout was complete, he sat up, straightened the ends of his open collar and then with flat hands pressed down on his hair, either side of the parting. 'She has, it would appear, left me some money.'

'Oh.'

'They haven't quite cleared everything up, they say, but my legacy will be at the least one hundred and fifty thousand pounds.'

'My goodness. That's a lot of money.' He did not reply. 'Are you the main legatee?'

'I don't know.'

Now he handed over the letter which she read. It gave the news briefly, and a slightly longer paragraph apologized for the delay, and described, complacently, their attempts to trace him.

'Since we divorced I've heard nothing of Janet. She made no attempt to get in touch with me.'

'Did she marry again?'

'Not by the look of this letter.' This had referred to her as Janet Kerr Anne Foulkes, (Mrs T. F. Tyler.)

'It's from her solicitor? Not from her own firm?'

'No. It appears not. I don't know if that's usual. She did not use a member of her own group for the divorce.'

'Did you expect a legacy from her?'

'I didn't expect her to die. She's only two years older than I am. The whole thing's beyond me. I don't know, I think I told you this, whether it was the result of illness or accident. Her mother died quite young, in her forties, with cancer.'

'She'd no brothers or sisters?'

'No.'

'Relatives?'

'I've no idea. Her father was still alive when we divorced. If he still is, he'll be in his eighties now. He made no attempt to get in touch with me at the time we parted.'

'Was he rich?'

'Not particularly. He'd a very nice house in Yorkshire. He was a country GP. I don't suppose he's the source of Janet's wealth, if wealth it is. If she's left her all to me, then it wouldn't buy much of a house in London. And she had an eye for property. Both aesthetic and financial.'

'You're puzzled?'

'I am. I did not expect to hear anything more of Janet except by chance. She chose to divorce me. I didn't want it, didn't see the necessity, but she was adamant. According to her our marriage was over. She wanted me when she first went to London to look for a job up there, but I wasn't willing. I'd just taken over the history department at Beechnall Grammar, and I wanted to get that straight. Perhaps if I'd agreed things would have been different. I don't know. I doubt it.'

'She was devoted to her work?' Elizabeth asked.

'Yes. She was. Dedicated. She put her work first even when we were in Beechnall.'

'But you were happy?'

'Yes. If she wasn't back on time, there'd be sensible reasons. She wanted to get on, and get on she did. For a woman, and from the provinces, to be offered a place and then a partnership in a large London office is unusual. Somebody must have judged and talked about her to her advantage.'

'Who?'

'For a start, the head of Houldsworth's, where she worked in Beechnall. He had influential connections. He held some fairly senior place on the councils, the Law Society. He was often in town.'

'Was he an old man?'

'No. Forties. Fifty at the outside. But he had a lot of energy, involved himself in all sorts of activities. And he liked his young people to get on, to improve themselves. It all happened rather quickly. Looking back on it now I guess this London firm for whatever reason wanted a fairly experienced youngish woman lawyer, and Howard Houldsworth put Janet's name in the hat. It didn't take long. I'd say two months from the time she first mentioned it to me to the transfer. Solicitors can get a move on when they feel like it.'

'You didn't argue against it?'

'No, why should I? Our marriage seemed to be stable, everything going admirably. I had the job I wanted so why should I begrudge her advancement?'

'But you'd be living apart.'

'On the whole we only did things together on Saturdays and Sundays. We both had fairly demanding jobs. I didn't mind doing little extras about the house. And when she moved to London it was I who used to travel up there. I don't think she came down more than twice. She still continued to pay part of the mortgage on our Beechnall home.'

'Did that make any difference, do you think?'

'I don't think so. But them I may be wrong. She *was* paying for her London flat, an uncomfortable dump in my eyes. It came as a surprise when she announced she wanted a divorce.'

'Was she a balanced sort of woman? Or given to these quick decisions?'

'Eminently sane, I'd have said. Of course, when an opportunity presented itself she weighed it all up, and took her chance.

Quite ruthless. But perhaps I'm biased against her. She knew her mind. Once it was sorted out that was that.'

'Things like marriage aren't so easily weighed up, are they?' Elizabeth asked.

'Janet thought so. As I've told you, it came as a complete surprise to me. Between one visit and the next, a matter of weeks, if I remember properly, and during that period I'd phoned several times and had written twice.'

'There was nobody else? No other man?'

'Not as far as I know.'

'And you'd done or said nothing to drive her to this?'

'Not at all. Except for my refusal to move to London.'

'On the occasion when she broke it to you, did she seem distressed, or angry?'

'No. I remember clearly. That day's etched into my mind, I can tell you. It was fearfully cold, January. And snowing slightly when I reached the flat. It struck beautifully warm inside. She made me a cup of tea, and sat me down. She seemed as normal. She wasn't ever an effusive sort, but she was as welcoming as she usually was. She dodged in and out, preparing for the evening meal, I thought, excusing herself. I didn't see anything out of the ordinary. After about half an hour she came in, sat down, and said there was something we ought to discuss.'

'Quietly?'

'I'd say so. Her usual lawyer's voice. To tell you the truth, I thought we'd be planning our summer holiday, that she'd outline some new idea she'd had. She sometimes did when we lived together. She'd spoken to somebody or read something and this had suggested itself. We went to India one year.'

Tom sat silent, uncertain of the effect he was making on his wife. Elizabeth waited for him, allowing him to bring it out in his own time. His expression and his posture both suggested unease. His left hand, clenched, hammered at the chair-arm, not violently, but in quick inch-high strokes. He breathed unevenly, stopping now and then to suck in air through the mouth.

'Did you argue?' Elizabeth asked.

'Yes. If you can call it that. I said I saw no reason for the break-up, that I wanted the marriage to continue. That was about the length and breadth of the argument. I said I loved her. As I did. We went on for perhaps an hour. She was in no hurry, and very polite. I said there should be a period of probation. She said we'd already had it. I asked for an extension. She agreed in principle as long as it was brief, but I could see nothing would change her mind. Then she left me, went off to her local shops, told me to sit and read or look at the television.'

'She didn't throw you out?'

'No. She obviously expected me to stay the night. That was the arrangement. I didn't think about it at the time, I was so shocked. She left me. I'll give her credit; she obviously expected me to put my case again. I wandered about the room like a madman. I can't explain how shaken I was. You might suspect there had been signs, indications. If there were, I had missed them. She had made this sudden statement out of the blue that our marriage was over, irretrievably wrecked. I had seen it as indissoluble. I never thought otherwise. I walked about that nasty room, more and more agitated. In the end I scribbled a short note, went out to the hall, put my scarf and overcoat on, picked my bag up, it was unopened where I'd left it, and let myself out into the street. The flowers I'd bought were still on the hall table. I caught the Tube to St Pancras, though I don't recall that clearly. I had to wait nearly an hour for a train; I'd just missed one. It was dark and the journey was a nightmare. My head knocked and banged and ached; I couldn't put two coherent thoughts together. When I got home I didn't eat, though I'd not had a meal since breakfast. To all intents and purposes I had become another creature in those few hours. All the rules had been changed. Nothing made sense or was worth doing any more. I didn't understand myself. I'd seen myself up to that day as a balanced human, able to cope in time with any sort of bereavement or adversity. Not now. It frightened me utterly. I had lost myself and found a raving madman.'

Tom rolled in his chair. Sweat glistened on his forehead. His mouth twisted. It was as if he recreated those first days of rejection. He seemed not in the room, almost unaware of her presence. He groaned aloud, grimaced, clenched fists murderously. Elizabeth had never seen him so disturbed. She found herself afraid.

'And that was the last you heard of her?'

'No. She wrote in about a week's time drawing up a proposed division of what we owned, for my comment. I'd already sent two letters, putting my case again, that I loved her, that I didn't want a divorce. She ignored those. When I began to come round a bit, I wondered if I wouldn't have done better if I'd stayed that night. It was perhaps a test. If I'd raped her or beaten her that might have changed things.'

'Would it?'

'I don't think so. She knew her man well enough. It never crossed my mind at the time. In the end she set about the divorce. Her lawyers outlined the division of our belongings and the alteration of the mortgage and so forth. I just signed, and that was that.'

'You didn't contest anything?'

'No. It wouldn't have done any good. I saw my solicitor. He said that the division was fair, more than fair, and so I let the whole thing go through without contest.' He rubbed his forehead as if to remove the pain.

Elizabeth, nervous now, allowed him to talk or keep silent as he thought fit. The agitating force of his memories shook her, because she had not realised that they could affect him so strongly. After all, it was now twelve years since his divorce. He had never before shown such obvious anxiety, though he had spoken, if briefly, of his former wife from time to time.

'What happened?' she asked, dully by choice.

'I tried to get on with my work. I suppose I managed it. But I was different. I knew I had to clear out of that house. I talked to the High Master at Beechnall BGS. He was sympathetic, but advised me to hang on where I was. This job at the Albert Ball came up. He told me not to apply, but when I did he gave me strong support. He made his views plain. "You'll be wasted on that place," he said. "Good teachers, scholarly teachers are rarer by the day." But I applied. When the job started I was still living in my Beechnall house. I acted sensibly in my financial transactions. I bought this cottage, and set about making it habitable. I could afford it. I had sold our Beechnall place to advantage. I did some of the work myself. I thought it might be therapeutic.'

'Was it?'

'I don't know. It filled the holidays. I kept my WEA class going. I visited the record office in the evening or at weekends. I had this longer drive to work; that suited me. I ate and slept and worked. I came to terms with it all. People I met didn't immediately write me off as a man driven near to insanity by a divorce. I occupied my time. But I was uncertain of myself. This had happened and it caused me to act and feel in ways I thought I was incapable of. That's why, all this time later, when the headship of Albert Ball came up, I thought twice, a dozen times, about it. I wondered whether I'd be faced with situations that might well change me again, that would lead me to do things that were wrong.'

'Is that likely?'

'Yes. A headmaster has to choose, let's say, between two good men for a promotion. Whichever he picks he'll do wrong, as well as right. Or he has to punish some child, perhaps unjustly, to deter others. It could tear me apart.'

'You'll get used to such decisions,' she said, evenly.

'I'm not sure that I want to.'

'No. I see that. But all this with Janet happened long enough ago.'

'But you see how it's affected me. She leaves me money, and that tears me apart. I've a beautiful, gifted wife, a reasonable job, a house I like, and yet here I am acting like an adolescent.'

Elizabeth kissed him on his forehead. He looked up, half gratefully. They sat silently together for a few minutes. He now appeared lethargic, chin down to chest.

'Why did she leave you this money?' Elizabeth asked. 'It's too big just to be some minor bequest left in by chance from some earlier will.'

He did not answer. She determined to pursue the matter, get what could be found out into the open.

'Do you think she felt guilty about her behaviour? And this is a reparation? She'd treated you badly, and now is making amends?'

Tom shook his head.

'I don't know when the will was made, whether it was recent or not. I sent her my pamphlet on Nottinghamshire clergy in the fourteenth century. I put a note in saying that I hoped she would enjoy it. She used to have quite an interest in my "antiquarian grubbing". That's what she called it. I said nothing about myself, just wished that she was well. I sent it to her office, but she never replied.'

'Did she get it?'

'I've no reason to think not. The postal service always seems efficient.' He sniffed. 'Perhaps it arrived at a busy time, and besides it's a pretty out-of-the-way subject, not to say dull as dishwater. I'd guess she meant to read it, and then reply, but never finished it.'

'Did you hope it might rekindle her interest?'

'Rekindle?' He raised a smile at the word. 'No. I didn't think so for a minute. She was a clever woman, and I thought she might appreciate the chance to read something I was working on when we were married.'

'But perhaps it was that which led her to think again about the way she'd treated you.'

'We've no evidence of that. At all. And until I've seen the will I'd only be guessing.'

'What will you do? Write to the lawyer?'

Tom rose. He seemed the man she knew, had married. He slapped the back pockets of his trousers.

'I'll ring him and find out what he's got to say, if anything. I might even go to London. We'll see.' He stroked his chin, put an arm about his wife's shoulders, kissed her. 'Thanks, Liz. You're a life-saver. You're the making of me.'

11

Elizabeth and her husband walked the paths round the back of their house, and the village, ending up in the churchyard. This, the first Monday of their summer holiday, blazed warmer by the second. Not a cloud calmed the sky.

'By God, it's hot,' he said, mopping his brow. In shirtsleeves, collar wide open, he stuffed his handkerchief away and wiped his broad hands on the backside of his corduroy trousers. He stretched his legs once he'd flopped to the ground.

'Have you been here before?' she asked.

'Yes. I've been into the church several times.'

'Did you trace the parsons?'

'To some extent.'

Easily, he explained the difficulties of a researcher. She half listened. The still day seemed alive with birds, chattering or darting low.

'When was the church built?'

'Thirteenth century. The first part. Probably.'

'Who was the king then?'

'Henry the Third.'

'I don't know anything about him. He's not one of your notables, is he?'

'A very interesting man. King John's son. Had a long reign.' He tapped his brogue ends with a finger. To complete the picture of a holidaying schoolmaster he should have played about lighting a pipe. Tom did not smoke. 'He came to the throne as a boy.'

'Is the thirteenth century interesting?'

'Yes. Aquinas lived then. Dante was born 1265. Giotto much the same time. Roger Bacon. Duns Scotus. Plenty going on.'

'Nobody local?'

'Robert Grosseteste.'

'I've never heard of him.'

'An Oxford scholar. Became Bishop of Lincoln. A power in the land. Clever and forceful man. Interesting views on

135

marriage and legitimacy.' He mentioned the words without a tremor. 'He'd seem modern to you. Canon, that's church, and common law didn't coincide at that time. Have you heard the phrase "under-the-mantle children"?'

At that moment three shadows fell across the lounging figures. George de la Tour, Ellen Woodcock and a third, a young woman in black, a Mediterranean type, stepped from behind, lined up comically in front, as if reporting their presence.

'So this is how you spend your holidays?' George laughed. 'Lying in graveyards?' The painter's clothes were casual, collarless shirt, trousers held up by a length of rope, sandals and no socks.

'Good morning,' Tom answered, scrambling to his feet to welcome the women. Elizabeth sat up slightly annoyed that her idyll had been interrupted. George surprisingly introduced them to the Italian woman, who formally shook hands. Neither caught her name.

'A lovely morning,' Elizabeth ventured. 'Almost perfect.'

'What does it lack?' George asked.

'It's too hot. Or will be in an hour.'

'Nothing like as bad as Italy.'

'But you're ready for it there. You expect it.'

The woman in black spoke in fluent but strongly accented English about Roman weather. She loved it here. She raised both arms and clasped her hands above her head. Black hair curled in her armpits. She continued the monologue, as if determined to improve her already excellent English.

'We didn't know you were coming over,' Tom broke into a pause.

'I've come to look out a few pictures for my agent. He'll be here next week.'

'This week,' Ellen contradicted him.

'This week, then. He's set up, he says, a bit of a run on my pictures. In America. And there are one or two wealthy Japanese interested. Things are looking up.'

'Will it make much difference?' Elizabeth asked. George twisted his face in surprise.

'It's already done so. I've sold a few things, or he has, very profitably. And he pays me in ways that save me money.'

'Will you be staying here long?' Tom asked, smiling at Ellen.

'I don't suppose so. It depends. If I start a picture here and it's going well, then I'll stop long enough to finish it.'

'You've some ideas?'

'Never short.'

Elizabeth thanked him for the two sketches he had sent her, and said he must come round to see them as they graced her walls. Tom took this up immediately. This was the first week of their holiday, and next week he and Elizabeth were making for Scotland, so was it possible for them to walk across to New Orchard Cottage for coffee next morning? He meandered on, headmasterly, explaining how these first day or two of their vacation were profitably spent idling.

George de la Tour spoke in Italian to his visitor, rapidly and with unaccustomedly animated hand movements. She replied in slow, deliberate English, and to Tom.

'We'd be delighted. George says yours is a typically English house.'

'You shall see.' Tom, preternaturally delighted.

Ellen had moved over and sat by Elizabeth. She seemed determined to cut herself off from her walking companions.

'Do you want me to come?' she asked.

'Yes, most of all,' Elizabeth answered. Both spoke in whispers. Ellen's face broke from severity into a wide smile, and she laid a hand on the other's arm. The Italian woman was making some sort of inquiry about the church from the men. Both offered replies stodgily to the flying questions.

'Have you touched your stone?' Elizabeth asked.

'Yes, but I didn't let them see me.'

'Are you glad he's back?'

'With her here?' The others had moved towards the church and had taken up a position by a large holly tree. Their bright clothes showed to advantage.

'Who is she?'

'She's supposed to be some sort of lecturer in Fine Art in Italy.'

'Does she seem knowledgeable?' It seemed a stupid question immediately Elizabeth had posed it.

'She doesn't waste her knowledge on me, if she has any. She praises George; I've been round the studio with her. When the three of us are together she prefers to speak Italian, though she knows English as well as I do. That's a bad sign.'

'Is it?'

'Yes. We sleep in three different bedrooms.'

Elizabeth made no comment. The other three were returning. George nodded to her, and led his party away, ahead of the two women.

'Ellen's not pleased?' Tom asked, casually.

'I don't think so.'

'The dottora's a bit of a powerful character. I wonder if they'll bring Ellen with them tomorrow.'

All three appeared, not more than half an hour late. The dottora wore the most elegant of trouser suits, in black, which emphasised her slenderness. Ellen's frock, white and nurses' blue seemed shapeless, ready for work at the kitchen sink or with the rolling-pin and pastry-board. George de la Tour's shirt was open to the waist exposing a hairily black body. He grinned broadly, but sat formally, buttoning up his shirt.

'Is this house old?' the Italian woman asked.

'Eighteenth century, I guess,' Tom answered. 'But much altered. Some of it by me. It was two labourers' cottages for a start, and then a little farmstead. That's why it's called "New Orchard Cottage". This room was made up from the complete lower rooms. They took the stairs out, put them in at the end and built a hallway. The deeds are by no means complete. They didn't bother with tenants' names. The owner was a man over in Whysall, and then a woman who lived in The Hollies, and she sold it off to the orchard man who knocked it about in between market gardening.'

'Did he make a go of it?' Ellen asked, out of turn.

'Well, he stayed there thirty years. I don't know what happened to him. He retired elsewhere, and a couple called Randall came in. They sold off the orchard and the market gardens.'

'You haven't much land, then?' the Italian asked. Her questions stabbed like rapier thrusts.

'Two acres. Quite enough for me.'

'You look after it? Without help?'

'I do.'

'Thomas is hopeless as a landowner,' Elizabeth laughed.

'I'm no peasant if that's what you mean.' Thomas sounded truculent.

After coffee, and much cross-talk during which Ellen said

not a word, they set about a tour of the house. The Italian lady whose name, they discovered, was Despina, 'like the skivvy in "Così Fan Tutte",' George explained, spoke freely about the pictures on the walls, whereas the painter kept quiet. She stood long enough in front of the first of the drawings of Elizabeth which was hanging in the dining-room.

'Place of honour,' she said. 'Quite rightly.'

'Oh, yes.' Tom, modestly. He seemed slightly overwhelmed by Despina's colourful personality. 'It's a beautiful likeness.'

'Yes. Not that that will matter in a hundred years. It is very well drawn. Not one pencil mark too many.'

They progressed at snail's pace into the music room, where they admired the economy of furnishing. Despina made immediately for the second drawing, Elizabeth as Eurydice.

'A work of strong imagination,' Dr Despina pronounced.

'But beautiful.'

'Both model and execution.'

George de la Tour had settled on to a hard wooden chair where he perched upright with feet well apart. He looked like some riding-master about to castigate his pupils, though he sat in silence.

'Would you play for us?' Despina asked Elizabeth. The others buzzed agreement.

'What would you like?' Elizabeth inquired, still standing. There followed a pause before George said in a loud voice,

'A fugue.'

This surprised them all, Ellen most so that she laughed out loud. George scowled.

Quietly Elizabeth opened the lid of the Steinway and began immediately on the B minor, the last fugue of Book One of the Forty-Eight, Tom and Despina silently took to seats side by side on the small settee. Only Ellen remained standing. Elizabeth played with intensity, lifted away from the rest by Bach's counterpoint, his suspensions, his magnificence of conception.

The fugue stretched too lengthy for the audience. They would have preferred some short catchy brilliance, virtuosity. Bach's powerful architecture baffled them. They had not expected this. They had looked for a small coloured flash of a window and were faced with the whole towering cathedral. They fidgeted slightly, adopting facial expressions denoting interest or enchantment, but did not glance at each other, sat frozen in the warmth of the room. Elizabeth brought the fugue to its final tierce, strongly but without force. The room expanded for her with ensuing silence. She dropped her hands together to her lap and told them what she had played.

'Not quite what I expected,' George announced, rudely.

'What do you mean?' Despina rebuked.

'I know when I'm out of my depth. The tune, theme whatever you call it seemed odd.'

'The subject,' Elizabeth said. 'In what way?'

'Well.' George rubbed his jaw. 'I thought it had to be something short and memorable so that every time it returned you spotted it.'

'Yes.' Elizabeth was smiling, delighted with George's objection. 'There's something in that.'

'But this seemed, to my untutored ear, a kind of slap in the face, "remember me if you can." Just play it again, would you?'

She repeated it, phrasing carefully.

'I couldn't sing that,' George said. Elizabeth, smiling, sang it at once in a clear voice without hesitation.

'The whole thing's like a great abstract painting.' Despina, healing.

'But moving,' Elizabeth said.

'An abstract painting can affect your emotions. Very greatly. Can't it, George?'

'Yes.' He offered the one word, uncertainly.

'Expound, then,' Tom, the host, encouraged them.

'Despina will tell you,' George answered, 'if you really want to know.'

'Please.' Tom turned to his companion.

'If you see an abstract painting, you admire the shapes and how they have been assembled, how they contrast or harmonise with the others and how they make up together the whole of the canvas. Then you can grasp how the shapes relate to the colours which have been used, and the gradations of colour. I've stood spellbound many a time by a marvellous interplay of colour and shape, the varieties of ways space has been filled. It really interests me. And of course you can admire the way paint has been applied.'

'You're not supposed to read stories into it?' Tom inquired. 'I can't look into a fire without seeing faces, and trees, and rocks.

140

And every time I look at the floral pattern on the bedroom curtains I can make out the skull of a bird. My imagination seems stimulated. But it's not what the artist or designer or even fire-maker intended.'

'No,' Despina answered, 'but all works of art do need the collaboration of the viewer or listener. And . . . but I don't know. What do you think, Giorgio?'

'Nothing much.' He sounded depressed.

'But you used to do abstracts.'

'If somebody,' Tom from the settee, 'looked at one of your pictures and it made him imagine something . . .'

'Such as what?' Glumly.

'A face or a dragon or,' the smile broadened, 'the Israelites crossing the Red Sea.'

'And such ideas had not been in your head when you did the picture?' Despina felt bound to support her companion. 'Would you object?'

'I can't stop people thinking,' George said.

'Even wrongly?' Tom, in excitement after the truth. George made no answer.

'An abstract painting is rather like music. We listen, and we are moved, but one can't be precise. What did you think about when Elizabeth was playing, Ellen?' Despina again.

'I don't know. Nothing out of the way.'

'Didn't you like it?'

'Not much.'

Now there were two with long faces.

'Tom?' Despina did not give up easily.

'It trailed along rather slowly. I wouldn't say it was grief, exactly, but it somehow seemed serious. Like a church service or a court of law where important matters are being considered.'

'You'd say it was musically interesting, wouldn't you?' Despina questioned Elizabeth for the first time. 'Bach overcomes all kinds of technical problems he'd set himself.'

'That's part. But I can imagine a piece of music which solved all sorts of puzzles, but was unsatisfactory as music. It's not mere ingenuity. Nor is it the movement from key to key, or rhythmical devices or difference of textures. It is a kind of . . . Israelites crossing the Red, no, but the state of mind of Moses . . . No. That's all too fanciful.'

'If I painted Israelites you'd be able to point to some bits and

141

say "they're Israelites" and other bits, and say, "that's sea".'
George's beard bristled. 'I might distort, but you'd know which
was which.'

'But the shapes and colours would be interesting,' Despina.

'That's for you critics to chunter on and argue about. My
eye, not words, would tell me.'

'But we'd be bringing something of ourselves to the picture.
In this case our knowledge of the story of the Israelites, our
belief or disbelief in it, other pictures on that subject, and
other Biblical epics.' Tom was enjoying himself, at ease on
the settee close to Despina. 'We shouldn't be able to do this
to an abstract.'

'No,' Despina argued, 'but you'd bring something else of
yourself. Your preoccupations, disappointments, fears, loves.'

'Money troubles,' George de la Tour grumbled.

'Indeed. But in some way the picture would affect them.
You'd temporarily forget the unpleasant thoughts, put them
aside, or have them magnified. And I expect this effect would
vary every time you saw the picture. But that's not the artist's
concern.'

'What is, then?'

'To use the skills he's acquired over years of looking, and
painting and drawing, to make an object, in this case a painting,
that fulfils the desires, satisfies the criteria that are the result of
the long period of training.'

'And where do you get these criteria from?' Tom asked.

'Ah, that's another, very long story.'

They brightened at this. George had now been pleased; he
seemed sadly out of sorts this morning. Elizabeth sat primly
at the keyboard. Ellen shifted uncomfortably from foot to foot.
Only Tom and Despina had found pleasure.

'What sort of music do you like, Ellen?' Tom asked.

The woman started at the question, shrugged, kept her mouth
shut.

'Do you like a good tune?' he persisted.

'Yes, I do. And simple harmony.'

'Now,' said Tom, master of ceremonies, 'there's the challenge, Elizabeth my girl. Can you provide us with a simple tune
and satisfying, uncomplicated harmonies?'

Elizabeth looked up at him as if her mind floated elsewhere.
She could not be sure that they were making a success of the

142

occasion. Ellen gloomed, black as thunder. It would not have surprised anyone if the woman had flung herself out of the room. Tom was doing his teaching act, encouraging his best pupil to step out and perform to the satisfaction of all. Elizabeth did not mind; it seemed stupid, but just about acceptable.

She lifted her hands and began to play the G major Schubert Impromptu. She performed without fuss, the accompaniment subdued, the static tune lingering, the quiet slow-moving harmony all-important. The balance she achieved seemed perfect; she smiled, eyebrows slightly lifted as she played, the still perfection of the music matched by the stillness of her body.

Oddly she did not complete the piece.

'Is that it?' she asked Ellen, who nodded. De la Tour looked quizzical. Tom had something of the impressario about him as he perched upright. Despina, equally still at his side, wept silently, almost proudly. George's expression changed immediately, as if her tears made demands on him which he would not satisfy. The atmosphere changed, from polite drawing-room to drama.

'What's that called?' Ellen asked. Elizabeth told her. 'I've heard it before.'

'Why is it so beautiful?' Tom inquired. He shook a finger warning them not to come up with any easy answers.

George scowled, made a sound of dismay, a sighing groan, and clapped both hands down hard on the arms of his chair.

Despina shrugged herself upright and wiped her eyes with a scrap of lace handkerchief.

'My mother used to play that at home when I was a child,' she said. 'She was a concert pianist, but gave it up. It's beautiful of itself, but my memories made it even more poignant.' Her voice lacked tremor, and she had cleared the tears from her face. Her remarks were delivered without force, scientifically dull.

George de la Tour pursed his lips. Despina gave an opinion.

'We don't know what Schubert's preoccupations were at the time of writing this.' Elizabeth, listening, tapped her keyboard. 'I'd be hard-pressed to say whether it was sad or tranquil.'

'There's nothing desperate about it,' Tom offered.

'Nor am I sure why that particular series of notes recommends itself to me as essentially beautiful.' Despina again. 'But it is, and I've no doubt about it. I suppose I am comparing it with other slow, calm melodies I know.'

'Such as?' George snappy.

143

'The Air on the G String, the Adagio from Beethoven's Pathétique, Haydn's Largo from Symphony 88, Mozart's Piano Concerto Köchel 488. I could go on,' Despina answered.

'And which is best?'

'I couldn't begin to tell you.'

'How would you find out?'

'Play each one over and over again,' Tom suggested.

They thought that out.

'I think one would tire of any melody, however beautiful, if one played it over and over,' Elizabeth said. 'That's not what's intended. It's like eating chocolate after chocolate until you're sick. And there are many other beauties in music besides simple melodies with attractive harmonies.'

'If you three women would group yourselves together I'd like to make a sketch or two.'

Despina came over to Elizabeth who had stood. Ellen did not move.

'Come on, Ellen,' George encouraged, sketch-pad open. 'Line up.'

Despina put out a hand towards Ellen who allowed herself to be drawn towards the others.

'How shall we stand?' Despina asked.

'Close together. Arms round waists. That'll do.'

He immersed himself immediately in his book, frantically drawing, mumbling at speed. Elizabeth in the middle felt the warm proximity of the other two, but found the position hard to maintain. Ellen seemed particularly to lean on her, while Despina, though close, seemed poised to pull away. She juddered with energy, while Ellen sagged almost dead-weight.

'Great,' George called. 'Superb.' He still sketched. 'Wriggle about, girls. Give yourselves a rest. Change places, if you wish. Ellie in the middle.'

They did as they were bidden, and he beavered on.

'The Three Graces,' Tom said, pleased with the development.

'If they'd all strip off I'd put you in as well,' George said, 'and do the Judgement of Paris.'

'No fear,' said Despina.

'That's right,' Ellen said. 'Keep your clothes on when he's about.'

'Don't be filthy,' George called out jovially, still hard at it with his book. 'Right,' he said in the end. 'That'll do. Break it up, girls.' They moved away, not quickly, while he worked at a new sketch.

Despina walked round the room, almost as if she owned it, then returning took Elizabeth by the arm.

'Show us your treasures,' she ordered.

'Treasures.' Elizabeth pointed to her Steinway. 'My father bought me that. He couldn't afford to, but he did. "There are some occasions," he said, "when money and prudence don't count."'

'Was it for a special occasion?' Ellen asked.

'It was just when I first came up here. He had the chance to buy this at a decent price from a friend who was moving, going abroad, I think. Daddy knew I was down in the mouth . . .'

'Why?' Ellen, surprisingly.

'I wanted to stay in London to continue my career as a pianist. There were more opportunities there than here. I wasn't keen on being a full-time teacher.' She smiled round her audience. George continued furiously sketching. 'Anyway, that's what he did. It was typical of him. I'd nowhere to keep it in my little flat. He hadn't really the space for it either, but he cleared some of the furniture from his drawing-room. He made out, in his joking way, that it was for his benefit.'

'He was going to learn, was he?' Despina, in a childish voice.

'No. He said I'd go down to see him more often so that I could practise on my piano.'

'And did you?'

'I went down, yes. Perhaps more than I would have done. I don't know. Then when Tom and I married, Tom had been preparing this room, and had decided that it would be my music-room. And when it was ready, up came the Steinway.'

'Did you have to get it tuned?' Ellen with her unexpected question.

'Oh, yes. I had the man who does the college pianos out here. Both to this, and to the upright. That came from Tom's grandmother's house.'

'Your forebears did you well,' George said, not lifting his eyes from his sketch-book.

'And the rest of the furniture?' Despina asked.

'This was going to be another large sitting-room at first. Tom had been working on it for years. And he'd acquired things. New curtains, now, he left to me, but he'd installed the two settees and the armchairs. That,' she pointed to a table, covered, if neatly, with her books and papers,' is my work-desk. Tom picked it up at an auction. It's an eighteenth-century piece of farmhouse furniture, they claim. He bought it for next to nothing. It just suits my needs.'

'You don't work down here, Tom, do you?'

'No. This is Madame's realm. I have a studio upstairs in the main house. This was going to be my library. Or that was one of the ideas. It's two outbuildings knocked together, and then joined to the end wall of the house. It means we each can work out of the other's way. But the bookcases are a reminder of the library it was intended to be.'

'Tom made them himself,' Elizabeth said.

'Do you regret not having the library?' Despina asked.

'Regret? No. It's ideal for Elizabeth. I can just about hear her from the house. These are thick walls. And it reminds me of my good fortune. The library would just have been a second, longer, and largely unused sitting-room.'

'Your marriage made a difference to your plans?' Despina asked. George laughed satirically.

'In a thousand and one ways. But it made up my mind about this room as a music studio. That seemed perfect, a real use of the space. It's not often that happens with me. I gradually build things up, and hope they're right in the end.'

'And are they?'

'Sometimes. Sometimes not.'

'Are you pleased?' Ellen asked Elizabeth.

'Very. It was a lovely wedding present. I can come in here and thump away to my heart's content, and I'm not disturbing Tom or neighbours or anybody else.'

Despina back at the piano asked Elizabeth to play the Schubert Impromptu for them again. She did so, but broke off. Despina seemed rapt. Elizabeth took Ellen by the arm and led her back to the house, where the women talked about marriage. Ellen, suddenly responsive, described her husband's devious life.

'Why did you marry him?' Despina, always in the lead.

'He was attractive. Very handsome. Wasn't he, George?'

'Who?'

'Archie. My husband.'

'Oh, yes. I suppose so.' George was engaged again with his sketch-book, puffing, making small exclamations of exasperation, jerking his head about.

'Are we going to see those?' Tom asked, pointing.

'No.' Blunt. Loudly rude enough to quieten the rest.

'George,' Despina. He looked up, noticed the extent of their surprise.

'Sorry,' he said. He closed his book and slipped it away into the bag which he carried on a shoulder-strap. The press-studs were snapped shut as a tender afterthought, slowly, carefully apologetically. Five minutes later, he stood, barked out to his ladies that they should vamoose and waste no more of the Tylers' time. They did not demur, though Despina had to break off in the middle of a disquisition on Raphael.

'Funny lot,' Tom ventured, when the visitors had gone.

'Did you like them?'

'Despina. She seems sociable enough. But Ellen was very subdued. And as for George well, he's no idea.'

'He perhaps felt he'd found some ideas.'

'They could wait,' Tom grumbled.

'Which do you consider more important: being polite to us or getting some good sketches on paper?'

'If he has to choose, then he should stay at home and work.'

'But perhaps it's making a trip out, seeing us and our house which gets him going.' Tom sat in his chair, fingers interlocked in front of him, the headmaster about to address his prefects. 'I was quite interested in the discussion you had about music and painting. And mainly so because neither of you seemed sure what the purpose of your art was. Oh, I knew you could say that it was to give pleasure. That's too vague. I can see that a painting used, at least, to have some narrative content – The Magi offer their presents to the baby Jesus, or Dante admires Beatrice as she passes in the street, or some classical myth or tale, Leda and the Swan, or Horatius Holds the Bridge. The viewer will be expected to know these stories, and will admire or deplore how well the artist has illustrated them, made them more vivid, introduced new notions. But there seemed to be some notion of form or colour that made painting rather akin to music.'

'We were talking about abstract art.'

'Yes, but I got the impression from somebody that these values also applied to assessment of narrative pictures.'

'From yourself,' she said, gently chiding.

'Probably. But what about music then?'

She pulled a thinker's face.

'I guess that some sort of canon has been set up, oh, over hundreds of years. It's based on tonality and accepted rhythms and shapes and variations of all sorts, and is gradually extended year by year. We learn by listening what Bach sounds like, well, roughly, and we widen our range by further listening. This is easier now than at any time before because we have all these excellent means of reproduction. Before you had to play it for yourself, or listen to somebody else in person. We have the greatest players in the world to perform for us, and we can make them repeat it for us as often as we like. And so we acquire our notions of music.'

'And?'

'When I sit down and play something on the piano, you listen and compare it with your CDs or tapes. You think perhaps I don't do it as well as Richter or Brendel or whoever your favourite is. Or that I do it quite differently.' She paused. Her husband had now placed his hands on the arms of his chair and sat eagerly, like a small child. 'And if I play something that is unfamiliar to you, like that B minor fugue, then you make such comparisons you can with works you already know, and if that isn't helpful you either get bored, as some of you did, or perhaps enlarge your range, add that, after a few hearings, to your canon. That's my hope.'

'Good, good,' Tom said. 'I've enjoyed this.'

'Did you never discuss things with Janet?' Elizabeth asked, delighted.

'Yes. Often. But not artistic matters. No, that's not right. We'd talk about a play we'd seen or an exhibition or concert, but we were amateurs. Janet was very intelligent, but I had the impression that to her one musical performance was as valuable as another. Within reason, of course. Not if one was full of wrong notes.'

'She'd notice that?'

'Oh, yes. More so than I would. She was sharp at whatever she put her mind to. But aesthetic matters were not a primary concern. She liked something about which she could give a reasoned or legal judgement. She saw that eloquent court performances by barristers could win cases, but I think she recognised that as a weakness of the system, especially if the decision ran contrary to what the law laid down or common sense suggested.'

'You make her sound rather, well, cold, bloodless.'

'That's not right. She could be very animated. And she was a good talker.'

'Did she laugh much?'

'She wasn't without a sense of humour. In that respect she was a bit like me. Not very fond of the silly or childish, and got little out of the filthy. And I have seen her giggly when she's indulged a little too freely in alcohol. But that wasn't too often. No, I think she was very like me in that respect. And I'm hardly a barrel of laughs.'

'Odd expression.'

'I overheard some girl use it on the corridors at school.'

'I take it that you've heard no more from her solicitors?'

'No. I acknowledged the letter. That's all. They don't move very fast, and I had the impression that they had some further work to do before the estate is cleared up. So I'll give him a bit of time. I may even call in on him. Do you fancy a day or two in London? We'll see. It's not important, is it? We're not short of money. And we've no great spending sprees planned, have we?'

'What about a Christmas cruise?'

'Would you like that?'

'I'd hate it.'

They both laughed.

'When I talk to you you seem much nearer to my pupils than they are to me.'

'Good or bad?' she asked.

'Oh, good. You won't let me lord it over you as I can over them.' He touched her. 'But you seem young and lively as they are and I'm not.'

'I'm a proper little sobersides,' she said.

In these ways their marriage appeared successful, by sudden leaps of understanding.

12

The day after the Tylers returned from their fortnight's Scottish holiday Elizabeth walking down to the village glimpsed Ellen Woodcock in the drive of 'The Hollies'. The woman seemed to be staggering. Elizabeth stopped, but Ellen paid no attention. Elizabeth approached the gate, and called out; again she was ignored. She called louder, and Ellen looked up raising her head like a startled hare, before she shuffled over. They exchanged dull pleasantries, and Elizabeth explained that she was walking down to the village to renew their order for bread.

'Don't you make your own?' Ellen asked.

'No.'

'I thought you would.' Ellen grimaced. 'Could I walk down with you?' she asked.

They set off at a sharp pace. Elizabeth was glad of the company, for her husband had gone off to the school to check on developments while he'd been away. Why a phone call to the utterly efficient secretary wouldn't suffice Elizabeth did not know, but she guessed that Tom needed time to himself again after an uxorious fortnight. The holiday had been perfect, but he was the sort who needed to rescue his own personality from time to time, to be occasionally a bachelor, a medieval historian, a schoolmaster. She appreciated this and had told him to spend a whole day or two in his office, while she got down to serious practice. He'd gone off gratefully, if expressing regret.

George and Despina had returned, it appeared, to London a week before and were soon to go to Italy.

'He went round the studio looking for things. I don't know how much he took. He hired a van. He left the studio in a mess. That I can tell you.'

'Did he do any painting?'

'No. Some sketching. When she gave him time on his own.'

'She wanted to look round, did she?'

'God knows. I don't think she's very interested in the house here. "What an awkward, ugly place," she said. "But clean," he told her, "which is more than you can say when I'm living here."'

'Will he be coming back?'

'No. He's going to live in Italy a good part of the year.'

'For tax purposes? Now he's making a lot of money?'

'I've no idea. I don't know what his plans are. I don't suppose he knows, either. He'd never take it on himself to discuss it with me, anyway.'

'Wasn't he friendly?' Elizabeth asked.

'That's not a word anybody'd apply to him. He acts as he thinks fit for his own good. "I'm a painter, Ellie," he says to me. "Not a human being very often." And that's about right. He does his work. Even his pleasures are connected with it.'

They paced it hard along the road, not talking, enjoying the summer fields. Just as they stopped in front of the cottage where Elizabeth bought her bread, (there was no shop in the village), Ellen put a detaining hand on the crook of her companion's left arm.

'They're going to get married, y' know,' she said in a dull, strong voice.

'When?'

'They haven't mentioned a date. They haven't even said that they are.'

Ellen turned away, as if from human kind, and stared hard at the sky over the houses on the other side of the road. Elizabeth went in, reset the order for bread, chatted for two minutes about holidays and was delighted that the woman said she was pleased to see her back and looking so well. She asked after Tom. Her oldest granddaughter was due to start at his school in September. 'She's really looking forward to it. She hasn't half grown up these last few months.' Elizabeth felt accepted. Mr Tyler's wife.

Outside she found that Ellen had walked down the street and stood now, shaking her arms like wings, fifty yards away. She caught a glimpse of Elizabeth, immediately ceased her antics and returned, not hurrying, an independent woman.

'All done?' she called from a few feet.

'Yes. We're about ready for winter.'

'Bloody hell.' The pain in Ellen's voice was almost palpable, but she straightened herself up. 'Are we walking back now?'

'I think so.'

As they set off, Elizabeth asked,

'What makes you so sure that they are going to get married?'

'Oh, I know him. He's caught. She's entangled him.'

Elizabeth murmured her surprise at the information.

'Didn't he want to get married, then?'

'He never knows what he does want. But she's a lady, a countess, contessa or something.'

'Doesn't she teach somewhere?'

'At a university in Rome. She's clever. She knows all the words and the ideas.'

'And he likes that?'

'Yes. He knows about actually putting paint on to canvas, but she's a philosopher, he says. She's knowledgeable miles beyond him. "I'd no time to be educated," he said to me many a time. "I had to learn to paint." He likes the way she can explain. I think it makes him feel he is somebody.'

'Well, he is, isn't he?'

'He's never sure. He's always grumbling that he's not got it right, and, anyway, nobody knows what he's trying for. He feels better at times like the present when people are paying all this money for his stuff.'

'And she keeps him cheerful?'

'She? She? Well. I don't know. I'm not ever sure that Despina's her real name. She's got half a dozen handles like all these foreign aristocrats; I saw them all printed out once, and I don't know whether Despina was one of them, even.'

'It's a kind of nickname, is it?'

'Possible. They, or at least, she talks about a Mozart opera.'

They were now mounting an incline in the road, but their pace did not slacken. Both seemed driven by their thoughts.

'Will he sell up here? At "The Hollies"?' Elizabeth gasped. They pressed hard as if racing. Not for some yards did Ellen stop, butterfly her arms again and, breathing heavily, answer,

'I don't suppose he's considered it for a moment. He's got money to burn so what he pays into the bank for me here he doesn't miss. But if she makes him buy some palazzo, or chase round the world, he'll see that this place does no good to him. Then he won't come back. So he'll sell it, and stop my allowance. "She's had it easy for long enough. She'll have to fend for herself." That'll be his argument.'

'That's not very generous,' Elizabeth said, gently.

'He'll think, if he thinks at all, that he's kept me here with a roof over my head for a year or more, while he's been away, and that'll be that.'

'But it was here . . .'

'He won't brood about any consequences for me. Not for a minute. I'm somebody who lives miles away in England. I've been paid while I was useful, and I'll have to be satisfied with that.'

'But,' Elizabeth continued with the point she had been making before Ellen interrupted, 'it was here that he did those pictures that have made so much money.'

'He won't bother his head about small matters like that. He thinks it doesn't make much difference where he works. He'd do just as well in a cowshed.'

'Why's he moved to Italy then?'

'The weather's better. There's lovely light for painting, he says. He feels comfortable. And there's Dottora Despina stroking his fevered brow.' Ellen laughed, ugly as sin.

They now began to walk again, but at a more leisurely pace, and without speaking. When they reached the side-lane to the lych-gate, Elizabeth asked if her companion would like to turn down and to the churchyard.

'No,' Ellen snapped.

'I always associate you with that spot now.'

She received no reply to that. Their easy way continued until they reached 'The Hollies'. The light was dim there in the shadows of the copse even on this bright day.

'That's it, then,' Elizabeth said. 'Come and have coffee with me one morning. Tomorrow if that's convenient.'

'Will you come in with me now?' Seeing Elizabeth's hesitation Ellen touched her arm. 'Just for a brief while.'

'It will have to be short.'

'I shan't keep you. I promise you.'

Ellen seemed to make a big performance of unlocking both doors to the house.

'I'm all thumbs this morning,' she said.

Inside it was shadowy, cool, closed up.

'Will you walk up to the studio with me?' Ellen asked. 'I don't like going in on my own.'

'Why not?'

'Superstition. But I have to check every so often to see everything's as it should be.'

'Isn't that likely?'

'You never know. Somebody could get a ladder and I'd be none the wiser. Or a leak might develop and then it would all be damp, and with all those paintings and sketches about that wouldn't do.'

Again Ellen went through the clumsy drill of unlocking and unbolting the door. The studio appeared dim compared with the stairs.

'I keep the blinds drawn,' Ellen explaining, advancing on the large window, running up the blind, and opening the frame. 'That's better.'

'It all looks very tidy,' Elizabeth commented, staring about her.

'I've been up a time or two since they left. I have to force myself. I dragged the vacuum up one morning to shift the dust. You could have buried yourself in it. I had to change the bag.'

They walked round the room twice. Now and then Ellen pulled a canvas from a pile. She seemed to know what she looked for. Once she held up a portrait of herself as a young woman dressed regally in a voluminous scarlet robe. Her tidy hair crowned a face that seemed arrogant with a sense of her beauty or status. The bold eyes despised the world. 'He used to call that the Queen of Sheba,' Ellen glossed.

'Why doesn't he exhibit it, or sell it?'

'It's not finished.'

'It looks perfect to me.'

'You can't see the body under the clothes. Or, at least, so he said.'

'That's the idea of a great formal costume like that. It hides the humanity. And the parts that are left naked, the shoulders and the arms are the more striking on that account.'

'I wish you were here to argue with him.'

'Would it do any good?'

Ellen replaced the canvas, and they took a third turn about the room. This time the housekeeper poked in a corner and produced a small framed oil-painting of herself and her master standing stark naked, but hand in hand. Both looked youthful, in face and body, and George was clean-shaven, but the breadth

154

of his frame, the barrel chest, the wide shoulders, the powerful biceps dwarfed his companion's frailty. Ellen stood delicately painted, pale, but shy, not of her nudity, but of her place in the harsh hierarchy of the world. "The harebell". That's what he called me.'

'It's beautiful,' Elizabeth said.

'He's made himself thinner than he was. He always had a bit of a beer belly.'

Jovially she held the picture at arm's length in the air and then kissed it comically with a satirical smack of the lips somewhere in the region of the man's genitals. Still smirking she wrapped the painting in its protective cover and again put it carefully away.

'Goodbye, the lovers,' Elizabeth said. Ellen looked at her with surprise. They both laughed and Ellen threw her arms round her friend. She clung for a moment and then released the other. 'Come and look at these.'

She led Elizabeth to a large bureau, and began to jerk out the drawers. She took out sketch-books, loose papers and laid them out for inspection. Some were pencil, some charcoal; many were coloured, with water-paints or pastel. Elizabeth examined landscapes, buildings, skies, but mostly figures. People worked, ran, harangued, or lay nakedly listless. One or two, silently pointed out by Ellen with a blunt forefinger, were erotic, copulating couples in frenzied motions of ecstasy. One naked woman, on her back, legs wide, had Elizabeth's face; she smiled serenely upwards, exposing herself, head calmly raised.

'Who's that supposed to be?' Elizabeth said, angrily, instantly afraid. Her mood had violently changed.

'You know quite well. And it's typical of him. He'll put you in and make up what he hasn't seen. He won't care. If your husband saw this he'd think George had used you as a model.' Ellen waved a hand, for no reason. 'And it might have repercussions.' She drew in breath after her chosen word. 'But he wouldn't care. Or even, he'd be pleased to cause trouble. Do you know what he'd say? "To the pure all things are pure", and he'd laugh, and pinch you you know where. That's the famous George.'

Elizabeth turned away, still fuming, anxious, aggressive.

'If he turned you out you could sell some of these,' she said. Ellen was packing the sketches neatly away, her fingers nimble.

155

'They aren't mine. These are done in the last year.'

'Will he use them?'

'Quite possibly. He had his sketches of me with him when he did that big bathroom thing out in Italy, though it's possible he might have used some local model or even the learned Dr Despina to revive his memory.'

'Is that failing, then?' Elizabeth asked her question with genuine concern.

'Not for women it isn't.'

Ellen slammed and locked the drawer, then led Elizabeth out, not looking back. She bolted the door with resentment, noisily, and ferociously took the lead downstairs. When they reached the ground floor she flounced across the hall floor. Deliberately Elizabeth took her time over the descent, making her companion wait. Anger burnt.

'Cup of coffee?' Ellen almost shouted from the door.

'No thanks, but you come and have one with me tomorrow. Eleven o'clock.'

'Whereabouts are you in such a hurry to go?' Ellen held the door open. Elizabeth sailed past her, annoyed by Ellen's behaviour, waving like a queen.

'I have to play a concert in three days' time for the aristocracy, gentry and clergy of the county at Leicester House. I need to practise.'

'Especially for the nobs. Especially.'

Elizabeth marched away. She needed to settle to her keyboard to rid herself of her ill-temper. Ellen Woodcock had taken her own anger out on her visitor; she had deliberately shown Elizabeth the obscene sketch. She had prepared the shock, to rid herself of her animosity against George and the Italian woman. She had been selfish, determined to drag Elizabeth down with her into her own vexations, and had succeeded. As Elizabeth walked quickly along the road, she felt her indignation grow so that by the time she reached the house she was in tears.

The home seemed quiet, cool, restful, every piece of furniture in its place. She rushed out to the kitchen and filled a glass from the tap. As she sipped she stared out at the sun, bright plants, at the solid double row of Tom's runner-beans, at the apples on the trees, at two daturas in huge earthenware pots, at the blue stretches of sky, the beginnings of autumn colour. The acid of wrath burnt in her. She put down her glass, and rushed back into the house and immediately out into the music room. There the blinds were already drawn. She dragged back the piano stool. She hated Ellen Woodcock, sat down, rushed up two scales, A major, B major. She repeated them, but not to her satisfaction. The seat was set at a wrong height, though nobody could have touched it since she had used it yesterday. With a quick hand she wiped a tear from her cheek, adjusted the seat from one position of discomfort to another, and began on Bach's Prelude in E flat minor, from Book One. She played without error, from memory and yet her mood allowed of no satisfaction with the performance. She rattled off more scales, major and minor, looking for perfection, as if she was preparing for an examination, then arpeggios, running thirds. Anger strengthened her fingers, but she could stand away from the execution, know when she made a slip, correct it three times, then pass on to the next exercise, determined to make her shortcomings the cause of brilliance. In the end, content with success, she played the Bach Prelude again, and this time it sang, and soothed. Did the Master feel grief as he wrote? She did not know. He must have experienced sorrow, distress in his life, the death of his first wife, of children, disappointment at failure on the ladder of promotion. 'To attention, gentlemen,' a great ruler had said. 'Old Bach is here.' Did Bach feel irony or condescension in the compliment? Was he merely his gifted son's father to the king? Elizabeth glanced across at a print on her wall of Haussmann's portrait. The expression was pleasant, the eyes, to be blind within three years, lively. Wigs seemed to throw a cloak of anonymity about eighteenth century notables; Handel and Bach seemed much the same man, double-chinned, self-satisfied, bland. But Bach returning one summer from a journey with his prince had found his wife Maria Barbara not only dead but already buried. Bland? She played again thoughtfully through the prelude, but this time triumphantly crowned it with the fugue.

Now she began on the Leicester House music, purged, not exactly in the world. The last two days before the first concert, on Saturday next, she would rehearse with the Smithsons, but she'd be more than prepared. She was ready now. She practised with careful pleasure. She did not stop to eat properly, but her mind was at ease.

By the time Tom arrived home (he had rung with the exact

time of arrival) she had the evening meal well on the way to completion.

'Good day?' she asked.

'Excellent. One or two little problems, and then I got on with Edward the Third.' She had guessed as much, and it gladdened her.

'In again tomorrow?'

'If you don't mind.'

He had also been in touch with Janet's solicitors, and had arranged to go up to London on the Monday of next week.

'Perhaps you'd like to come with me. You needn't call in on the solicitor unless you want to. Just think about it. You'll have had those two Leicester House concerts over and done with. We'll stay overnight if you wish. I must be back by Wednesday when the A levels results will be in.'

'Was the solicitor forthcoming?'

'Yes. He's called Hedges. They haven't quite cleared everything up. I didn't speak to him, but to some understrapper.' One of Victor's words. 'He seemed to know something about it. But I've an arrangement to see Hedges, the great man himself, on Monday, and we'll learn what's to be known.'

'Are there snags, then?'

'Not that I gathered.'

'Why does he want to see you, then? Lawyers aren't very generous with their time.'

'I expect he'll charge me. But I asked a few questions, and they said they'd do their best to clear them up. Not that they promised anything.'

Tom sat expansively at the table. He looked exactly the headmaster, she thought, and it pleased her. She wondered what small part she had played making him the man he had become.

'Are you really interested?' she asked. 'Or is the legacy just something that's likely to be inexplicable, and not worth pursuing?'

'No. I'm as curious as the next man. Janet gave me a good half-share of the home when we parted, and I expected to hear no more from her. I didn't think sentimental memories or guilt would trouble her much.'

'Suppose you found she thought she'd done wrong parting from you?'

'Done wrong? In what way?'

158

'Either she felt she had treated you badly, or it was borne upon her, she began to realise, that she missed you, that she should never have dismissed you in the summary way she did.'

'Well, it wouldn't improve things for her to leave me her money, now would it? I might easily die first.'

'It might have eased her conscience?'

'It doesn't seem much like her.' He stroked his hair flat. 'It's an interesting question, but one I don't expect a complete answer to. Lawyers don't usually ask their clients why they are leaving this bequest or that unless they see it might cause trouble. Nor do I think Janet would be there talking freely about her motives. If I knew her, she'd have put down on a piece of paper exactly what she wanted. I don't suppose making wills was new to her.'

'The mystery deepens.' Elizabeth laughed. She had changed from the morning's disgruntlement and outrage.

'What I suggest is that you come with me. And then if there are any questions I fail to ask, you can raise them.'

'I will,' she said. 'I think I will.'

'Agreed.'

13

The Tylers decided that they would travel to London by train.

They enjoyed their journey, surprised at the number of businessmen in the first-class carriages at this time of summer.

'They're keeping the country on an even keel,' Tom said, facetiously.

'Or the crest of the wave.' She vied with him in cliché.

Once in town they made by underground to the solicitor's office in Bloomsbury. The office was by no means palatial, down a rather shabby side-street off a square. The majority of the Victorian buildings had shops on the ground floor, but Temple and Hedges were reached by a rather grand door and occupied all six floors. As they walked along they made up suitable titles for the partners. Hedges and Ditches. Banks and Hedges. Dyke, Hedges and Fields. Hedges, Betts and Prospers. They went soberly giggling along the street, like children let early out of school.

'Where shall we have lunch?' Tom asked. 'I was thinking of a pub.'

'We'd better wait until we see how much you've inherited, hadn't we?'

They straightened their faces to be shown to a waiting-room on the first floor. The room, carpeted, had straight-backed chairs where they perched uncomfortably together. Almost at once a delicately-scented young woman with silken legs led them into Hedges' room. The solicitor, already on his feet, was, Elizabeth claimed afterwards, exactly what she expected: grey-haired, dark-suited with silk tie and polished black shoes. He smiled them to their new chairs, already in place, over his half-moon glasses. Tom introduced his wife; Hedges graciously inclined his head before he shook hands. Once he was seated on the other side of his desk, an opened file before him, he remarked on the beauty of the weather, and its effect on his roses. A small cluster filled an elegant silver vase on the vast top of his desk.

'My Mr Douane spoke to you the other morning. I felt I must

160

give you some kind of explanation of the delay in bringing this business to a conclusion.' One felt that the inheritance was insignificant amongst his 'vast concerns'.

Elizabeth's spirits rose. As she sat in this clean, comfortless office where the shining furniture smelt of polish, her spirits rose. The two performances at Leicester Hall had been warmly received; two large audiences in a beautiful place had been more enthusiastic than she expected. People had congratulated her, gone out of their aristocratic way to do so. She and her partners had played well. Tom had been greatly impressed sitting there, as he said in joy, 'like a pouter pigeon' in his dress suit. He had insisted that she brought new outfits to suit the occasion, saying that his father's favourite pianist was a gorgeous lady called Eileen Joyce who changed clothes for each set of pieces in her recital. The organizers said that their charities had made a great deal of money; the local newspaper gave a long and favourable review of the concert, and this morning's *Daily Telegraph* offered a short report of the event mentioning her playing with particular pleasure. Now in Hedges' office she felt complete, a person of consequence, one worthy of receiving the news of her husband's good fortune as her right.

Hedges outlined the present position.

The bequest would be more than they had the right to expect, somewhere in the region of a quarter of a million pounds. He waited for the provincials to gape. Tom did not oblige, forcing the solicitor to outline his difficulties in realizing the estate.

'We had to sell her house,' he said. 'Sometimes that is left to the heirs, but we were instructed to put it on the market, and to accept nothing less than a named price. If your wife had lived for a few years more,' Hedges instructed, 'she would have been a very rich woman.'

'So her death was unexpected?' Tom asked.

Hedges looked at him in surprise.

'She was killed in an electrical accident abroad. North Africa. Negotiations are still going on about the payment of compensation. These may well in the end swell your coffers to some large extent.' He smiled presumably at his own archaic phraseology, perspicuous but not mean. 'Her insurance company's lawyers are pursuing these matters, and I am following their work with close interest.'

Tom asked a few questions, but Hedges had no detailed

161

knowledge of the manner of her death, except that it entailed an unprotected cable at a swimming pool. It had all been most unfortunate, and the hotel's contractors were absolutely to blame.

'Was she killed outright?' Tom asked.

'I believe so.' Her body had been cremated in England, and the ashes had been scattered in Wharfedale near where she was born: That was the extent of his knowledge.

'How long has the will been made.'

'You have seen it, Mr Tyler. Or a copy. Just over three years.'

'And it replaces earlier wills.'

'Yes. It says so.'

Tom explained why he felt surprise not only at the size of Janet's bequest, but that anything had been bequeathed to him at all.

'We have been divorced now for twelve years. During that time we have had no contact, apart from my sending on of correspondence to her office in the first year or so. You can see this. I have been at my present school for nearly ten years, and yet she had no idea. I have lived in my present house for nearly that length of time, but clearly she did not know my present whereabouts, and had made no attempt to find out. She gave my address as the one where we lived together and my occupation as the position I held at the time of the divorce.'

'That was enough,' Hedges hummed. 'It cost some little time and money to locate you, but it was managed. Now, I can see your puzzlement, but in my experience of the making of wills we find some real eccentricities. It would seem that your former wife from the time of making her first will in London, and that would be twelve years ago, some three years, let us say, after the decree absolute, had determined to leave you one third of her estate.'

'But you've no idea why?' Tom persisted.

'I haven't. I wasn't concerned with drawing up the earlier wills. And when this last one was made, she gave no inkling of what was in her mind. The estate was to be divided into three. One third to you; one third to relatives. To this latter category she added two more names in her last will, making eleven people in all, as you know. The final third went to what we could call charities.'

162

'I never saw Janet as a charitable person,' Tom said.

'No.' Mr Hedges expressed no opinion one way or another with his monosyllable. 'No.'

'Though the Tate Gallery or the National Trust are not exactly what I'd call charities.'

'You think that only societies intending to help the very unfortunate should be so designated?'

Tom hitched his well-cut trousers.

'Thank you. That will have to do,' he said.

'I'm sorry I can't be more informative,' Hedges said, as cheerfully as he could. 'You and I, in your profession and mine, find people acting in ways we can't explain. Human beings are very various. As are their motives. If I tried to suggest what your ex-wife was doing and why, it would be purely guesswork on my part. Especially as I did not know her personally. She was known to me as a very successful commercial lawyer, but not at all as a woman. When she came into this office, and she sat the last time she was here, Mr Tyler,' Hedges smiled at Elizabeth, making sure she did not feel ignored, 'she sat in the chair, in the place you now occupy, our dealings were short and businesslike. There was no social intercourse, beyond the usual courtesies. She had written down what she wanted, had it typed, and passed it over.'

'I see.'

'She would have been barely fifty when the will was made.' Elizabeth wondered how Hedges knew that. 'And probably expected to live another, say, thirty years. It may have been in her mind that she would outlive you, so that you'd never receive the bequest. Later she might have altered the will again. She kept it up to date, as you've seen. But at least over a period of something like ten or more years, she made you the major beneficiary of this will. If she died, you would profit. And that suggests she felt that you deserved this, or that she was in some way in your debt. But that was never discussed.'

'Did she seem happy when she was in here?' Tom asked.

'I formed no opinion.'

Tom stood. Hedges said that he hoped to complete the whole transaction inside two months. He apologised for the delay, but said such affairs were far from straightforward. Hands were shaken. His grip was firm and warm. They were shown out to the street by the silk-calved secretary. The crowded traffic and

163

the pedestrians had now become different. The blue sky fluffed with white cloud seemed more cheerful over tall, forbidding buildings. They made for Regent's Park along the Euston Road hand in hand. Twice they were stopped by strangers asking for directions. Tom on each occasion took his 'streetfinder' from his pocket and gave schoolmasterly guidance. On the second time the recipient of his advice, a thickset man with a north country accent, thanked him and said what a pleasure it was to meet somebody who knew something and spoke English. 'Every single body along here I've stopped to ask is a foreigner. And I only picked them out because they looked British.'

'Are you here on holiday?' Tom asked.

'Just five days. We haven't brought the car. We've holed up near King's Cross. That's where we came in from Doncaster. We live just outside. And we're having a stroll up and down here. We've had a look at St Pancras, first, lovely station that, some style about it, a cathedral from the outside, and then Euston. I'm interested in railways. My grandad worked on them. An old Great Northern man. He drove expresses, not that he ever called them that, fasts, he called them, "fasts" not "farsts". I love to see those big electrics drive into King's Cross; the power, the strength and the control.'

'Would your grandfather have liked them?' Tom asked.

'I think so. The old steam locomotives took some driving. It was a skilled occupation. But yes, he'd have revelled in the ease and the speed. Perhaps it isn't as exciting as being on the old-time, open footplate, draughty and noisy, and you could feel the power under your feet, but he was a practical man.'

'Your father wasn't a railwayman?'

'No. He was like me. Didn't fancy getting his hands dirty. Grandad used to give me bits of what he called "waste" when I was a boy. The drivers and firemen wiped the oil and muck from their hands with it. I used to rub my hands on the stuff. I felt grown-up.'

Tom questioned him. Elizabeth could see that his mild inquisition sprang from his pleasure at the holiday, the lawyer's news, pride in her groomed appearance. The north-countryman's wife, a thin woman with a carrier bag, had listened intently but without a word suddenly interrupted her husband's expansive answer to dismiss his enthusiasm and confide to Elizabeth. 'They never grow up,' she said. 'They're like boys all their lives.'

164

The men did not disagree, nor resent her interference. They laughed as though her comment had some spurious accuracy about it, but missed the deeper reality. But the interlude was over. They shook hands all round, expressing mutual regard. 'I've enjoyed that,' the man said. 'I hope we run across each other again while we're down here. In one of the main line stations.'

'In these foreign parts,' Tom said.

They parted, all laughing, the Yorkshire wife especially.

'I wonder what he does for a living?' Tom mused.

'You guess.'

'In business of some sort. He's well educated. At least he doesn't make grammatical mistakes.'

'Well-dressed,' Elizabeth said. 'Both of them.'

'Not short of a bob or two, then. But still with his grandfather on the footplate of The Flying Scotsman.'

They walked leisurely along to Regent's Park, commenting on the people they met, as if the rest of the pedestrians paraded the streets for their amusement. They ate a substantial lunch at a pub, examined the Nash Terraces, wondering,

'I have never seen anybody inside those houses,' Tom said. 'Not even coming out.'

'You haven't put enough time in in surveillance.'

'I suppose not.'

They parted reluctantly, she to visit a friend who lived near the Royal Academy. Tom, who refused to accompany her, made for Bloomsbury to visit a friend of his father's who was confined to a nursing home, and then to mooch round. He claimed that when he'd finished with Edward the Third he'd read all the books about the Woolfs and Stracheys, 'just for pleasure'.

'I shall sit there in an armchair. I won't take a note or mark a passage. I'll remember what I can, and what I forget doesn't matter.'

'Why?'

'They're an interesting lot. Quite unlike me. Another age. They kept busy even when there was no need.'

'But you never read what they wrote, *Mrs Dalloway* or *The Waves*.'

'Have you?'

'No,' Elizabeth mocked him. 'But I know some who have. This girl I'm going to see. She had a Virginia Woolf craze when

165

we were at the RCM. It was unusual. Most students didn't read anything much. We were too busy. Or the serious ones were.'

'And your friend was not serious?'

'Oh, beyond belief. But she's an academic. She should have gone to university first. She did a B.Mus, and later a doctorate. She teaches at the Academy now and at University College.'

'What did she play? What was her instrument?'

'The organ. She was very good. Could easily have been a full-time recitalist. Women are taking over in that department, you know. But she wanted to be a scholar, and that was that.'

'And she's managed it?'

'Yes. And happy as a king with it. She has two children, and does enough work for a dozen.'

'Would you like children?' he asked, gravely.

That was Tom, her Tom. He looked you and life in the eye, asked the straight question.

'I'm happy as I am,' she said.

'But in future?' he persisted.

'That I don't know. But I don't want to start a family just yet. What about you?'

'I've never felt so well. I don't want this to come between us.'

At her friend's home, Elizabeth suddenly realized how ordered her life had become. Tania Metcalfe, two years older than she, looked worried, almost bedraggled. She lived in a large Victorian house, in a run-down district. Her two children were now at school; she had three students, girls, in the attic bedrooms; her husband worked in a bank.

'Won't the bank authorities move him about?'

'Not outside London. For one thing he's good at his job, and secondly they can't get sensible people to move into town even on promotion.'

The two women sat together at first in a large, dark room, lit by one sash-window. The high walls were lined with books. There were two desks, three chairs, and the carpet was piled with papers, books, magazines, all desperately untidy. In the darkest corner on a small deal table Tania brewed up coffee, strong as death, she said, then parked herself at the desk by the window; the surface lay hidden deep in unsorted litter at which Tania pointed and claimed, laughing a little hysterically, that she knew the whereabouts of every paper-clip.

166

'Where's the piano?' Elizabeth asked.

'In the drawing-room. That leaves me room to walk about when I'm giving private lessons. I do organ lessons at a big Methodist chapel at the end of the street.'

'And your own practice?'

'No. I have an electronic organ here. And that serves me to keep in trim. I don't make too much noise, because I can use earphones. So that's possible at night when Paul and Emma are in bed.'

'Are they musical?'

'I guess so. They hear a certain amount here, and the school puts on some very good shows to which we take them.'

Tania questioned Elizabeth about her appearances with the Lombard Quartet. 'You must be in pretty good fettle.'

'You learn a great deal playing with them.'

'Would you like to do it all the time? Solo and chamber work?'

'There's not enough to live on. It was the biggest slice of luck I got the Lombard.'

'You must have played well for them to ask you again.'

'A pretty lady is always an attraction.'

'Do you like your teaching?' Tania asked. 'Would you miss it if you gave it up?'

'I like it some of the time. I'm easily bored. And my pupils will be nothing like as gifted as yours.'

'Oh, I don't know. I'm pretty near the bottom of everybody's lists, both at the Academy and UCL. I get lumbered with those nobody else wants to teach.'

They grumbled and laughed together. They seemed to themselves very little different from the two girls eleven years ago at the Royal College. Both, as they talked, caught something of their old enthusiasm, when they had seemed to themselves capable of any heights. They laughed now as they did then, at length and uncontrollably, unsure of themselves and their place, but full of hope so that the world and its setbacks seemed matters for wild mirth. Now in this dark room, two women aged thirty threw away a dozen years and were glad of it.

At three-forty Elizabeth accompanied her friend in the car as they set out to collect the children from a school outing. Paul was seven and Emma now five. Both wore uniform, blazers with emblazoned pockets and Emma a round felt hat with ribbon and upturned brim. They had plenty to say to their mother about the expedition they had been on. Emma had been awarded two stars for her answers and Paul's team had won some difficult race on the grass. After a minute's shyness they spoke as much to Elizabeth as to their mother. She showered them with questions.

'I thought Daddy was picking us up,' Paul said.

'No. But he'll be at home early. You'll get plenty of Daddy tonight.'

'And that means you're going out,' the boy said. 'To the West End.'

'Lord forbid.'

'Not with your friend?'

'Not even with her.'

Elizabeth helped in the kitchen with the preparation for an evening meal. She had ordered a taxi for six so that she'd have time for a quick bath before her own dinner. Richard appeared soon after five, changed from his city suit into T-shirt and shorts, made five minutes pleasant conversation with his wife's guest and then took to the floor with his children and building blocks.

'Whenever he gets an early evening,' Tania glossed, 'he spends it on the children. "We only get one chance with them" is what he says.'

'And is that right?'

'Sure it is. Mrs Seddon, the head of their school, had to cancel a trip for the junior part of the school last term. A sudden-death inspection which the authorities wouldn't cancel. So she laid the trip on in the middle of the holidays. Some of the children were away, but most could manage this day. There was no need for her to do it; it wasn't her fault, but she'd promised this end of term treat to the children and she kept her word. She made the authority pay for the bus. They wanted a good school to let the inspectors loose on, and they must fork out for their interference. She's an outstanding woman, but if she does these things for our children, then all the more reason why we should.'

'Where did they go?'

'To a farm somewhere. Out beyond Windsor. Where the headmistress comes from. She'd also lined the village hall up as a standby, in case it rained. She's a good organizer.'

'Do the children enjoy it?'

168

'I guess so. "It'll be a break for them from holidays. They do sometimes get bored." And two of the teachers volunteered, and a few parents.'

'She seems on top of her job. I suppose that's necessary with small children.'

'I guess she'd arranged covering insurance and all the rest of it. No time for improvisation these days. People sue if anything goes wrong.'

'How have you managed?'

'With Paul and Em? I just had to sort myself out. I had to give up some things. I was offered a super job as organist and choirmaster not far from here, but I had to turn it down.'

'Will it or an equivalent come up again?'

'I don't suppose so. Gone for good. But you can't have everything. You have to make your mind up.'

'Is it a rush? Life? The daily round?'

'Um. Once they get on their feet, yes. Dashing about, and if you think about it, boring as well. I used to think about it. Was it any duller than teaching, say, four part counterpoint? It ought not to be. You're watching and guiding the development of two bright children. It ought to be more exciting than teaching even gifted pupils old-fashioned disciplines. But you only get musical pupils an hour at a time. I don't know. It's physically very debilitating. You don't have a minute to yourself, not even to go to the loo.'

'Would you have missed it?'

'We'd decided we wanted a family. Richard's very good with them, and spends as much time as he can. And so far both have been healthy. If they had been disabled or disadvantaged or even ill quite often, it would have been different. Very different. As it is, we've managed, and we've not neglected them. Or so we feel.'

'And?'

'So far, so good. If when they're grown ups or teenagers they are murderers or drug addicts or criminals of one sort or another then we'll have failed. But most people don't turn out that way, and time and trouble spent on them when they're little is something of an insurance against such development. Or so I believe.'

'So you're pleased?'

'I wouldn't be without them. Not now. We miss out. If I were away as a recital organist a great deal then I couldn't have had children. As it is, I'm glad.'

'Tom, my husband, is fifty. Does that make any difference?'

Tania laughed.

'You look well enough on marriage, so presumably he's all right sexually. The older men are, the more likely there are to be variations in their genetic codes.'

'Might that be always bad?'

'Don't ask me. Would you like children? Do you like children?'

'I've no idea.'

'Neither had I. I wouldn't change now, though it's put back my career as a recitalist. But I've started an academic line that might be just as interesting. Once you get older the life of a peripatetic player is less attractive. Though I am preparing for a Messiaen recital now, in London and at St Sulpice in Paris . . .'

'I say.'

'Well, I've been lucky there. And have influential friends. And Messiaen seems to suit my style.'

'Not my cup of tea. Have you given a recital in France before?'

'Yes. Twice in Paris. And in Belgium, Bruges and Ghent. That's why I need this practice-organ at home so that I can get new things up quickly, if they're required.'

'It takes it out of you?'

'When the children were smaller I seemed in a giddy whirl all the time. I got other things done. I don't know how. Red mist half the day. Enervation half the night. Richard took a big share of responsibility. But I kept well, in health, I mean, and it allowed me to do all these things at once. I wonder now how I did it. Luck. Strong constitution. Real training. Help.'

'So you'd choose to do it again?'

'Yes. I would. Because I realise now it can be done. I'm not the only one. Thousands of women manage.'

'Have I left it too late?' Elizabeth asked, wondering to herself if this were the right question.

'You're only a chicken.'

The taxi arrived on time just as the Metcalfe family sat down to their evening meal. The occasion seemed quiet, but intense; four people round a table, all marvels in themselves, all joined.

170

Consubstantial and utterly different. Later that evening she described it to her husband as the equivalent of a late Beethoven quartet. Tom looked at her in adoration. This young woman, who could say such things out loud, had transformed his life, exalted the dull schoolmaster, melted the dross of middle-aged lethargy away.

The next day they visited the National Gallery, strolled in St James's Park, went to a violin recital at St John's, Smith Square and heard the Kreutzer Sonata. They felt both exhausted and exhilarated, and set off early next morning for home so that Tom could attend a meeting in the afternoon. He studied papers on the train, smiling up at her. She watched the speeding hedges, and toyed with a pamphlet which Tania Metcalfe had signed and presented to her on the organ music of Olivier Messaien. The confident tone of the text seemed to proceed from a certainty of knowledge that she would never match. And yet it had been hammered out on a keyboard, her word processor, by a mother of two, a housewife, a lover of crowded life. Elizabeth did not in any sense envy Tania, that clever friend; they'd been rivals of a sort at the RCM, but now were parted, widely so; one had forged ahead of the other, but for the moment it did not matter. Elizabeth lifted her eyes tolerantly from Messiaen, Olivier Eugène Prosper Charles, born Avignon, 10 December 1908, to the flying telegraph poles.

14

Tom Tyler returned from the scrutiny of A level results. In reply to his wife's inquiry, he answered, gruffly delighted,

'Better than I expected. And by a long chalk.'

'You're pleased.'

'The Albert Ball is on the way up.'

'Is there good reason for the improvement? Or is it just a statistical blip?'

He pulled a comical face at her.

'No. At long last we've got the lower school in better order, and that means we are much more likely to profit at "A". We've some good teachers in the sixth, but they don't want to be held back by having to spend the first term making sure that their pupils know the things that should have been drilled into them at GCSE level.'

'Who's responsible? Stephen?'

'Yes. To some extent. To a large degree. He's appointed some well-qualified people. We're beginning to get something of a name, and teachers seem, or some of them, to prefer to work in places like ours where the children are more amenable. And the better we do, the better the job applicants.'

'And you're expecting good GCSEs in a week's time, or whenever it is?'

'Yes. I shall be disappointed if we don't. Very disappointed.'

He walked tall, chest inflated, humming, conducting himself. Elizabeth chilled a bottle of champagne she had secretly bought for such occasions. As she was preparing the evening meal, Tom came into the kitchen.

'Anything I can do to help?' he asked.

'No. It's all under control. You sit down and rest on your laurels.'

He kissed her, turned away and then at the door swung back.

'One other thing came up today?' he said, solemnly glum.

'Good or bad?' She did not even turn from her working surface.

'Giles Thackeray rang me up.'

'Thackeray? Thackeray?'

'The High Master at Beechnall Grammar.'

'Oh, yes. I remember now. What did he want?'

Tom came a step or two further into the room.

'He rang, he said, because he expected I'd be in for A level results as he was.' He paused, walked about in a circle as if collecting his wits or his words. 'He's decided to retire at the end of the next academic year.'

'How old is he?'

'Early sixties. But he says, jokingly of course, that he must be the oldest serving headmaster in the country. And,' again the wait, the deeply inhaled breath, 'he suggested that I think seriously of applying for his job.'

'You've only just taken the headship here?'

'That's what I told him. He said he realised that, and that he couldn't expect me to give an answer immediately. But he insisted I should seriously consider it.'

'And will you?'

'Oh, yes. I was very flattered, as I told him. Beechnall Grammar is an outstanding school. I would never have considered putting in for the headship there. At my age, and my CV, I didn't think I'd get as far as a short list.'

'Then why is your Dr Thackeray pressing you?'

'He said they needed somebody on the arts side. He's a physicist, and his predecessor was a mathematician. And however all-round they may be, a change in the High Master's main subject is an advantage. He's done his best for Classics and Modern Languages and History and English as well as Economics but I should watch their development with a more understanding eye. Maths and Science is very strong. The historian who replaced me has been, so Thackeray said, slightly disappointing.

'Why's that?'

'Doesn't understand young people. Makes it all too dull. Oh, his results are well up to standard, but he can't hold the brightest ones, as he claims Matthew Dodd and I did.'

'You won't be able to alter that, will you?'

'I don't suppose so.' He dragged out a stool, and sat down.

173

'Well, then. And will he have much influence over the appointment of his successor?'

'On paper, no.' Tom smiled to himself. 'But our Dr Thackeray has spent all his life pushing and scheming to get his own way. They won't ask him directly, but he can spend the next year, he says, planting seeds.'

'But won't there be an enormous number in for such a prestigious job?' she asked.

'I expect so,' Tom answered. 'And one can't guess who'll finally come up trumps. But Thackeray said he'd thought hard about the sort of man he'd want. And time and time again I forced myself into his mind. I was a good teacher and something of a scholar. I'd spent most of my life in the classroom, and that wasn't a bad thing these days. This is a period of steadiness, of looking over and setting right mistakes. We don't need brilliant new deviations. We're on the right course for once, and we need to make sure we get as much out of the system as we can. Perhaps in twenty years we'll need a radical change.'

'How does he decide all this?'

'He says that with the publication of educational results, people now see that the selective schools, mostly private, with their emphasis on knowing a great deal are seen to be winning hands down, so that the state comprehensives are now falling into line to try to compete.'

'Is this all true?'

'I honestly don't know. His school has always done well. And with the competitive entry examinations and a well-run preparatory department, that's not surprising. I sometimes thought when I was there that we drilled the initiative, the flights of fancy or originality out of our people, but I don't know. They went to the universities they wanted, and did well enough there. And I see them in public life making a success of their careers, so perhaps that's what's needed these days. I'm baffled. I'm the sort of do-as-you're-told man, grubbing into old records.'

'You're not. You have to draw some conclusions when you've dug out all your facts.'

'I wonder.'

Tom appeared to muse on this, to be engaged elsewhere. His wife watched him knit his forehead, nod, clamp his teeth together, breathe ponderously in, then out, touch his face with fingers that he hardly seemed to guide.

'Anyhow, Thackeray thinks I'm the sort of man to hold the tiller steady for the present. I've been in the state sector. He'd like to attract clever boys from the other side.'

'That's less likely than ever now, isn't it?'

'He thinks that somebody like me who's worked outside our charmed circle will realise what it is that these state-school boys need, or at least will know how to make them comfortable.'

'Do you?'

'Only vaguely. Expense and accent and peer pressure. What chance will they have? Unless they're very gifted?'

Tom struggled up from his stool, and walked about the room, almost as if she weren't there watching him. She allowed him his moments of movement and recovery.

'Have you spoken to anybody else about this?' she asked.

'No. I've had no time. But in any case I'll keep this to myself for a month or two. One of the advantages of staying on at Albert Ball is that it gives *you* more chance to move about. I'm here. I know the ropes. I can get local help for the house. You can flit about the world.'

'Some hopes.'

'You don't know. Suppose the Lombard decide on you as number one pianist? You could throw up your job at Cavendish, or demand extended leave from them, and do what you want as a recitalist.'

'Thank you,' she said. She went out, returned with champagne and glasses. 'Could you do this. I've kept it on ice for your triumphant return.'

'Suppose we'd done badly?'

'Quietly put away until you do win.'

He opened the bottle, efficiently as always, poured, handed her a glass. She proposed the toast. 'To the future,' she said.

'Yes,' he said. 'Not bad. Not the fizz, the future, our future.' He put his glass down, grasped her round the buttocks and hoisted her. She squealed, spilling some champagne, hanging on to his head. Held high, whirled round the gleaming windows, she raised her glass confidently.

On the next day Elizabeth rang Ellen Woodcock. Tom had driven back to school to interview pupils. 'I'll make a day of it,' he said. 'I've some stuff on Edward the Third I want to work over, and I can do it there, out of the way. Nothing to be heard but the clank of caretakers' buckets.'

'Won't they interrupt you? Or the secretaries?'

'No. I have a hidey-hole. They can get at it by phone but they won't unless there's an emergency. I've trained them.'

The first time she called Ellen nobody answered. The second time immediately after she'd cleared away and washed the few lunch cups and plates she found Mrs Woodcock at home but laconic.

'Am I interrupting anything?'

'No. What can you? I was out in the garden when you rang this morning. I checked up who it was, but I didn't like to ring you. You might be practising or going out.'

'Would you like to come over this afternoon for a cup of tea?'

'Could you come here?'

'Yes, if it's no trouble.'

'I should like to see you. I don't exactly know where I am.'

'That sounds exciting.'

'You wouldn't think so if you were here.'

Elizabeth knew she had said the wrong thing, but an hour later Ellen showed her in cheerfully enough.

'Look at this bloody mess,' she shouted as they pushed into the hall.

Two lines of canvas on stretchers had been neatly placed, thick newspaper underneath. There'd be perhaps eighteen.

'What are they?' Elizabeth asked. She could see only the back.

'Oil paintings.'

'They're complete?'

With a gesture not far from contempt, she lifted the first picture out and held it up. The difference between the bright surface and the plain wooden back with grey canvas flashed startling. Elizabeth had not known what to expect: a nude perhaps. This was a landscape, a path between tall birch trees in the early morning. One looked eastwards at the shining clarity of sky, new-risen sun, white bark, blue shadows. Elizabeth had not seen a de la Tour painting like this; it consisted of irregular shapes, none very large, dabs or short brush strokes of colour which together completed a scintillating reality, a dance at once solid but light, utterly dazzling.

Elizabeth took a step or two back.

176

'It's marvellous,' she said. 'Exciting and real. When did he do this?'

Holding the picture in one hand, Ellen tapped the bottom right hand corner.

'Thirty years ago.'

'It's lovely,' Elizabeth said. 'It's almost alive. It, it shines, doesn't it?'

Ellen nodded, sniffed, blew dust off the top.

'You'd be surprised the amount of muck and dust I had to get off this lot.'

'You know how to do it?'

'I've done it often enough for him.'

'I meant without spoiling the pictures. One has to be careful.' Elizabeth, receiving no answer but a half-shrug, asked, 'Why have you brought these down? I take it they're from the studio?'

'Genuine de la Tour small pictures. Nothing above twenty inches square. His agent reckons he can sell them. Eurydice and two of the bathroom nudes have been on public exhibition, in America, in Britain and in Italy. They've made an impression.' She was clearly quoting George, a surprisingly good imitation. 'He's in now. The Tate has fished out, or prominently displayed one of his things. So has the Metropolitan in New York, and some gallery in Chicago. And the magazines have taken him up again. He sent me a pile, with the bathroom nudes in them, some in languages I didn't understand, German and French and something else, Hungarian. He rang me up and said, "Here's your bum featured all over the world."'

'Were you pleased?'

'I don't think anybody would recognise me. But it's odd to see pictures I remember being painted in all these magazines. The colours are quite different.'

'From the original?'

'Yes, and from one another.'

Ellen returned the picture to its line, eyeing it, straightening one other straggler.

'George sent me a list of the pictures I was not to let this agent have. But he's careless and doesn't remember. There are certain to be rows, so I've kept his list and told him I've done so. This agent came up; he was on his way to Hardwick, and had a look at what was going. He picked out the ones he thought he

177

could handle and asked if I could clean them up before he came back. But he spotted the ones he couldn't have; I'd put 'em aside, and out of the way, I thought, but he saw them straight off. He wanted one or two of them, I can tell you, but I said he'd have to argue with George.'

'When will he pick them up?'

'Tomorrow. And if I know him he'll go up to the studio and poke about again. I've put my cleaning material up there to get the thick off. He won't touch 'em, not in his fancy suit.' She laughed. '"We have to play our cards right," he said. "We don't want to flood the market. Play 'em along." I suppose it's sensible. But I thought, and I don't know why I thought it, I'd like that Elizabeth Tyler to see them before they go. So when you rang up, it turned out just right.'

Ellen went out to make coffee instructing Elizabeth to look at the other paintings.

'You can pick them up. They're not dirty now.'

Elizabeth began at one end, lifting each canvas and moving with it towards the light. There were half a dozen landscapes done of mountainous country in winter, Scotland or the Lakes, grey and craggy, ugly and awkward in shape but beautiful in the artist's execution. Spring pictures depicted a house in trees, one of a pond, another of the sylvan path with birch trees, but this time in snow. An almost comical daub showed Ellen walking cock-a-hoop across a field arm in arm with a scowling, handsome man, presumably Archie. Three nudes of a girl unknown to Elizabeth flaunting her body on a multicoloured mattress, two of a young Ellen dressed like a gypsy pointing arrogantly down to the earth as if ordering the artist to his knees, two of a London street in mist, a half-ruined Greek temple painted from above with distant mountains completed the tally.

Elizabeth dusted her hands, wondered how much each would fetch at auction, decided that framing would marvellously improve even these pictures. If she had the choice of one, which would it be? The Greek temple with its slender circle of broken pillars defiant amongst the frown of rocky cliffs, distant touches of villages, an implacable blue of sky. Men would choose the one of the girl on the bed with her thighs half open. Would Tom? She did not know, but would not be afraid to ask. Ellen was long enough brewing two cups of instant coffee.

The hostess returned, wringing her hands.

'Every time I go in that bloody kitchen I break something.'

'What was it this time?'

'A sugar-basin.'

'But we neither of us take sugar.'

Ellen shrugged so violently that she seemed almost to struggle out of her dress. Elizabeth followed her into one of the small sitting rooms near the kitchen.

'This is where I watch telly at night,' Ellen said, 'in the winter.'

They occupied the two big ramshackle armchairs. Elizabeth felt herself to be lying almost on the ground. She asked about the pictures and Ellen answered plainly, only becoming animated when she described how George made his own stretchers, 'good and strong'.

'Did he ever frame his own pictures?'

'When he was younger. He's always had some money coming in. There was always some well-to-do fellow with a commission, or a newspaper or magazine.'

'Did he enjoy being told what to do?'

'He said not. But he'd get on with it. He reckoned you were not likely to find a decent idea amongst any of these patrons. They didn't know what they were after. He preferred dealing with their agents who'd go away and convince these Midases that what they'd bought was what they wanted.'

'Did he ever do portraits?'

'He'd do anything. But, yes, he did.'

'And did the subjects like them?'

'Not always.'

Ellen seemed to grow cheerful as she talked. Elizabeth looked round the bare room with its one radiator and small gas fire. The single window, narrow, bordered with stained glass, vaguely gothic, demonstrated the thickness of the walls.

'Do you ever get lonely here all on your own?' Elizabeth asked still staring round. There was one picture only, cut from a magazine, glazed and mounted but framed with some black tape. It was not large, but seemed to show an unremarkable house.

'I'm used to it. He was often away. Teaching or painting.

179

He went to Italy or Greece or Cornwall and left me and Archie behind. And Archie was never at home while he'd got money and women to spend it on. I've been unlucky with men.'

'You sound quite cheerful about it.' Elizabeth feared she'd said the wrong thing.

'I don't think about it. Not now. Why should I? When I do I just get mad with myself. What am I doing hanging about this house all on my own without too much to do in winter except clean? The garden keeps me going from Spring onwards. If I look at it all rationally, that used to be one of George's favourite words, I'm just hanging on here waiting to be slung out when he sells the house.'

'Will he?'

'I would. What good is it to him? It seemed just right when he'd started on a new lot of work. I could cook his dinners, and wash his clothes, and satisfy his sex. You don't like that, do you? It's true. And the house was within his means, and gave him a big studio, and me a big garden, and we could keep out of each other's way when we couldn't go out. But now money's pouring in. Or it is according to him, so he's invested in this Italian place and he's got his Despina and his name in all the papers. What use is this dump to him? They're in America now.'

'Doing what?'

'Talking about a companion picture to Eurydice. He's going to look where they've put the original, and see if there's anything he can do to match it.'

'Will there be?'

'You don't know with him. And since he's been going about with Despina he follows her ideas to an extent. She's certain to say what can be done and not done.'

'Doesn't he know by himself?'

'Well, in a way. He knows what he can paint when he's got a brush in his hands. He lays down the law when he hasn't, but then comes this Countess with her big ideas and he's impressed.'

Elizabeth left soon after, puzzling over what she'd learnt. Ellen said she'd potter in the garden all afternoon, and not eat until the evening. She had a beef casserole that she'd started yesterday.

'It'll last me for days.'

'And you won't get tired of it?'

'No. It fills me up. I'll change the vegetables. Peas, beans, potatoes, even rice, if I can be bothered.'

'And then what?'

'I'll wash the dishes, have a bath, and watch the telly.'

When Elizabeth discussed this with Tom, he listened and asked,

'Would you say she's unhappy?'

'She says not.'

'But basically? When you forget all about the performance she's putting on for you?'

'I don't honestly know. She's enough to occupy her, out in the garden, and with this agent, and quite frequent phone calls and instructions from George or his people in America. But what happens when winter's on her, and there's nowhere to go, nobody to talk to, and it's dark by four-thirty on the brightest days?'

'That's the test, is it?' he asked.

'It would be for me.'

'You have your piano. You can sit down to that.'

'Even that's not so easy if you've got nothing in view. I like specific, limited aims. It's only human.'

That evening they walked down to the Fox and Grapes but they did not stay long. As Tom said, it seemed a shame to sit indoors with chrome and darts and fancy bottles with the air outside so calmly warm and inviting.

Three mornings later the leader of the Lombard 'phoned to ask if they could call in for a run-through of the Brahms on the way back from Durham. No sooner had she made a note of arrangements than the phone squalled again asking if she would give two recitals in Glasgow in January. Feeling particularly pleased she was not surprised that the telephone interrupted her practice a third time. She cursed, but without venom knowing it didn't matter. This was one of those days, making life interesting.

Ellen spoke in her deliberately reduced, dull voice.

'Is that you, Elizabeth?'

'Yes.'

'It didn't sound like you.'

There followed an awkward pause.

181

'Could you come over and see me? Something dreadful's happened.'

'I'm so sorry. To you?'

'I don't want to talk about it over the phone. You never know who's listening.' She spoke rudely, crudely.

'Do you want me to come over now?'

'If you can.'

'I'll get the car out.' She'd miss time she'd allocated to practice, but Tom was away all day at his school.

Ellen had left the gate of 'The Hollies' open so that Elizabeth could park on the drive. She rang the front doorbell, but was kept waiting. Here, with the trees close, it seemed darker and colder than on the open ground of New Orchard Cottage. Elizabeth, slightly angry, leaned on the bell again, hearing it peal distantly indoors, but it was a minute or two before Ellen made her appearance.

'Come in,' she said. She was dressed for housework, and led Elizabeth immediately into the largest of the sitting rooms, where she ordered her guest to sit at a polished table. She seated herself on the other side of the room at least six metres away. 'I've had some bad news,' she began. 'Very bad.'

Elizabeth made a murmur of sympathy.

'Despina's dead.'

Ellen left it there, desperately silent.

'Was it an accident?' Elizabeth dredged the question up; she could barely make herself audible.

'Yes.'

'How did you find out?'

'Some man rang. From America.'

Silence hung between them.

'Is George all right?' Elizabeth tried again but feebly.

'Yes. Physically he is.' Ellen now made an effort. 'The man who rang was some sort of lawyer, I think. I didn't quite catch all he was saying. He seemed to be connected with Mr Muller, the millionaire who commissioned Eurydice. But George had told him to let me know.'

'Were they together when it happened?'

'No. She was away. At the seaside. She was drowned. Or that's what I gathered. I was so shaken I couldn't take it in properly. The man said George was too upset to ring me himself,

but he wanted me to know. So I could tell other people, perhaps.
It turned me into ice. I couldn't take in half the man was telling
me. And he had a queer accent.'

'They were going to get married, weren't they?'

'They can't now.'

'Where is George?' Elizabeth asked.

'I don't know. The man did mention where Despina was
when it happened, but it meant nothing to me, and I've forgotten.'

'Was it in bad weather, or some bathing accident?'

'Don't ask me.' Ellen straightened herself. 'I didn't seem to
take it in. I was so knocked over. I mean, she was a young
woman, years younger than me. Not that I liked her. I didn't.
But here she'd been not long ago throwing her weight about,
laying the law down. And George took some notice of her.
Obsessed with her. Not like himself. Hung on her words.
And now she's dead, gone, can't say yea or nay, not to him
or anybody else.'

'He'll be heartbroken.' Elizabeth said the trite words slowly,
heavily.

'He will. And that's not like him.'

'Where is he now? With this Mr Muller?'

'No idea. Why weren't they together? I didn't think he could
bear her out of his sight for a minute. And he was usually
gruff with people. But not with her. I mean, he'd shout at
her occasionally. He couldn't help it. That was his way. But
he looked frightened when he did as if he'd lose her if he put
a word too many out of place. Not that she minded. She could
give as good as she'd taken from him. That's what he liked,
perhaps. She was a clever woman.'

'When did this happen?'

'I didn't ask questions. I couldn't think. It was some time
this week.'

'I'm sorry to hear this, Ellen. She seemed a very forceful
personality.'

The two women sat in awkward silence. One had given
the message and the other had received it. Now both were
damaged by what was told and heard. Neither made any
attempt to speak; both raked round sore and empty minds.
Elizabeth had entered this house a few minutes ago with
apprehension; now she sat reduced, curiosity dispersed as the

numbness of knowledge unsettled her. She placed a hand, leaving an ephemeral print, on the polished surface of the table. Beneath the sad news worse lurked. Ellen had done badly in collecting the detail; the tragedy grew because one lacked defining limits. They would see nothing more of Despina; that exotic bird would not descend again on this village, dazzling them all, scintillating and brave. But what would George do?

'What do you think will happen?' Elizabeth asked. She must keep talk alive between the two of them. 'Will he come back here?'

'I don't know. Why should he?'

'He has you waiting, and a house and studio all ready for him.'

'He's bought this place in Italy where they were going to live. That'll be warmer when winter comes. And he'll remember the time he was here with her. He looked ready to settle down. He's not a young man any more. He's sixty-one.'

'You think they would have been suited?'

'How can I know that? George soon gets tired of things or people, and drops them pretty quickly. Just doesn't bother with them any more. Forgets all about them. That's why I was surprised he made money over to me to keep the house in order. It might have been Despina getting on at him. It didn't seem like him.'

'Unless having an enormous amount of money has changed him.'

Ellen grimaced, but did not answer. The two women sat guarding their awkward silence. Elizabeth made a further effort.

'Didn't this lawyer give you any idea of what was going to happen?'

'How could he? He wouldn't know. All he knew was that she had died.'

'And he gave no further hint about George's state?'

'No.'

'He didn't give you instructions? About informing other people?'

'No. He'd have been told to ring certain people to tell them about Despina. Probably by his employer, Mr Muller or some connection.'

184

Another pause. Ellen sat slightly skewed in her chair.

'And what are you going to do?'

'Hang on here. Until I get instructions to do otherwise. I can't do anything else. I've nowhere to go, and nothing else to do.'

Elizabeth invited Ellen over to lunch, but the offer was refused.

'I shall be all right, now I've told somebody about it.'

'You'll give me a ring if you need any help, won't you?'

'Yes.'

'Let us know. Whatever it is. We're on holiday now for the next week or two. We shall have a bit of free time.'

Ellen thanked her. No offer of refreshment seemed forthcoming so that Elizabeth after one or two further attempts at conversation, pushed herself to her feet, said she must go. Again she offered to provide lunch, and again Ellen refused, almost graciously this time. Both stood. Ellen advanced, threw her arms around her friend, and kissed her full on the mouth. The force of the embrace toppled Elizabeth, but Ellen pulled her steady, held her secure. The woman's arms were strong. For a second time she kissed Elizabeth. Her mouth was soft, seemed eloquent after the grudging sentences she'd been offering.

They walked out together to Elizabeth's car in the drive. A second invitation to lunch was refused. No, she wouldn't change her mind or spoil Elizabeth's day with her miseries. She raised a crooked smile as the guest backed out into the road.

Elizabeth discussed the news with Tom before dinner. He had reported a poor day with nothing but interruptions. He'd give up working in school; it had seemed a good idea. He could push on with his own research, and deal with the one or two queries that came up and so save himself much trouble later. It had not turned out like that. The director, the area education officer, members of staff, parents, students had all received the message from somewhere that he was at the Albert Ball and available to them. Even his secretary, the model of efficiency, had twice come running in to him with matters she would effortlessly have dealt with on her own, had he not been there. He'd got nothing of his research done, and sounded thoroughly disgruntled.

When Elizabeth reported Despina's death, he straightened himself.

'That puts my bloody grousing into place,' he said. 'She was a really vivid personality. George will be shattered.'

'Ellen's not been in touch with him personally. Only with some lawyer.'

'About legal matters?'

'No. Just to tell her that Despina had died. Ellen didn't seem to know how it had affected George.'

'How was she?'

'She asked me to go down, wouldn't tell me why on the phone. I went straightaway, but she didn't seem very willing to talk, once she'd told me what the trouble was.'

'But surely you could tell from her demeanour how she was taking it?'

'I couldn't. She seemed to have locked it up inside her, frozen it. She'd no idea what was going to happen to her, or to George. She told me that, after a bit of probing on my part, and with a glum face and in a flat voice. I guess she was upset, though she said she didn't much like Despina. She'd no idea how it would affect her in the long run, whether George would sell the house, put her on the streets. She spoke as if he hadn't much forethought or compassion. He'd get rid of the house if it saved him a pound or two, and not consider her.'

'And this troubled her?'

'I suppose so. The uncertainty. She's always been a dependant.'

'Yes.' His face had grown grim. 'I hope George de la Tour treats her properly, especially now he's so rich.'

'He's been a very long time making big money. Perhaps he's got into habits of scrimping and saving.'

Tom nodded, cleared his throat, his face angry still.

'That's two of them,' he said. Elizabeth did not follow him. 'Women. Killed on holiday when they should have been enjoying themselves.'

Elizabeth had not made the connection between the deaths of Janet and Despina before. She felt ashamed that this was so. What troubled her husband was not Ellen's plight but the sudden deaths of two gifted women at a time when they should have been revelling in their success and their deserved leisure. She ought to have thought about it, but she had not.

Tom recovered quickly. His distress, he had noted, registered with his wife, and now he had put it on one side. Perhaps that was the result of his professional skills. As a headmaster he had to be, or was by temperament, sensitive, but the pains were then duly dismissed, or hidden, so that life, and the life of a thousand or more pupils could go steadily on.

She told him about the flying visit of the Lombard Quartet, and he marked his diary carefully.

'I don't want to be out at some useless, boring committee meeting when I can be listening to your practising here with them.'

'They'll come in the afternoon on their way back from Durham.'

'I'll take an hour or two off. I have my own education to see to.'

He smiled, himself again, ready for the world.

15

The last few weeks of her holiday Elizabeth spent in serious practice. Tom warned her not to overdo it, that she mustn't start the new term at Cavendish College jaded and out of sorts. She paid no attention, as he knew she would not, but the week before the new term started they elected to spend five days in Paris, looking at pictures, at Frenchmen and each other as he put it to her. He had insisted on this break, and she found, to her surprise, that she liked him in this dominant mood.

In this time she had seen Ellen Woodcock only once. She had rung 'The Hollies' two or three times, had found nobody at home, left a message on the answering machine but had not been contacted. Against her practice of never calling on anyone without prior warning, she drew up one morning on the verge outside Ellen's house on her way back from the supermarket in town. Ellen answered the door, seemed genuinely glad to see her, invited her into the kitchen, boiled the kettle.

'It's so nice to see a friendly face,' Ellen enthused.

'Nothing but enemies round here?'

'I haven't seen anybody.'

'I've left you a message or two on the answering machine,' Elizabeth objected.

'I know. I'm not blaming you. It's my own fault. I can't bring myself round to seeking company. I just hang about here, doing nothing in particular, waiting for winter.'

She banged down a mug of instant coffee and a big rock bun on the table in front of Elizabeth.

'Aren't you busy in the garden?'

'Yes, I am; I enjoy that, especially when the weather's good. But I keep thinking to myself that somebody else will reap the benefit when the house is sold.'

'Is he going to sell it, then? Have you heard?'

'Not a cheep from anybody since that lawyer rang from America.'

'So you don't know where George is or what he's doing?'

188

'No. All I know is that money is still being paid into the bank. I ring on the first of the month to find out how the account stands, and I spend as little as possible in case of emergencies. Of course there are things I've no control over, such as gas and electricity and phone and council tax. They're paid off by direct debit straight out from the bank. As to the rest, I'm going steady with it. I've put some of it into a building society. It doesn't earn much interest, but at least it's mine.'

'You're not starving yourself, are you?'

'No. I've a garden.'

'And trips out?'

'Where would I want to go?'

Elizabeth described their Parisian jaunt; Ellen looked jaundiced.

'Sounds marvellous, but I'd have to travel on my own.' Elizabeth congratulated Ellen on her rock cakes, was given two more in a bag, and extracted a promise that as soon as Ellen heard anything she'd let them know. 'If you get lonely,' she said, 'you know where we live.' The offer sounded generous.

Term started at the Albert Ball Comprehensive and four days later at the Cavendish College. Tom reported to his wife that the sorting-out of new students had gone well. The sixth form, especially the Science sixth, had grown quite extraordinarily. The number of applicants for first-form entry from outside the catchment area was large.

'Could you take them all?'

'No. Not really. In the end it depended on things over which I have no control. Well, parents who have cars and are prepared to bring them in.'

'Are they good entrants?'

'So I'm told. We insisted on full reports from the junior schools. Robert Furniss the new deputy in charge of the junior school has worked like a Trojan, interviewing parents, ringing head teachers of feeder schools, looking at exam results.' Tom had insisted that the governors promoted Furniss to this new post, and he'd made his mark already.

'Suits his name?' she asked.

'Eh?' Tom's mind darted elsewhere.

'Furniss. Like a refiner's fire.'

'Not spelt right.' He was in no mood for lower school jokes.

Later he inquired about Ellen Woodcock.

'What do we do about her?' he asked.

'What do you mean?'

'We ought to keep an eye on her. But I guess she won't brook interference, so how do we go on?'

'I've told her to keep in contact with us, and I'll give her a bell from time to time.'

'A bell?' he said, as if he didn't follow. 'I don't like to think of her hanging round in that big, empty house with nobody to talk to. Or to turn to if something goes wrong.'

'She seems pretty competent.'

'Seems. Hmm. She called us in that first time we met her because she was scared.'

'Yes. But the weather's still good, and she can go out and work in her garden.'

Elizabeth drew the conclusion that Tom, appearances to the contrary, was nervous about the Albert Ball. Everything seemed to be shaping well according to his own evidence, but she guessed from his concern over Ellen that he feared some unseen difficulty with his school. When she questioned him, as she did frequently, he denied that he was in any way troubled.

Early in October she returned one Saturday from her first recital of the season in Liverpool. It had gone perfectly, better than she could have hoped, and two secretaries of Lancastrian music societies who attended her performance had attempted to book her for the new year. She knew she had done well, and as she travelled back on a sprinter train she recalled the fine Steinway she had played, the enthusiasm of the audience, her three encores. The weather was sunny and warm; just before she left home Tom, at long last, had received the final settlement of Janet's estate. When all the legal bills had been paid, he found himself almost three hundred thousand pounds the richer.

'What are we going to do with this?' he asked.

'I've not given it a thought.'

'Wouldn't you like to live elsewhere?'

'No.'

'Are you sure? It doesn't seem exactly right to have all this spare money washing about and not doing anything with it. We can pay our way, and easily, without it. And yet there it is. We could expand into a new house.'

'Why should we? I'm barely used to this one yet.'

'I thought you might like something bigger. We could buy it outright with this little lot.'

'No, thanks. This is ideal.'

His beaming face rewarded her.

On this Saturday morning he met her at the station. All was well at home. Lunch was in preparation. She in turn gave him a happy account of her recital. He asked his usual, pertinent few questions, then said,

'Guess who I saw.'

'Go on.'

'Yesterday as I was driving home from school,' he was dragging it out, 'just as I was passing "The Hollies" there was George de la Tour large as life.'

'Doing what?'

'Leaning on the outside gate.'

'Did you stop?'

'No. I was past before I realised. I hadn't even waved. Or sounded the horn.'

'Did he see you?'

'I've no idea. I mean he'd see me, but I don't know if he'd recognise my car.'

'Was Ellen with him?'

'Not that I could make out.'

'Did he look well?'

'I was driving too fast. I wanted to get home.'

They left it there after a conjecture or two about the loss of Despina. Next morning at breakfast he asked if they should telephone 'The Hollies'.

'We don't know how long he's been back. He might only just have arrived. I think we should give them a day or two to get themselves sorted out, to say to each other whatever it is that it is that they have to say.'

'You don't want to ring, do you?' he asked.

'I don't want to interfere needlessly.'

'I wonder what I'd do if I suddenly lost you,' he said. 'They seemed such good partners. She was so quick, exotic, positive. And then, suddenly, she's wiped out. It does not seem right.'

'No.'

They sat for a few moments in melancholy silence, but were too happy in themselves to extend the grief. Soon they were dancing hand in hand round the garden together.

'I wonder what your pupils would say if they saw us now?'
she asked.

'I could tell you. At least, what some of the boys would say.
But it's not fit for polite company, so I'll leave it.'

'How wise,' she mocked.

On Wednesday, her half-day free this year, she rang Ellen,
hoping no one would answer. Ellen must have been standing
close to the telephone. Elizabeth asked how things were.

'George is back. Did you know?'

'Tom thought he saw him as he drove past.'

'Well, he is. He came a week ago.'

'And how is he?'

There followed a pause and the sound of the phone being
laid down and a door shut.

'He's gloomy. That's about the word. He's not like himself.
He doesn't talk much, and never laughs.'

'Have you spoken to him about Despina?'

'I've tried to. Once or twice. I thought it might do him good.
But he didn't want it. "She's dead, Ell," he said. "That's all
there is to it." And he turned away. Either as if I'd insulted
him or as if it didn't mean anything to him. When I tried again,
I had to because he seemed so bad, he just muttered, "Shut up,
Ell. I don't want it. It's happened." And again he turned to the
door, but he stopped and put his hand on the edge and said,
"It's bloody happened, Ell," and cleared off.'

'Is he painting or drawing?'

'I don't think so. He goes up to the studio, but what he does
there I don't know. He's drinking quite a lot.'

'Does he go out at all?'

'Sometimes. For a walk. I don't know where. Mainly at late
evening time. I think he just tramps about. He hasn't got a car
here. He doesn't go into Beechnall or any other town as far as
I know.'

'Does he eat well?'

'No. I tell him when the next meal is, and he turns up on time.
But he doesn't eat heartily. Not a half of what he used to.'

'Does he talk to you at mealtimes?'

'No. Not much. He says things. But he doesn't always answer
what I'm telling him. And he plays with his food. I'm worried.
He's lost weight. And he's like a man that's only half alive. He
shuffles about.'

192

'Is he clean?'

'He trims his beard and has baths, if that's what you mean. He's about in the house now, but I can't hear him. Well, not moving about.'

'Would he come with you to see us? For coffee this weekend? Or a meal? Will you ask him?'

'I will. It would do him good to see somebody else, but I reckon I understand how he feels.'

'Will you go and ask him?'

'No, not now. I don't want to spring things on him. It might do him harm. Or me. But I'll put it to him at lunchtime. I'll tell him you were on the phone. And if . . . Oh, no, never mind. I'll give you a ring tonight. When he's gone out. It won't be too late. He usually sets off about nine o'clock.'

'And how are you?'

'Me? I'm me. I don't understand it. I'd feel better if only he'd eat.'

'Or paint?'

'I can't make him. When I do say anything he just says, "Oh, shut up, Ell," not angrily.' She drew in breath. 'I just keep myself going by doing things, cleaning and gardening. And I'm whitewashing one of the larders.'

Ellen kept her promise and rang at about a quarter to ten that evening. George had gone for his walk. She had spoken to him, and after three attempts on her part he had agreed that they should be invited for coffee on Saturday.

'He wasn't keen?' Elizabeth asked.

'He was not. You'd stir up all the memories he wants to bury. Besides, he's a bit wary of the pair of you. He thinks you're beautiful, and know about music, as he doesn't. And he always refers to your husband as "the schoolmaster" or "that bloody schoolmaster".'

'Is that how you think of him?'

'Perhaps a bit. But George says that your husband seems to know it all, to be so sure of himself.' Ellen cleared her throat, giving herself time. 'He's no confidence in himself, you know.'

'But he's so successful now. His name's regularly in the papers. And he's sold his picture for all this money.'

'I guess he thinks he's deserved all that. He's better, in his view, than anybody else painting, but once he's convinced himself of that he begins to wonder what he'll do next. He said to me years ago, "When I was young, I could set about painting one damn thing after another. Once one was done, I'd be off on the next. Some were better than others. But I wasn't staring reputation in the face all the time." He often used to tell me this.'

'I see.' Elizabeth was amazed that Ellen had remembered so well. The woman had even managed something of de la Tour's accent. Ellen suddenly lost heart, then, and wished Elizabeth goodbye, ridding herself of the phone.

Tom listened to his wife's account, (she missed out George's strictures on the schoolmaster), and agreed to go with her on Saturday morning. On each of the intervening days he raised the question of de la Tour's lack of self-confidence.

'He's well known,' he said, wondering, 'really famous. He gets as much publicity as Lucien Freud or Hockney. They're mounting an exhibition of his stuff in Australia. I read that only yesterday in *The Times*. He must begin to believe what they say about him.'

'And?'

'And it inhibits him. Usually it's lack of appreciation or adverse criticism or complete lack of success that stops one doing one's work.'

'I see.' She tempted him on.

'It's my considered view,' Elizabeth tittered at his expression, 'that if one is any good, and it's not only a matter of talent, but of character, one continues in and even profits from adversity. Things run against you, and you make from those obstacles the inspiration for your work.'

'I don't think I'd say that to him.'

'No. Perhaps not. But then you see he may not be of the highest quality. I'm not in any position to judge.'

'It seems queer to me that somebody as famous as he is,' she said, 'with pictures in all the major galleries in the world, and discussed in newspapers should be sitting not a mile away from us here, mooning about, depressed.'

'Even the famous have to sit somewhere.'

'Yes. It doesn't seem exactly right.'

'That's because you rate the arts so highly. The best pianist in the world, the greatest composer has to eat his breakfast, or open his bowels like the rest of us poor mortals.'

194

They set off Saturday morning on foot in the bright St Luke's sunshine.

'It's marvellous weather for the first week in October,' Tom said, swishing his unnecessary walking stick. He appeared very smart, with a pale blue open necked shirt, a knotted silk scarf, an alpaca jacket, old-fashioned flannels with turn-ups and polished brogues. Elizabeth had dressed simply, in a flowered summer dress, 'like the vicar's wife', she told him.

Ellen led them into the largest of the drawing rooms. The place, recently decorated, smelt of furniture polish. Windows and picture-glasses gleamed.

'Sit down,' she invited. 'The percolator's on.'

She left them, shutting the door. They could hear nothing from inside the house or outside.

'She's taking her time,' Tom complained. He had risen from his chair and walked over to a window which overlooked a small path, a stretch of lawn at one side of an ornate greenhouse, and at some distance a fruit-cage. 'I wonder what she's got in there.'

'Raspberries, currants,' Elizabeth guessed. She now stood by him. 'I can't see from here.'

'It all looks in decent order.'

'Ellen's an energetic woman. She says she follows the procedures which she learnt from the old men on the allotments near where they lived before. By doing this she can just keep up, whereas if she was always trying new things out she'd fall miles behind.'

Tom fiddled with the change in his trouser pockets. Elizabeth had noticed before that he did not like being kept waiting. Now he almost writhed with impatience. He wanted to get his meeting with George over.

'She's in no hurry this morning,' he said, teeth together.

'Perhaps she's trying to get George to come down.'

'We're here on his invitation, aren't we?'

'He may have changed his mind.'

Tom turned back to the window and its sunlit stretch of garden. He tapped at the carpet with his left foot.

'I can't see any de la Tours on the wall,' she said.

'Would you recognise them?' he asked.

'I think so. These look dull. A job lot. Or left behind by the last owner.'

'Colonel Fothergill?'

'Or his predecessors.'

Both were now thoroughly uncomfortable, walking round the walls. Still the room seemed sealed off in silence from the rest of the house.

'I'm surprised,' Tom ventured, 'that George left these pictures. I thought he'd just throw them into the dustbin.'

'I don't think he'd bother. There they are, and there they stay if that's what Ellen wants. He'd never even notice them. I don't think he bothers much about the circumstances he lives in.'

'Oh. It seems odd that a painter doesn't notice pictures. You'd be annoyed if you heard somebody playing the piano and constantly repeating wrong notes.'

'Perhaps he doesn't come in here.'

'He'd prowl round. He's that sort.'

'I don't know.'

The edge of impatience cut into their exchanges. Both were now considerably ill at ease. Tom blew his lips out, but had sat down again when they heard the knob of the door being turned. The walls and doors were solid. The door opened cautiously and Ellen entered with a trolley, coffee cups, a pot, sugar and milk, a plate of home-made buns, heavy and laced with demerara sugar. Ellen looked round.

'Where's George?' she asked, as if the visitors were at fault. They did not reply. 'I thought he'd be down by now. I'll pour our coffee, and he'll have to tag along as best he can. If his is cold, it's nobody's fault but his own.'

She poured out three large cups. Elizabeth refused milk, perhaps to fortify herself against this ordeal. Plates and cakes were issued, cheering Tom who congratulated Ellen on her cooking.

'Straightforward,' she said. 'Plain.'

'They have,' he laid down the law, 'both weight and lightness. That's unusual.'

'That's because they were done this morning,' Ellen said dismissively. Elizabeth noticed, with pleasure, that her bun was still slightly warm. Tom's remark exactly summarised the quality of the confection. His diplomacy as usual merged with shrewdness.

While they were still talking about cookery and the great numbers of television programmes on the subject, and the reasons for this fashion, the door was quietly opened and George de la Tour entered.

To Elizabeth he looked exactly as when she had last seen him. His clothes were neat but old; his shirt-collar was left Byronically unfastened. Chest hair bushed greyly. He had recently washed and trimmed his beard. He bowed his head in her direction, and wished her good morning in a low, firm voice.

Tom sprang up from his chair, held out his hand. George shook it, murmured a greeting. Elizabeth concentrated on her cup wondering why and in what ways she had expected him to be different. He wore trainers, she saw, splashed with mud or paint. Ellen was on her feet pouring his coffee.

'We thought you were lost,' she said. She pushed the buns towards him. 'Have one. Your favourites.'

'Thank you.' His voice he kept low, and polite.

Tom, still standing, spoke.

'We were terribly sorry to hear about Despina. It was a tragedy. She seemed so full of life.'

George de la Tour was raising his coffee to his lips, but paused and with immense care replaced cup and saucer on the table beside him.

'Yes,' he said. 'Yes. Thank you.'

'It seems unjust,' Tom ventured. 'An injustice.'

'You'll miss her. Terribly,' Elizabeth said. It sounded trite, but she at least had spoken.

'Yes.' George's head nodded. 'Yes, I shall.'

'She was so young,' Tom said. 'So lively.'

'And beautiful,' Elizabeth added. 'We hardly saw her, but I shan't ever forget her. She seemed different.'

George made no reply, but stared at the floor. He, preoccupied, seemed to have dismissed the others, with their lame condolences, from his mind. They had said their pieces, raised the unmentionable, and he had thanked them. Tom took a hurried sip of his coffee, determination to continue etched on his face.

'She was a gifted art historian,' Tom said, 'so I hear. I read a short article by her in the *Burlington Magazine*. On Masaccio. It seemed very enlightening. Not that I am any sort of expert. But it not only told me much that I didn't know, but seemed to open up ideas on the subject.'

Elizabeth had no idea that he had taken trouble to look out the essay. He had not mentioned it to her.

'Ideas,' he continued, 'that would have been useful, fruitful had I known the facts already. That is the best sort of criticism. I expect you found what she had to say about your paintings very helpful.'

George raised his sad head, looked briefly across at Tom.

'No. Not really,' he answered. There was no force behind the delivery; a mere conveyance of denial sufficed.

'No?' Tom, taken aback, struggled on. 'I thought any exchange of ideas might lead profitably on.'

'It leads to argument,' George said.

'And that has no part in a painter's production?'

'Not in this painter's. I search out my own way, such as it is. I don't find what journalists say anything but ignorant. One stroke of the brush is as good as another to them.'

'You surprise me,' Tom exclaimed, and sat back to be enlightened. George offered nothing more, but swivelled to reach for his coffee. Tom waited, without reward. Elizabeth felt sorry for him, but proud of his effort. She must now try.

'Are you painting much?' she asked.

'No.'

'Anything?'

'No. Nothing.'

'That's a pity.'

George blew out breath as if to confirm her belief, but did not speak. They sat in awkward silence for a time, eating and sipping, making heavy weather of the occasion. In the end it was Tom, the public figure, who broke the silence.

'Are you staying here long?' he asked.

George vouchsafed no answer, did not appear to have heard the question.

'I thought that while you were here, you and Ellen might like to come and have a meal with us up at New Orchard Cottage. Is that possible?'

George nodded, though Tom had no idea whether he answered the question or merely acknowledged its existence. He writhed in his chair.

'I'm not sure of my future plans.'

'No, I can understand that.'

George scratched his head noisily; his face showed malicious pleasure, a crooked smile, but at what Elizabeth could not guess.

'Perhaps Ellen would let us know,' Tom continued, now directly facing the woman who did not herself speak. She suddenly stood, so quickly that Elizabeth thought she was about to run from the room.

'Anyone for more coffee?' she asked. She swooped on Elizabeth, removed her cup. Tom drained his, held it politely forward in her direction. The visitors watched the refilling.

'George?' she asked. He shook his head soundlessly. 'Another bun, Mr Tyler?' as she delivered his coffee. He accepted her offer; she brought the plate over.

'I shan't need any lunch,' he said.

'Think of the money you'll save,' she answered.

She approached Elizabeth with the plate, but the visitor shook her head. When the buns had been returned to the table, before Tom could speak, George pushed himself stiffly to his feet. He supported himself with one hand on the surface of the table, perilously near his empty cup.

'Thank you for coming,' he said, in the same low, colourless voice. 'It was most kind of you. You must excuse me now.' He made a jerky obeisance in the direction of Elizabeth, turned on his heel, reached the door which he opened and closed without noise. The guests sat in silence.

'You see what he's like,' Ellen said.

'The bereavement has affected him badly,' Tom answered. 'That's clear.'

'He seems so quiet,' Elizabeth added. She remembered his forcefulness, his loud voice, the vulgarity which had perhaps indicated creative energy unable to contain itself, spilling out into other spheres. Now he was like some church deacon, some undertaker's mute, the personality dissolved in the solemnity of the occasion.

'Is there anything we can do?' Elizabeth asked. 'To help.'

'I wish I knew,' Ellen answered.

'How does he spend his time?' Tom spoke slowly.

'Again I don't know. He's either up in his bedroom or in the studio. It's pretty warm up there now the sun's out. But what he's doing I haven't the faintest.'

'Sorting things out?' Tom suggested.

'For all I know. He doesn't say much. He might go out for an hour at night to the pub.'

'Does he eat more now?' Elizabeth asked.

'Better. But without enjoyment. He clears his plate. Let's put it like that. But he shows no pleasure, nor appreciation. He might thank me or he might not.'

'Doesn't he talk over meals?'

'No. Not much. If I have things to ask he'll answer. About payments. Or the next meal. But you've seen what he's like. You question him and more often than not he just ignores you.'

'And if you repeat it?'

'He still doesn't bother to answer. It's hard work I can tell you. I've never seen him like this before. He used to be awkward sometimes and lose his temper and swear and throw things about, but now he's a nothing. All he seems to want is to hide himself away.'

'You've no idea what his future plans are?'

'No more than you have.'

'He's not spoken about going?'

'No.'

They talked for another twenty minutes. Tom pressed Ellen to try again, however great the discouragement, with George. 'You never know.' Ellen, face sour now, was unimpressed. She showed them round her garden, where she recovered something of cheerfulness, and, once the circuit was complete, quickly to their car.

'What do we do about that pair, then?' Tom asked, back at New Orchard Cottage.

'I don't know. There's nothing we can do. Except keep in touch. Intermittently.'

'He needs shock tactics,' Tom said.

'Not from us,' she retorted.

'No. You're right.'

16

October became November, and the air remained mild. Elizabeth telephoned Ellen Woodcock several times, but spoke to her only twice. Either the call went unanswered, or the receiver was left off its cradle. On the successful occasions Ellen claimed that she had not yet managed to persuade George to accompany her to a meal at the Tylers'. He was still with her, though on the second time he had gone that morning to London for a few days.

'Is that a good sign?' Elizabeth asked.

'He's a bit more human than he was, but no more sensible. He's still doing nothing, art-wise, I mean, and still keeping out of my way.'

'Who's he meeting? In London?'

'He hasn't said, nor left either an address or a phone number. He only told me late last night that he was going. I asked him straight out for a name or address, but I might as well have been speaking Chinese. He just stared at me as if I'd said something so ridiculous it was not worth answering.'

'How long is he staying?'

'When I asked him he said, "A few days." "What's that mean?" I asked him, and he just replied, "You've as much idea as I have." That's typical of him these days. He won't make up his mind, and he tries to keep me at arm's length from him.'

'He's said nothing about moving?'

'No. But I'm not surprised. It'll be all sealed, signed and delivered before he says anything to me about it.'

'Are you keeping well?'

'I'm glad he's gone off. That I can tell you. Looking after him's too much like hard work. It's being his keeper, if that's what they're called, in a lunatic asylum. You don't know what he'll do next.'

'Would you like to come up? On your own?'

'That's kind of you, but if you don't mind I'd like a bit of time to myself.'

'Very good.' Elizabeth smiled, was relieved at the decision.

Tom, the headmaster, seemed to grow in confidence. He spent long hours at the school, and attended evening meetings, but took all in his stride, mocked himself. 'My whole day's spent listening to or settling trivialities.' He enjoyed the handling of finances, but took rather less pleasure in adjudicating rival claims between individuals. 'Some of the staff,' he grumbled, 'seem to lose all sense of judgement as soon as they open my study door.'

'And this surprises you.'

'In a way, yes. I knew there were crackpots enough amongst my colleagues before this. I couldn't help noticing. But what I didn't realise was how cracked some of them were.'

'Do you go round the school?' she asked. 'What my H.O.D. calls "creeping the corridors".'

'I do. And I let 'em know that I'm there.'

'Do you go over to the junior block every day?'

'Not quite. I take a couple of assemblies there. And look in on the new teachers. Occasionally. Bob Furniss keeps 'em up to scratch. That was a first-rate appointment.'

'He's as good as you thought?'

'Better. They could sack me, and put him in charge, and the school would benefit, I reckon.'

'Will he leave?'

'For promotion? Very likely. But not just yet. He's not too ambitious, and he has young children he won't want to shunt about too often. I'm looking for a new head of science. Bloxham has told me he wants to retire in the summer.'

'What's his subject?'

'Chemistry.'

'And there's no one in the school to replace him.'

'No. Unfortunately not. Bloxham's a decent old stick, does a respectable job. But I'd like somebody younger, some live wire. Whether such a person exists I don't know, nor whether he'd want to throw his lot in with the Albert Ball. We can but hope.'

'You say "he". Mayn't women apply?'

'Possible, but unlikely. I don't know why. Perhaps it's prejudice on my part. We're trying to persuade more girls to do sciences in the sixth form. A senior science mistress might encourage this.'

'And how's discipline?' she asked. 'I hear such horrifying tales.'

'It's good. They all wear school uniform. They have to walk sedately along the corridors.'

'And they're willing to accept these restrictions?'

'Seems so. I'm not saying that there are no lawbreakers, or clodhoppers, but they're trained to act sensibly from the first form. That's to my predecessor's credit. And our sort of children aren't too bolshy.'

'If you get a bad case? A real villain?'

'Out. Send for the parents and tell them to take their monster away.'

'And if they won't?'

'They've no option. They're allowed to plead their cause. And I, or one of the deputies, will listen. And we're getting a reputation for academic success. That's what parents want to see these days, their children with qualifications. They'll back me if I want to get rid of disruptives.'

'And is it dull?' she asked, mischievously.

'The very opposite, I'd say. When there's a good work ethic in the place, it's easier for the teachers to make their lessons more interesting. And we're a goodish staff. It's partly by chance, but mainly due to Stephen's sharp eye.'

'Is it trickier than you anticipated?'

'You ask just the right questions. No, it's easier, less stressful. But I'm a bit inclined to pessimism.'

'Why?'

'I'm never sure how long the calm will last. It needs only one lunatic to bring a knife or an airgun to school and use it, and there we are in the Press, with adverse publicity, the whole place in uproar.'

'And what will you do?'

'It's not happened yet. Act sensibly, I suppose. Try to get the school settled down as soon as possible. I think we'd manage it, but one never knows from which direction the devastating blow will fall.' He screwed his eyes. 'I felt the same about our marriage. It didn't seem proper that we should be so happy.'

'The blow's not fallen yet,' she said, strongly, but laughing.

'No.' Tom took her in his arms.

In the middle of the month she went away to do her week of recitals in Durham, Newcastle and Edinburgh with the Lombard Quartet. She found the short period very heavy work, and did not sleep well. She had prepared herself carefully for the six events, but the members of the quartet seemed out of sorts so that the rehearsals before the tour started were uninspiring. They did nothing to encourage her, niggled uncomfortably at each other, made no helpful suggestions to her. She played well, in her own judgement, but could not help suspecting that she in some way disappointed them.

The first recital at Durham University went without a hitch. The authorities had provided her with an excellent piano which suited her admirably in the Brahms. The audience received the performance most warmly, and at the short social gathering afterwards she received much congratulation. She, by prior arrangement, was driven back to her hotel by a woman professor of music who said she could not recall the Brahms Op 34 being better performed. The quartet had sloped off earlier, separately, rather silently; they had spoken to her in the interval just after the Brahms and again after the concert, but without marked enthusiasm. They had played well, but their reception of her, of their own performance had seemed lukewarm.

On the second night the Schubert 'Trout', thoroughly rehearsed in the afternoon, was encored. They had played outstandingly; Elizabeth had no doubt about that, but the quartet spoke to her as they might have thanked a casual plumber, brought in to do a simple job they could not do for themselves. They were polite; they answered questions, but they would have done as much for anybody else. Elizabeth tried to comfort herself by saying that they considered her now as a fellow professional. At their first performance in Beechnall they had seen her as a gifted amateur, to be coaxed along, coached even. Not now. Her explanation did not convince, and on her arrival in Newcastle, (she went by train, then car,) she cornered Hugh Donald, the leader.

'How do you think we're doing?' she asked. She'd start amiably enough.

'Very well,' he answered. They were walking the street in the sunshine on the way to the hall for a rehearsal. She shivered.

'Are you certain?'

'Yes. Absolutely. Why?'

'I'm not so sure.'

Hugh pulled a wry face.

'Um. What makes you say that?' He stopped almost rudely to look at a row of fashionable men's suits in a wide shop window.

Elizabeth, caught out, had taken a step or two past him, and had a sidle back.

'It's not that we did badly,' she said. 'We didn't. And perhaps I've misjudged it all, but when we played before you all seemed, well, enthusiastic, encouraging me and each other. And, it may be me, of course, it's all very subjective, but now it's as if we've been picked and assembled at random, against our better judgement, and told to get on with it.'

'Which we do,' he said.

He turned from the men's wear and began to walk again.

'Let me say first,' he began once they had established a steady pace, 'that you played quite beautifully. There is no doubt at all. I thought I'd said as much, but not apparently with enough emphasis. To tell you the truth I prefer your interpretation both of the Brahms as well as the Schubert to that of John Dutton.'

'That's flattering.'

'Dutton's a first-rate soloist, make no mistake. But you play with us, as he doesn't always.' They walked along in silence. He seemed to lengthen his stride. 'It's true that we're having something of a crisis. I hoped you weren't going to notice. But there's no hiding anything from women.' He speeded up to such an extent that she thought he was trying to escape before he was forced to reveal the nature of the trouble. 'Julian Davis is at the bottom of it.' The second violin. 'He has a wife and a young family, and she's beginning to complain about the length of time he has to spend away from home. She ought to have known about this. She was an orchestral player herself, a violinist like him, so it couldn't have come as a surprise to her. What did upset her was the stress of looking after small children. They've been a touch unlucky, with illness and accident, but Jules is a thoroughly conscientious man. Whenever he's at home he puts himself out to take his share of childcare and cleaning.'

They continued walking but Hugh Donald kept silent until they crossed the road at traffic lights. Then he touched Elizabeth's arm before he resumed.

'It's all come to a head just recently because Jules has been offered a professorship at the Royal College.'

'Was he working towards this? Such people usually are.'

'No. Not as far as I can gather. It came out of the blue. I'm not surprised. Jules is not only a very good player, but he'd make a good teacher. And somebody there had noticed this, they don't always and they don't always want competition, and had got the college authorities to make him a firm offer.'

'Was it financially viable?'

'He wouldn't earn as much as he would with us. We're beginning to do well now. We're up to the eyes with engagements, some of them abroad and valuable. That's perhaps the trouble with Tessa. We are away a great deal, and all through the year. And there's some jealousy involved. She thinks she's just as good a musician as he is, but all she is allowed to do is feed and wash babies and clean the house.'

'Is there any truth in it?'

'She's nowhere near his class, in my view. He's very good and getting better. That's why we don't want to lose him. He is a beautiful player.'

'What does he want to do?'

'I'm pretty certain he wants to stay with us. We're making money, and we're playing better and better.'

'But?' she asked.

'His wife's forceful. And he feels guilty. Both about leaving us or not pulling his weight at home. If he was less tender-hearted he'd tell her to get lost. She's not the only woman in the world whose husband works away or isn't home until late.'

'You want him to stay?'

'He's a very good player, that's the first thing. And he's undemanding, in the sense that he doesn't put his own concerns first. He's no temperamental virtuoso. Moreover, he's a good musician. When we're faced with some modern composition, he'll make sound suggestions, help us to see some sense in what at first shot seems meaningless noise. He feels his way quickly into things, and that's very helpful to me. I'm the diplomat in this little lot. It's not always the case. Sometimes the leader's a dictator. What he says goes. And always. With us I sometimes have to put my foot down, but less often than I might because Julian Davis is there, doing his stuff.'

'And the others?' she asked.

'They get on well with him. Both of them are forceful characters, Matthew especially.' The cello. 'And they argue now that he should tell his wife to shut her mouth and get on with her own work. They put it to him with considerable force, and that makes it worse for him. And that's what the trouble is.

That's the reason why we can't even be polite enough to tell you how well you've played.'

'And what will happen?'

'I honestly don't know. Nor does anybody. Not Julian even. That's what makes it worse. We're on the lookout for a new second fiddle.'

'You have somebody in mind?'

'Oh, half a dozen. There's no shortage of good players. But the new man, or woman, will have to learn to fit in. And it takes some doing.'

'But mayn't you get somebody even better?'

'Just possible. Very unlikely, though.'

'I'm sorry, Hugh, that I've bothered you with all this brewing up round you.'

'Don't worry. I thrive on interesting crises. We all do, except Jules, and he's the cause of it. The other two are on to him all the time, but he just seems to shrug it off. And that makes them worse.' He turned as they walked, waved a left hand in her direction, towards the passing traffic, the boring October sky. 'Oh, the perils of the artistic life.'

He said no more, but smirked the last few yards of his way into the rehearsal hall. There, it was Julian Davis who inquired whether she was being properly looked after. He had brown eyes, she noticed for the first time, and hadn't shaved too closely. He at once set carefully about the task of mastering a difficult passage. He played it beautifully the first time, but shook his head and tried again.

The rest of the week proved extremely successful. Large audiences cheered and encored them. The Press praised beyond expectation. In Edinburgh they laid on a bogus rehearsal of the Schubert Quintet. The 'cello, Matthew Schlesinger, excelled himself, clowning, charming the students. Jules Davis said barely a word, though once Hugh asked him to demonstrate a passage. He complied, without show. Hugh asked for a repeat. 'Too good to be true,' said Matthew to the students in the rows in front of him. 'I wish I could play like that without practice.'

On the morning after the last recital she caught a London express. The quartet were flying over to Germany for a recital that same evening. She enjoyed the speeding swing of the carriage, stretched her weary legs. Tom would be there on

207

the platform at Retford, ready to carry her cases, drive her the last miles home.

Man and wife embraced briefly on the platform. He carted her luggage away with something of a swagger. 'I read this week that Sir Adrian Boult wouldn't allow Denis Matthews, his soloist, to ruin his fingers lugging bags about. You haven't been wasting your time while I've been flitting about the world,' she said mockingly. Once Tom had reassured himself about the success of her recitals, he talked about his school, where all had progressed smoothly.

'You've had the time to put in,' she said. 'No wives to interrupt you.'

'Surely, surely.' His crooning voice pleased her. She felt comfortable, coddled by his presence. It had been announced he said, that the school would have an inspection in the spring of the next year. This had come as a surprise to him. 'I thought they'd give me a full year to set my mark on the place before they appeared.'

He had no idea why they had decided to descend on him thus early. He did not mind, because things were shaping well.

'But will it do any good?' she asked.

'On the whole, yes. Inspections suit some people: the show-offs and bullshitters. And it distresses some decent, nervous teachers. Most of us are somewhere in between. We wonder if we are doing the job properly. And that can cause problems. But teaching is always an occupation which involves stress, and I guess that it does no harm to add to that as long as it's not too great, and not too often. You recitalists thrive on it.'

'Yes, but we're the show-offs.'

He had told the staff and the heads of department at short staff-meetings, junior and senior, that he was ready to discuss any facet of the inspection with them. The ways of OFSTED were not as mysterious as all that, and he wanted them all to know what the inspectors would be looking for. Tom sat straighter at the wheel as he explained this to her; she realised he felt this as a challenge that would do him good. He was confident and competitive; the more she saw of him, the more it became plain. In his school he was a strong man, but rational and compassionate with it. She kissed him on his ear as he drove.

Near home as they passed The Hollies she asked if he had seen anything of George de la Tour or Ellen Woodcock.

'I knew you'd ask that,' he said. As he removed her luggage from the boot at New Orchard Cottage he continued. 'I telephoned twice while you were away, hung about, but still got no answer. Last night as I came back from school I stopped, got out, rang the bell. Nothing. Nobody about. It was dark, especially in the wood, but there were no lights on anywhere in the house. I made sure; I knew how to get round to the back even with all the side gates fastened and I walked all round the place.'

'Staring in through the windows?'

'Of course. There were no curtains drawn.'

'And?'

'And nothing. The rooms seemed tidy enough, as if they had been recently occupied. The kitchen was well supplied with cleaning powders and soap.'

'The bedrooms?'

'I didn't climb the drainpipes in the dark. No. I shone my big car torch in at the downstairs windows, and saw nothing amiss.'

They were now inside and in each other's arms. When they broke away he made for the kitchen and the kettle.

'This morning,' he continued, setting out teapot and cups, 'I asked about them in the village when I collected the bread and paid for the newspapers. They had seen nothing.' Mrs White, the newsagent, had shouted to her husband asking him if he had spoken to Mr Delly, that's what they called him, in the pub recently. White himself appeared, did elaborately frowning calculations in his head and said it must have been, oh, a fortnight since he'd seen any thing of him. 'O'course,' he concluded, 'he may have changed pubs. The Plough's not all that brilliant, and Mr Delly didn't go out of his way to be sociable. He sat near the bar, and drank a half-pint or two, and didn't say much.'

'Did people like him?' Tom had asked.

'They knew who he was,' White answered, and shrugged, spreading his arms. 'I mean, his picture's been in the paper.'

Tom had met the postman in the village, and he had been delivering letters at The Hollies for the past fortnight without seeing anybody. They hadn't asked for anything to be forwarded elsewhere, so he'd taken it that they had gone on holiday somewhere. No, they had not said anything, but Mr de la Tour was often away, wasn't he?, and the lady wasn't exactly a great talker. 'She'd speak sometimes, but as likely as not she would just nod towards the door if she was outside as if to tell me to put the letters into the box. I don't know what else she'd expect me to do. Eat 'em, perhaps.' Clearly Ellen was no favourite.

Elizabeth made three vain phone calls, and once stopped her car outside 'The Hollies' and walked up to the house. She poked at the bell and, failing there, peered through the letter box. A pile of mail lay dustily in the porch.

'I wonder where they are,' she complained to Tom. 'You'd have thought they'd get in touch.'

'They didn't seem a couple very observant of the social niceties,' he said in his magisterial voice.

In December she travelled to Worcester, then Gloucester for the final recitals of the year. On the Saturday after her return she saw, went back to check, a For Sale notice outside the gate of 'The Hollies'.

'They must have decided to leave,' she told her husband.

'Not a very good time of year for selling,' he said. 'But I don't suppose that'll be a great part of his fortune.'

'I wonder what they're asking.'

'A hundred and ninety thousand,' he said at once, very confidently.

'How do you know?'

'I don't. I'm guessing.'

Later in the week he told her he'd been slightly out. Two hundred and ten was the figure. He had been in touch with the house agents.

'Is it worth it?' she asked.

'It's a bit out of the way, and rather ugly. But it's roomy, if a touch awkward. I guess it might be subject to damp, but the central heating could keep that at bay. You don't fancy living there, do you?' he asked, frightening her.

'I do not.'

'Good. The one big advantage is that huge upstairs studio. That's what would have attracted de la Tour. I thought you perhaps had designs on it as a music-room.'

'I'm perfectly satisfied with what I've got.'

'Good.' He kissed her.

'But supposing I had said "Yes", what would you have done?'

'We, you and I,' his arm was round her waist, 'would have

had a closer look, and decided how much alteration would be required, and so on.'

'You'd be willing to move?'

'If you could convince me you wanted it. But I'd be loth to pay that price. I'd try to beat them down,' he said, smacking his lips.

'Even for your beloved's dream home?'

He slapped her buttocks, and they fell to lovemaking. Later that evening Elizabeth confided that she was sorry that George and Ellen were leaving.

'I enjoyed having a famous neighbour. And Ellen was not like anybody I've ever known.'

'A sheltered life,' he answered.

'That's what I want.'

One afternoon on her way back from college for her half day she passed Ellen Woodcock on the road. She drew into the verge and waited for the woman to catch up.

'Lift?'

'Yes, please.'

'I thought we'd seen the last of you. I rang, oh, half a dozen times. And so did Tom. In fact he crept round your house, looking in at the windows to find out if there was anybody there.'

'And there wasn't. We've been away. Fitting ourselves up.'

They were now outside The Hollies. Elizabeth invited Ellen to go along with her to New Orchard Cottage for a drink or a sandwich. Ellen thanking her, agreed, said she could not ask Elizabeth into The Hollies which had now been denuded of all but a very few bits and pieces.

'I haven't even a table. I have to cut bread on the draining board.'

'No bed, then?'

'One small truckle-thing and mattress.'

Ellen then began to ask Elizabeth what she was doing. Only yesterday her agent had asked her to play two concerts in Germany and two in Switzerland in April and May with the Lombard. These had been arranged on their recent visit, and John Dutton could not or did not want to join them. Elizabeth had asked for leave from her college that morning. There seemed no snags. Her head of department expressed his delight. The principal had said that it brought fame to the college. Elizabeth doubted this. She was to play the Schubert Quintet, or part, at the Christmas concert with players from the college, and was already well on with rehearsal. She felt pleased with herself; from this provincial corner of the world, from the shackles of marriage she was making big progress. A good woman could not be kept down.

Over a sandwich, with salad, she and Ellen talked easily. Ellen spoke like a released prisoner. It was marvellous, she said, to sit in a comfortable armchair, to drink such lovely coffee. She was leaving very early in the morning of the day after next.

'Tomorrow the removal men come for the last time. I needn't have been here. They know what they have to do.'

'And what about George's pictures? All those he put aside, that the agent wasn't to touch.'

'The dealer's taken the lot. He went round the studio with George. They spent a whole day. They won't put the pictures on the market all together. But George wasn't interested any more. This is a slice of his life that's gone stale, he said.'

'Is that like him?' Elizabeth asked.

'It is. Sometimes. One day he's certain. Nothing's to be touched or altered. The next, it's do-as-you-like. He thinks about his painting, but not about his living. That's not quite true. He grumbles now and again that this agent or that dealer could have done better for him, and then the very next minute it doesn't matter. I don't suppose it does now he's making so much money. And this agent, this dealer has done him well. He's cunning and clever, George says.'

'Is he new?'

'He's had him some years now. Five. Six. And he's stepped up the value of George's painting enormously. By clever ruses. Don't ask me how.'

'Is George painting again?'

'Yes. So the dealer says.'

'Where is he?'

'What date is it?'

'December the Fourth.'

Ellen made a calculation, comically tapping her fingers, and repeating 'the fourth', then 'third, fourth, fifth'. Finally, when she had satisfied herself, she said,

'He's going to America. Today's the day he's flying.'

'Permanently?'

'Yes. So he says.'

'I wouldn't have thought he wanted to live there,' Elizabeth said. 'Not since that was where Despina was killed.' She felt comfortable now with Ellen, confident enough to raise such a point.

'It's a big place. He's gone to California. Right the other side. It's like Italy for light, he says.'

'And that's where he'll stay?'

'So he says.'

Ellen seemed philosophical about the matter, eating her sandwich with relish.

'And what about you?'

'He's bought me a flat. In Guildford. And got me a job. Well, he didn't. It's a long story. I'm going to be housekeeper to some old man. I shall spend the whole day there, eight in the morning until after dinner at night. Two days off a week.'

'Is he disabled?'

'Not very mobile. Doesn't go out much. I shall be able to drive him out in his car if that's what he wants. He's an ex-military man. I quite liked him. A major-general.'

They talked into the afternoon. Ellen said she wouldn't come back for dinner. They must say goodbye. As they did so, Ellen wept, powerfully squeezing her shorter companion.

'I shall miss you,' she said, dabbing at her cheeks. 'But not much else. It was very lonely when first we came. But you became a friend. I don't know why you've been so kind to me. But you have. I shall miss you. I'm certain of that.'

'Come up and visit us.'

'Thank you, Elizabeth, but I can't make promises. Not now. I'll have to see. And your husband won't want me here, cluttering the place up.' She kissed Elizabeth full on the mouth. Then straightened herself and walked to the door. Her hostess accompanied her to the end of the garden path and stood at the gate to watch the stiff figure make pace down the road. Perhaps they would never meet again. She was certain she'd remember Ellen from time to time. She would not be able to pass 'The Hollies' without recalling that first occasion, that night so early in the marriage, when Ellen had called them in. Or some magazine or newspaper would feature de la Tour's earlier pictures of the naked, vulnerable Ellen. Ellen had been, was, an ordinary woman caught up with a man of outstanding gifts who had preserved the beauty of her breasts, genitals, stance, features, hair, skin for posterity. Ellen would never be the goddess of George's canvasses; at best she was a woman who, faced with a new life, could walk bravely down the road. Elizabeth stood at the gate waiting for Ellen to turn her head, to raise her hand in a last gesture; it did not happen. The woman pursued her steady way.

When she discussed this with Tom in the next few weeks, he seemed not to understand her feelings.

'She was decent but limited,' he said. 'With an unusual man. And something like a petty criminal for a husband. But she'll be remembered as we're not because of the pictures George made of her.'

'That doesn't help her live her life, does it?'

'Not many of us are hankering after immortality, you mean?' he asked.

'Exactly.'

'No. I agree. We're both doing well just at present, but it may not last. If that's not too pessimistic.'

She laughed at his lugubrious face.

On the first day of her Christmas holiday Elizabeth walked out as if under compulsion to look at 'The Hollies'. She had seen no evidence of activity there; the For Sale sign stood in place. Tom's school was still at work with two more days to go. The weather had been unpromising all week with grey skies and a cold north-east wind. She told herself that she'd do better to stay at home and practise for her January concert or to make out Christmas lists, but she had promised herself, against reason, that her first morning would be spent on 'The Hollies' and its environs. She had no idea why this was important. In fact, she knew that it was not so, but she had determined to go, and that if she did otherwise she'd be unsettled. She shook her head at her obsession, even as she dressed to keep out the cold.

She reached the gate of 'The Hollies', and stood there, undecided. Wind whipped the high treetops. The five-barred gate had no padlock so that she walked in taking care, meticulous care (Tom had said that etymologically the word had to do with *metus* – fear) to make no noise. Why she did so she did not know, for hardly any traffic had passed her along the road as she walked. She tiptoed into the turn of the drive and when she reached the front door of the porch she shook the knob. The

214

place was securely locked, but the pile of letters, junk mail, even, all this way out of the village, free newspapers sprawled across the floor. Surely any prowler would see this as an invitation to break in. She walked round the house now, without hurry, peering in at the windows. The rooms stood empty, without furniture, though the curtains remained. On the floor of the kitchen sheets of newspaper had been deliberately spread. A rusty bucket symbolized the cold, unwelcoming place. Round the side she looked into the large sitting room where they had been entertained, to misuse the language, on their last visit. Tom confided later that he had much admired the black marble fireplace there, 'the only good thing about the room.' 'But it won't be marble,' he had complained. 'Disguised slate.' 'Not worth buying the house for?' she had facetiously inquired. 'No.' Now the room was dark; the carpet which had been left seemed shabby, faded near the windows, deeply marked where the heavy tables, chairs, sideboards had stood. Some darker stains suggested spillage, accident, quarrels even. The lighter rectangles of the positions of former pictures methodically disfigured the surface of the walls; quite unwelcoming, the room congealed with dust and chill. Elizabeth turned away, saddened. Put a professional decorator in, spend a few hundreds on a carpet, renew the curtains, return half of the furniture and polish it, turn on the central heating and within a day or two the room would be homely, warm, comfortably embracing, part of a home. She turned back, breathed heavily on the window, leaving a small cloud-shaped smear which she cleared immediately with the cuff of her coat.

She made strongly for the bottom of Ellen's garden. It looked neat enough to her, but perhaps this was no weed-growing weather. She pressed past the fruit-cages, the dividing hedges, down to the lane. Smoke rose from the chimney on the nurseryman's long greenhouse on the other side of the partitions. The air grew colder; the sky darker. She shuddered and made her way quickly back to the front of the house where she drew herself up by the gate, in the chill, under dark trees, uncertain where to move next.

Without much confidence she set off down the road towards the crossroads and the village, but turned sharply left towards the churchyard and the locked lych-gate. She clambered over the stile and made, as she and Ellen had done on their first visit, towards the church. The grass, heavy with moisture, overhung the narrow path. She paused by the south porch, took the iron ring of the latch in her hand, turned it a clanking inch. The place was shut. She moved on, skirting Arthur Horton, A.M., and reached the low grave of Ellen Annie Hoskin, 1855–1901, the favourite of her namesake. Crouching she searched for a mark on the stone where Ellen had touched the monument for luck. She failed in her scrutiny, for though she found weather-stains there was nothing that could be construed as the mark of a finger. Ellen would never see this grave, this talisman, again, would not walk superstitiously on this path which she had chosen out for herself in the past five years. She had disappeared. Elizabeth did not expect phone calls, letters, Christmas cards; that was not Ellen's crooked way. The young woman drew in a great, triumphant breath, not at any victory over circumstance, but at a recognition of things as they were, and reached out again to touch the chill stone with a forefinger, before rising to make for the other touchstone, the grand canopy of (she began to read) Sir Joseph Wainwright Thorpe, Bart, 1857–1931 and of Harriet Adelaide, wife of the above. This was the marble that Ellen Woodcock slapped, with the flat of her hand. Elizabeth did likewise. In the cold her hand stung from the blow. She examined it and grinned, nodded to the angel in his silent perusal of the blank page, noticed that the grass round the grave had been mown. The angel, she thought, looked rather sheepish, as if surprised, like her, on a pointless exercise. She buttoned the top of her coat and set out for home.

Once she had reached the road she noticed that her shoes were wet and quickened her step to warm herself. She did not pause as she passed 'The Hollies', merely glanced at the trees, hedges, shrubs as she made greater speed for the welcoming heat of her room. She wondered what Ellen was doing at that moment. Settling herself in the new flat in Guildford, or perhaps already there at the major-general's squaring up to or for the old man. Ellen had said that it was a long story, the way she'd acquired her new position, but had made no attempt to relate it. And George, he'd be safely in Californian sunshine, doing or not doing. He was as far away from this cold place as that other painter, Georges de La Tour. She wondered what his dates were. She must look him up when she reached home. She began to feel warmth spreading inside herself, though the wind pecked greedily at her face. Tom had promised to be back exactly on five, and had said he would like fish cakes for dinner, with parsley sauce, peas, potatoes boiled in their skins, and, he had laughed, vinegar on the table. 'A large plateful,' he had demanded. 'I shall be ravenous.'

She had no sooner entered the comfort of the house, made for the kitchen, filled and put on the kettle, than she noticed the post-van at the gate. The postman advanced jauntily along the path. He carried a parcel. The doorbell pealed.

'Registered parcel, madam. If you'd sign it, and print your name, if you please, underneath.'

The postman, a small, neat, West Indian of Asian origin, swayed smilingly with official form and biro. She fulfilled her obligations.

'The kettle's on, Ernest,' she said. 'Tea? Coffee?'

'I wouldn't say "No", madam. It's a bit parky this morning.'

He followed her in. They drank their coffee together. He accepted a chocolate biscuit. As she put her empty cup on the draining board she asked the postman if she should open her parcel.

'Yes, please. I don't often get to see what I've brought. I have to use my imagination.'

She picked up the slim package, balanced it on one hand, then passed it to the postman.

'What do you think this is?' she asked.

He put down his cup, turned the packet over, held it by thumb and forefinger.

'Light,' he pronounced. 'Stiffened. Not to be bent. Registered. Somebody thinks it's valuable. London, J. R. Dutt, New Bond Street, Dealers in Fine Art.' He hung the packet out again a yard in front of him. 'A picture, I'd say. Is that right?'

'I've no idea,' she answered.

'You've not ordered any?' he asked, handing it back.

'No.'

'We'd better open it,' he said, thin fingers round his cup.

She took a sharp kitchen knife from the drawer and without hurry slit the end of the package.

'Now,' she said.

The contents were so carefully wrapped and protected that she had difficulty in extracting them. She succeeded, and then used her scissors to open the last integument. One small pen-and-wash sketch of the Thorpe monument in the blue moonlight lay revealed. A note, impersonally typed and illegibly signed, said Mr de la Tour had asked that this be sent to her.

'Very good,' the postman said. 'Is it a tomb?'

'Yes,' she answered. 'It's in the churchyard here. I went to see it this morning.'

'A relative?' he asked. 'Buried there?'

'No. A baronet. Sir Joseph Thorpe.'

'No,' the postman muttered, shaking his head. 'It's good.' He moved his face nearer the paper, then tapped the bare table. 'That man can draw.' Then as if to excuse his impertinence, he added in a low voice, 'I used to attend art classes at the WEA in Beechnall.'

'It's from George de la Tour. He used to live at 'The Hollies', down the road.'

The postman shook his head, left his stool, placed his cup on the draining board, thanked her for her hospitality, and said he must get on. He paused for another long examination of the picture.

'Look after it, madam,' he said. 'But I don't need to tell you.'

She followed him to the door. He let himself out but on the path called back.

'It's good. Be worth something one of these fine days. It's very good, believe you me. Thank you, madam.'

Elizabeth made her way back to the picture, the good, the very good, the memorable.

218